THE LIBYAN

A MEMOIR

ESTHER KOFOD

This is my story, a work of creative non-fiction. Some names and identifying details have been changed to protect the privacy of the people involved.

ISBN: 0989054306
ISBN-13: 9780989054300

Library of Congress Control Number: 2013935365
Whitfield Press
Tallahassee, Florida

This book is dedicated to the men and women of Libya who have fought for peace and freedom...

And to the Libyans who will not live to see it happen.

To my children and grandchildren, the lights in my soul
And to my husband, the love of my life, my all...

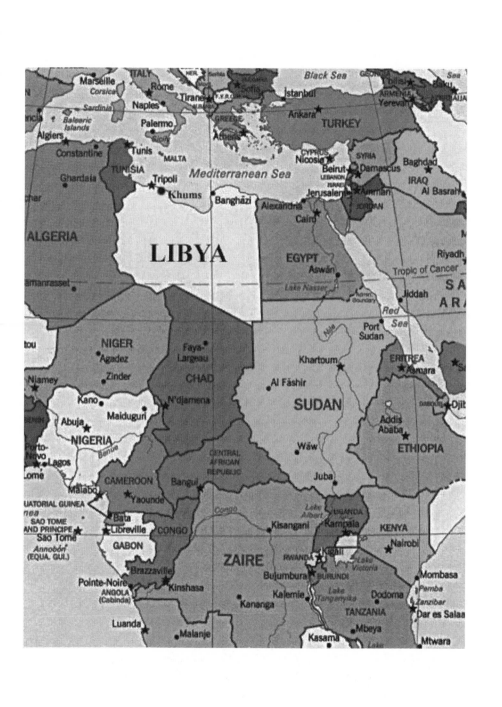

HISTORY OF LIBYA

ROMAN ERA .... 146 BC - 640 AD

ARAB RULE .... 640 - 1551

OTTOMAN RULE .... 1551 – 1911

ITALIAN COLONIZATION .... 1911 – 1934

ITALIAN LIBYA .... 1934 – 1943

ALLIED OCCUPATION .... 1943 – 1951

KINGDOM OF LIBYA .... 1951 – 1969

GADDAFI'S DICATATORSHIP .... 1969 – 2011

LIBYAN REVOLUTION .... February 2011

LIBYAN INDEPENDENCE .... October 2011

TABLE OF CONTENTS

PROLOGUE

As I walked into the American Embassy that spring morning, I glanced surreptitiously at the rooftop of the building
across the road. Libyan Secret Service men were perched
there like vultures, just as Kamal had warned, watching and
filming every person entering the embassy.

I was riddled with guilt for not telling my husband what
I was doing. I was sure he would tell me not to go—so I
hadn't asked, by rationalizing that the welfare of my unborn
child justified my defiance. By my doctor's calculations
back in Florida, the baby was due in June. It was already
April, and I had not seen a doctor since leaving the States in
December. Four months.

The embassy was housed in an old Italianate terracotta stucco villa in the city center, surrounded by modern buildings that already looked tired and aged due to
neglect. The reception room was packed with Libyans
and foreigners, all frantically vying for an official's attention. I idly wondered if any of the men there were also
secret police.

It was hot and stuffy inside, despite several window air
conditioners struggling to suffuse cool air into the close
quarters. The scores of all our hot bodies pressed closely
together defeated their tireless efforts.

I wiped the perspiration from my forehead and took deep breaths to overcome a creeping tide of claustrophobia, both from the surroundings as well as from the heaviness of my advanced pregnancy. I heaved a determined sigh and got to the back of one of three long lines.

It was obvious that most of the people were there to get visas to the United States. For some reason, I felt safe simply knowing that I was diplomatically on American soil. I just hoped I wasn't doing anything wrong by being there, and that Kamal wouldn't be too angry with me.

After standing in line for a while, I felt a soft touch on my arm and turned to see an attractive black woman with an overly friendly smile. Despite the heat, she looked impeccably crisp in a smart white linen suit with matching white pumps.

"May I help you, Madame?" the woman asked.

She was an American! My spirits lifted immediately. It was nice to hear an American voice.

"Oh, yes, please!" I replied with relief. "My name's Hiba Ben Ramadan. I'm American; I'm here to register."

"So nice to meet you, Mrs Ben Ramadan! My name's Lynn Pendleton. I'm the liaison for consular affairs."

Her accent hinted at Ivy League. She extended a bony, well-manicured hand, which I happily accepted and shook. Her smile widened, and I wondered if she already knew who I was. Using her other hand, Miss Pendleton lightly laid it on my shoulder.

"Please follow me," she said in a low voice, drawing me out of the line.

I was quite taken aback by this show of favoritism, and while relishing in it, I was also a little self-conscious. Her manner exuded such grace and hospitality that it made me feel more like an honored guest in her home. I noticed the questioning expressions of some people in the crowd as I was whisked away, but I didn't care. Often, because of my olive complexion, I would be mistaken for an Arab, so they were probably thinking I was in trouble.

I followed Miss Pendleton down a long narrow hallway into a room at the end. It was a small room, about twelve by twelve feet, but the walls were very unusual. They were completely covered in a metallic quilt-like fabric, including the ceiling. The temperature in the room was much cooler than the other rooms, almost cold. A low wooden round table stood in the middle, surrounded by four comfortable looking club chairs. The only other thing in the room was a large crystal ashtray on the table, overflowing with cigarette butts.

I sensed Miss Pendleton was watching my reactions very closely. With a gracious smile, she motioned for me to take a seat, simultaneously removing the ashtray.

"I'll be right back," she said reassuringly, as she made a move to leave the room. I settled into one of the chairs, marveling at how quiet the room was. It was nice to just sit and relax after standing in line for so long in the oppressive reception room. Miss Pendleton returned in about ten minutes with someone.

"Mrs Ben Ramadan, there's somebody here I'd like you to meet."

Before I could answer, a large man, wearing thick glasses, with sandy-colored hair and a bushy mustache walked into the room. He wore khaki trousers and a navy blue sports jacket over an open-neck white shirt. I suspected he was responsible for a lot of those cigarette butts in the ashtray. He too had a very big and friendly smile, eagerly extending a beefy hand followed by a firm handshake. He was average-looking, and if I had not known he was American, he could have passed for a fair-complexioned Libyan like my father-in-law. Despite his thinning hair, I suspected that he was only in his early forties.

"Mrs Ben Ramadan! I'm James Moore, delighted to meet you!" His exuberance seemed genuine.

"Very nice to meet you, too," I nodded, feeling somewhat confused and overwhelmed by this special treatment.

"Well, I've got to get back to work," Miss Pendleton interrupted with a demure smile, laying one hand on my arm. "If there's ever anything I can do to help you, anything at all, please let me know!"

"Thank you, Miss Pendleton. It was nice meeting you," I mumbled—uneasy by the curious exchange.

She left discreetly, closing the door carefully behind her. The room was so sound-proofed I could not even hear her heels clicking down the corridor.

I was now left alone with James Moore. I felt a little uncomfortable, realizing that Kamal would not be pleased to know that I had been alone in a room with a strange man. I knew enough about Libyan customs by now to know that I was in a compromised situation politically as well as culturally. Once again, I was torn between what I was and how I was supposed to behave. For now I was just glad to be in the company of an American-speaking person, yet I had a suspicious feeling there was something behind all this hospitality.

Mr Moore turned out to be a pleasant and engaging conversationalist. He told me he had been working in the Middle East for many years, and let on that he was a collector of Arabic art and artefacts. He asked if I spoke any

Arabic, and inquired about my family back home. I had the feeling he already knew the answers, because he was asking all the right questions. However, I was enjoying the conversation so much that I really didn't care.

Reluctantly, I decided to change the subject, and take the opportunity to gear it to the real purpose of my visit.

"Mr Moore, I..."

"Please, call me Jim."

"I'd like to have my baby delivered at the American Oil Clinic, but apparently only employees of oil companies are allowed. However, my husband and I are willing to pay whatever it costs." Kamal had said nothing of the sort.

"Is there any way the embassy can help me?" I sounded like I was begging, but for my baby's sake I could afford to be a little shameless.

"Consider it done!" He replied, without hesitation. "In fact," he continued, "I'll make sure that Dr Watson, Head of Obstetrics, will personally take your case. You'll have the best suite there!"

I couldn't believe it was that easy.

...

"Thank you so much, Mr Moore." I gushed, with relief and gratitude, trying not to sound too desperate, but I was thrilled!

...

"Mrs Ben Ramadan, if you would please give me your telephone number, I'll have someone from the hospital call you with details."

Without hesitation, and without thinking, I quickly wrote down my number with the pen and notepad Mr Moore had removed from his jacket pocket and happily handed it back. "I'll take care of this right away, Mrs Ben Ramadan. I promise you'll be hearing from someone by tomorrow, at the very latest."

I thanked him and started to get up to go, but Moore cleared his throat and subtly gestured for me to stay.

Looking me straight in the eye, with a more serious tone in his voice, he said, almost apologetically, "Mrs Ben Ramadan, I'd very much like to meet your husband, Dr Ben Ramadan. Do you think it would be all right for me to call him?"

Surprised at what he was asking, I was at a momentary loss for a reply. I also realized that, of course, now that I had given him our home number he could call anytime. I was starting to feel a little worried.

"Well…I'll have to ask him. I think our phones are bugged, and …"

I wondered if this man realized that a call from the American Embassy would put Kamal in a precarious position. There were eyes and ears everywhere, and Kamal could easily be accused of working with the Americans.

"Mrs Ben Ramadan, I absolutely understand your hesitation," he interrupted, in a sympathetic tone.

"But I want to assure you I have no intentions of putting your husband – or you," he paused and looked at me seriously, "in a compromising position. All I ask is if you would just please tell him that I would like very much to meet him."

"All right," I replied, uncertainly, and with some hesitation. "I'll tell him."

I was perplexed by this request, but I also wanted to try to be accommodating and not appear ungrateful. Despite everything, the hospital booking remained foremost in my mind.

"Mrs Ben Ramadan, I think there's something I should tell you," continued this big American with a gentle smile. "Nothing said in this room can be heard by anyone, anywhere, which is why we brought you in here. I want you to feel comfortable to say anything you want," he said, pausing for a second. "Do you understand what I'm trying to tell you?'

I nodded, his implication slowing sinking in. I thought quickly about the secret police monitoring who was coming and going, into and out of the embassy. However, I was an American citizen, and didn't see why I would get into trouble. In fact, I had not even registered my presence with the embassy, which was the required and perhaps sensible thing for all Americans who reside abroad to do.

Mr Moore let his words sink in before continuing.

"This room is totally isolated from any kind of sound or visual devise. We call it the Bubble Room."

It finally dawned on me that he was CIA!

How the hell was I ever going to explain this to Kamal?

CHAPTER 1

BIRTH IN THE DESERT, 1942

After the most intense and brutal battle fought by the Afrika Korps in the Second World War, the strategic port of Tobruk, on the northern shores of Libya, fell to the Germans under Rommel. It was 20 June 1942, and it was a grim outcome for the Libyans. After suffering for years under the Italians led by Rodolfo Graziani, otherwise known as "The Butcher of Libya", they were now under Nazi control.

In a small stone house in the coastal town of Khums, a very pregnant young woman and her husband were awakened by a loud knock on their front door.

Alarmed, Ibrahim told his frightened wife, "Stay here and don't move!"

He rushed to the next room and carried two sleeping boys to their mother, gently placing them beside her, nestled in sheep skins for bedding and woven Berber blankets for covers.

"I don't know who it is, so be very quiet," he whispered to his wife. He could see that she was scared, and he wanted to reassure her, but the knocking became more persistent. He left the room, closing the door behind him and locked it with the large key that always stayed in the keyhole.

Taking a deep breath, Ibrahim prepared to deal with whoever was outside his house in the middle of the night.

He wished now that he had taken Rogaya and his sons to Ramadi weeks ago.

The retreat of the British and the presence of German troops had spurred thousands of Libyans to flee into the desert, to seek refuge from the bombardment and killings. Rumors of atrocities committed by Italian and German troops spread fear and hatred among the people, helpless to protect themselves except by flight.

The Sahara desert to the south, far away from the towns along the Libyan coastline, provided a temporary sanctuary for many. Libyans from cities and towns along the coast returned to their Berber roots, to tribes they had left, who now welcomed them back with open hearts. Their families and tribes shared with them what little they were able to eke out of the arid land by growing barley and raising sheep and goats. Occasionally, even a camel would have to be slaughtered for food. The code of unconditional loyalty and hospitality within the tribes, which had fortified them throughout centuries of foreign domination, now protected them from the threat of atrocities by the Italian and German armies.

When Ibrahim opened the heavy wooden door, he was surprised to see Renato, the Italian who owned the small grocery store in town, standing there.

"It's okay, Ibrahim, I'm by myself," Renato quickly explained, his distinctive Roman features silhouetted against the shadows.

"Tobruk has fallen…the Germans are coming to Khums on their way to Tripoli. They could be here by tomorrow!"

Renato spoke in a hurried whisper, furtively looking around, listening.

"You're a good man, Ibrahim, and I don't want anything bad to happen to you or your family."

Ibrahim stood still, seemingly calm in his bedclothes, intently listening and absorbing the implications behind Renato's warning.

Renato had risked breaking the curfew imposed by the Italians to warn him, a man for whom he had utmost respect and admiration. He had seen Ibrahim help others over the years, regardless of who they were: Libyan or Italian. He was afraid his friend would not survive the Germans and their rumored cruelties towards the Libyans. He would be too proud and too stubborn to tolerate any form of injustice. Ibrahim was the undeclared Libyan "capo" or leader of Khums.

"You know they've killed many Libyans along the way, and taken whatever they wanted. That those who protested were tortured and killed..." Renato paused, seeing Ibrahim flinch in the little light afforded by a quarter moon.

"You must leave immediately, my friend, before it's too late."

Renato was sweating by now, fearing for his own life. Ibrahim knew it would not have been good for the Italian to be caught talking to a Libyan in the dead of night.

"*Grazi*, Signor Renato." Ibrahim was touched by the man's concern for him and his family. "I will, but first let me accompany you back to your house."

"No, Ibrahim, you are kind to offer, but I'll be safer without you. May God help you and your family and, *Inshallah*, I will see you again one day."

3

Quietly and quickly, Renato disappeared into the silence of the night.

After reassuring his wife that everything was going to be alright, Ibrahim Ben Ramadan went about making a pot of strong tea. He took it outside and drank it in the dark, looking up at the stars. His only concern was for his family, and he knew the time had come for him to take them to his familial village of Ramadi, in the desert to the south. Rogaya was eight months pregnant and food was becoming scarce. They had to leave immediately. The British would not give up easily, and Ibrahim feared that Rogaya would not have the strength to live through a birth under those circumstances.

As soon as he got his family to safety, he vowed, he would return to Khums to start a resistance movement to help defend his people against the Germans. Swallowing the last of his tea, his mind made up, Ibrahim started preparing for the journey. He gathered the stores they had been able to put by, including jars of olives and *Gideed*, sundried lamb preserved in olive oil, which Rogaya had saved for the celebration of the baby's birth. As the first of the sun's rays crept over the house, Ibrahim secured everything to the sides of the camel that he and his younger son, Ali, would ride. On the second camel, which he covered with carpets and sheep skins, he helped his wife settle as comfortably as she was able. Their elder son, Amir, rode with his mother so he could help keep her steady on the long bumpy ride.

"Are you sure you'll be able to make it?" Ibrahim asked Rogaya just before they set off. He knew they were doing the right thing, but to undertake this journey at such an advanced stage of pregnancy was an ordeal he wished with all his heart he could spare his wife.

"We have to leave, Ibrahim," the young woman assured him, "I would rather die this way than at the hands of the Germans."

Ibrahim had anticipated that the journey to Ramadi would take at least three days, but after only a few hours, he saw that the camel ride was already proving too strenuous for his wife, strong as she was. She had become quieter and paler, and he was starting to wonder if he had made the right decision.

Though familiar with the signs of labor, Rogaya tried hard to ignore the onset of the first contractions so as not to delay their journey. Struggling quietly with her burden, she silently prayed to Allah to help her deliver a healthy baby girl. Her first two children were healthy, handsome boys who brought immense pride and joy to her husband and herself. She thanked Allah again for all the blessings he had bestowed on her, most of all her husband and the good life he had provided for them. She had everything a woman could wish for, and she knew that she owed everything she had to Ibrahim. Theirs had been an arranged marriage, and, like all Libyan girls, she had known that her fate lay in the hands of the man who had been chosen for her. She had heard stories of women who had not been as fortunate. Many were married to men who were indifferent to their wives, husbands who barely acknowledged their existence. Their roles as wives was to produce male heirs and to satisfy their husband's personal needs and desires. The unlucky ones were married to men who treated them badly, sometimes abusing them for any or no reason, knowing that the women were at their mercy.

The pains were getting stronger and closer, and Rogaya knew that she would soon have to ask Ibrahim to stop the journey. As they approached an oasis, she decided that the baby was not going to wait any longer. She called out to her husband to stop. Ibrahim was shocked when he realized the baby was coming already. He quickly led his camel to an area under some date palms, which provided a little shade from the already scorching June sun. He silently prayed that his wife would not feel too much pain. Rogaya had delivered their other two children relatively easily, but had been assisted by the village midwife and several women from the family.

Ibrahim had married Rogaya when she was only fifteen years old, but now, after five years, she had become strong and matured beyond her age. He felt blessed to have such a rare woman for his wife, but he now blamed himself for not having left Khums sooner. The baby was not due for another month; since the other two had come on time, he had taken for granted that so would this one. He cursed himself for putting his wife in the position of birthing her own baby. It was not customary for men to aid in the delivery, and he knew that Rogaya would not expect nor want him to. However, if she asked him he would not refuse her.

After securing his camel, Ibrahim assisted his wife from hers and carried her to a shady spot. He spread some rugs on the sand and gently settled her into a comfortable position, leaving her with water and a clean knife. He then walked down to the water's edge with his sons, and slowly unfolded his prayer rug onto the rough surface. He could hear Rogaya moaning and wanted to go to her, but knew that she would be too embarrassed to let him see her in that condition. He silently said his prayers, imploring Allah to have mercy on his wife and their soon-to-be-born child. As her moaning increased in volume, Ibrahim prayed louder and with more intensity.

After what seemed a long time, but was in actuality only about an hour, he heard the sound of a newborn wailing. He first thanked his God, before reaching into his *holi,* a toga-like robe worn over pants and shirt, for the towel he had tucked in earlier. He wondered if it would be a daughter or another son, this one who was so impatient to be born. He secretly hoped for another boy, even though Rogaya wanted a girl this time. Libyan society was not always kind to women, and Ibrahim did not foresee major change for his children's generation.

He dipped the towel into the cool spring water and hurried back to his wife, all the while whispering prayers of gratitude. Rogaya was lying where he had left her, a pale figure on a blanket in the middle of the desert. A very wet and bloodied baby boy was resting on her stomach, already suckling from her breast. Rogaya had managed to cut and tie the umbilical cord herself, and handed the knife back to her husband.

Ibrahim fixed his eyes on his new son and felt as if his heart was going to explode with joy. There was something very different, he thought, something very special about this baby. He was not only perfectly formed, but there was a look of such purpose and determination on his little face. Ah, he thought to himself, smiling, this was going to be a stubborn one. For now, the newborn was totally concentrated on his first undertaking in the outside world. In one moment of precognition, Ibrahim saw that this was going to be the first of ventures and adventures, all of which this boy would be attacking with the same fervor.

With the pride of generations of Bedouin leaders behind him, and the pride of a Ben Ramadan and a father, Ibrahim gazed at his son with absolute happiness. He wiped the perspiration from his wife's face, gave her water from his own goatskin canteen, and quietly whispered words of gratitude in her ears. He kissed her forehead with love rushing from his soul, and with the same emotion he kissed his son, gently removing him from his mother's breast.

Holding his third son for the first time in his arms, he said, in a strong voice swollen with pride, "In the name of Allah, I name you Kamal Ibrahim Ben Ramadan."

About 200 miles to the east that same day, another baby boy was born in the desert south of Sirte. He was named Muammar Minyar Gaddafi.

Before sunrise the next morning, Ibrahim and his family slowly continued the journey to Ramadi, arriving there five days later. About a week after their arrival, Ibrahim returned to Khums to become part of the local resistance against the Italian and German occupiers.

It was two years later, after the Italians and Germans were forced out of Libya and the country came under British administration, when Ibrahim could return to Ramadi to take his wife and children back to Khums. His acts of defiance against the Italian and German occupation had cost him several severe beatings and incarceration, but had also earned him the respect of the Khums population.

Kamal was walking by now and already showing signs of precocious behavior, much to the delight of his father. After he had settled his family back at their home, Ibrahim set about establishing their future. Whatever money he was able to acquire through the sale of animals and produce, he would use to buy acreage surrounding the modest original plot he had inherited from his father. As the years went by and his family grew, so did Ibrahim's farm.

The Ben Ramadan land bordered the magnificent ancient Roman ruins of Leptis Magna, an example of some of the best preserved Roman ruins outside of Italy. Presumably, some of the Ben Ramadan property also sat on top of unexcavated sections. It was here that Kamal spent his childhood playing, digging in his father's land for scraps of pottery, pieces of mosaic, marble, and even sometimes finding coveted Roman coins. Whenever he found something, he would take it down to the small Italian grocery store owned by Renato, whose beautiful teenage daughter, Maria, was adored by little Kamal. Maria would teach him a few words of Italian every time he came by with a prize; in return, Maria would give him a few pieces of candy.

By the time he was seven years old, everyone in the village knew Kamal, and he knew everyone. He adored his older brothers, especially Amir, who sometimes treated him like his personal serf, but Kamal did not mind. Being the eldest son, Amir ran the Ben Ramadan household when his father was not around.

The highlight of Kamal's young life was at the age of eight, the day his father took him and his brothers to Tripoli for the first time. Tripoli was the capital and also the largest city in Libya. He felt as though he had stepped into another world. Never had he seen so many people, cars and shops in one place. The noise and smell of the city stimulated all his senses and overloaded his imagination. When they stopped at a small café for lunch in the Medina, the walled-in old city, Ibrahim gave his sons a brief history of Tripoli. He explained to them that "Tripoli" derived from the Greek word "Tripolis," which encompassed the three cities of Tripoli, Sabrata and Leptis Magna. For the little boy, whose mouth had been hanging open without a word from the time they entered Tripoli, the floodgates opened and the questioning began.

"What is Greek, Father?" What is, who is, where is… His curiosity turned into a barrage of questioning and heightened awareness of a whole new world. At first this pleased Ibrahim as a sign of Kamal's intelligence, but by the end of the day wore him out. When they left Tripoli at sunset, everyone was so exhausted by Kamal's questions that Ibrahim had to tell him to be quiet to prevent Amir from smacking him.

The visit to Tripoli was a life-changing event for Kamal. For the rest of his life he would be drawn to the world outside of Khums. Yet he would also be rooted by the unconditional love he received during his childhood, by the supportive villagers and by having grown up in such magnificent surroundings of historical significance.

Soon after that trip to Tripoli, Kamal realized that something was not the same at home. His mother didn't laugh as she used to, and she always seemed angry with his father—and sometimes even her children. He mentioned this to his brothers only after his mother got cross with him when he came home with a larger than usual amount of candy from Renato's shop.

"Why are you taking candy from those people!" She yelled at him.

"Don't you go to that shop again, you understand?"

He had never seen his mother so angry; he was afraid that she was going to hit him. Though he did not understand what he had done wrong, he was also not stupid enough to ask or argue.

When he told his brothers about it later, they got angry at him for cutting off their candy supply. When Kamal tried to guess what was wrong with their mother, they told him to mind his own business and go to sleep. As soon as his brothers fell asleep, Kamal sneaked out of the room he shared with them and stationed himself outside his parents' bedroom. Looking through the keyhole, he saw his father sitting on the mattress. His head was hanging down and his whole body slumped. Kamal's mother was talking to him in a steady, even tone, pointing her finger at him. Her defiance startled Kamal. Straining to hear, Kamal put his ear to the keyhole and heard her say in a threatening tone, like she used with him when he was naughty:

"Do what you want, but if you marry her I will take my children back to my father's house!"

His head spinning with shock and confusion, Kamal went back to his room and sat in the dark. Though he did not understand fully what he had witnessed, he sensed that life as he knew it was shifting under his feet. All he knew for certain was that he did not want to leave Khums. He quietly went to the kitchen and packed the leftover bread from supper into a cloth bag that used to hold sugar. He then crept back to his room and threw a pair of pants and a shirt into the sack. He gathered up his blanket and quietly left the house. He knew exactly where he was going, and started walking for almost a mile, the full moon helping to guide his way.

There was a crevasse hidden somewhere among the ruins, just slightly below the ground, which ran horizontal for about five feet. It looked like someone had started digging there at one time, or perhaps it was just a vacuum below the sand. He had found it when he was playing around there one day, and had covered up the entrance with rocks to make it his own secret hiding place. He found it easily in the bright moonlight, and methodically moved the rocks aside, putting them into a pile to use later.

Dragging his bag with him, he crawled into the hole and wrapped himself up in the blanket. Scared of being on his own, but determined not to go back, Kamal began to sing the lullaby his mother would sing when she wanted them to go to sleep. His face caked with tears and sand, Kamal finally fell asleep. The sound of the Mediterranean and the gentle desert breeze finished his mother's song.

The whole family and almost everyone from the town searched for Kamal. Even when it got dark, the search continued. People were looking up and down the road towards Tripoli and Leptis Magna, along the shores, and on every farm in Khums. It was not until very late the next night when Ibrahim found his son asleep in the crevasse, the blanket tightly wrapped around his small body for protection against the cold desert air. He sank to his knees, thanking and praising his God, over and over again, in the ancient scripts of the Koran, *"Allahu Akbar!"* God is Great.

He reached into the small hole and gently dragged his son out by his legs. The sleepy little boy snuggled in his father's arms, murmuring, "I don't want to go away…I don't want my mother to leave…"

In an instant, Ibrahim knew what had happened and why Kamal had run away.

The subject of a second wife or Kamal's escapade was never mentioned again after that night. Within a few months, Renato and his family left Libya to start a new life in Italy with the money Ibrahim had generously paid to buy his store.

In school, Kamal proved to be a brilliant and diligent student, with an insatiable thirst for knowledge and information, excelling in his studies, and always at the top of his class. As a teenager, he had a passion for history and developed a remarkable gift for remembering historical dates and events. His favorite hero was Omar Mukhtar, the leader of the Libyan resistance movement who fought the Italian colonists for over twenty years. Also known as the "Lion of the Desert," Omar Mukhtar was finally captured and executed by the Italians in 1931. Kamal never got tired of hearing stories about the Libyan legend. He made his father repeat stories of battles and his capture so many times over the years that sometimes it would even exasperate Ibrahim, but he was a very patient man who believed strongly in indulging his son's insatiable curiosity.

Kamal fantasized of becoming a modern day Omar Mukhtar. Whenever he said anything of the sort to Ibrahim, his father would smile and tell him, "The most important thing is to study well and get the best education you can, you understand? We must learn to fight with our hearts and our minds, not with swords and guns."

Ibrahim repeated his mantra to Kamal over the years, knowing that of all his sons, Kamal was the one who had the mind and natural charisma to be a leader.

When he finished high school in Khums, Kamal moved to Tripoli to stay with his eldest brother Amir while attending the University of Libya. After graduating at the top of his class at the university, he was awarded a scholarship by the government to study for a master's degree at the University of Alexandria in Egypt.

Before leaving for Egypt, Kamal returned to Khums for a visit to say goodbye to his parents and younger siblings. Just before sunset on his last evening in Khums, Ibrahim invited Kamal to take a walk with him to the ruins.

As they sat on the steps of the ancient theatre, looking at the last vestiges of the sun setting over the Mediterranean, Ibrahim turned to look at the strong profile of his handsome son. Here was the man his father had envisioned him to be on the day he was born in the desert. Ibrahim prayed that Kamal's life would be as fulfilling as his own.

Affectionately, he placed his arm around his son, and in a voice holding back tears, he gently said, "Wherever you go and whatever you do, my son, don't forget that you are a Ben Ramadan from Khums."

CHAPTER 2

ESTHER

I was born in colonial Singapore to a Chinese mother and a Danish-American father, at a time when intermarriage was frowned upon by the European as well as the Chinese community. My father, Ernst Kofod, was born on Bornholm, a rocky, windswept island in the Baltic Sea, between Denmark and Sweden. As a young man, he studied engineering at the University of Copenhagen. After finishing his studies, Ernst travelled steerage class aboard the Queen Elizabeth to America to seek his fortune and to earn his citizenship. It was ten years later, after he was sent by Frick, an American company, to be general manager for South East Asia in Singapore, when he met my mother.

My mother, Lian, was born in Ipoh, on the Malayan peninsula, the daughter of a wealthy tin mine owner. When the Japanese occupied Malaya during the Second World War, her life of ease and innocence came to an abrupt end when her father was tortured to death by Japanese soldiers for insubordination. After the war, what was left of my grandfather's properties was divided between my grandmother and the Malayan Government. My grandmother spent the next two decades gambling away her inheritance, leaving very little money towards the education of her children. She thought it was unnecessary for her daughters to be educated anyways, as they were expected to marry wealthy men who would take care of them.

Like many Chinese families in Malaya, my mother's sister and her husband moved to Singapore after the war, where opportunities for business flourished. A few years later, my mother went to live with them to begin a new life, happily adapting to the exciting post-war cosmopolitan city. She was an extraordinarily beautiful and vivacious girl who possessed a captivating charm that was quite unusual for an eighteen year old.

Lian's brother-in-law was a businessman who entertained a lot, and it was at one of these dinners where Lian met Ernst. They never spoke a word to each other that first time they met, not only because Lian hardly spoke any English, but mainly because it would not have been proper for them to overtly socialize. Ernst was a young, single foreigner, and though it was permitted for her to be present with him at dinner parties in the presence of her family, it was not acceptable for her to be romantically involved with such a man. However, Ernst made an effort to ingratiate himself to be invited more often.

Before long, Ernst and Lian started seeing each other surreptitiously in restaurants, cinemas and parks—anywhere she would not be recognized. Ernst fell head over heels in love with the Chinese beauty, and desperately wanted to marry her. Despite her boldness and determination to do what she wanted, Lian would not allow him to ask for her hand in marriage from her family because she knew he would be rejected, and she was determined to marry him. She decided to elope and marry him without their permission. After the private nuptials at City Hall, the newlyweds went to her family to announce their marriage and to ask for their forgiveness and their blessings. Instead, they were told to leave, and it was many years before Lian saw her family again.

16

Ernst was doing well financially, so he was able to afford to give his new wife the type of life that she had been accustomed to. He was proud to take her into the European society of Singapore, where she quickly learned to emulate the practices and mannerisms of westerners. She charmed Ernst's friends, and astutely coached him in the customs of dealing with his Asian business associates. When he found out that Lian was pregnant, Ernst bought a lovely British colonial style bungalow on Green Lane, which they decorated with a mixture of Chinese antiques and modern Danish furniture.

From the moment I was born, I was put in the care of a nanny, who became my surrogate mother, my companion, and my caretaker for the next fifteen years. My father frequently had to travel on business throughout Asia, India, and Australia, and my mother accompanied him on most of his trips. When they were home, they were either invited out or had guests for dinners and parties. Until I was twelve years old, I usually ate alone or with my nanny.

On Sundays, my parents would take me to the Singapore Island Club to swim or bowl, followed by a *Rijstaffel* curry lunch, and on special occasions they would take me out for dinner. I looked forward to those outings, even though my mother often made me feel like an unwelcomed guest. My father, on the other hand, wanted to expose me to everything and everyone, and always made me feel he was proud of me.

As a child, I led a lonely and isolated life, except for school and in my imagination. My companions were my nanny, another servant who was in charge of taking care of the house, and the Indian gardener. My mother was very strict with me, but my nanny was always there for me whenever my mother spanked or scolded me. She would hold me in her arms and sing Chinese songs quietly in my ears, reassuring me that I was a good girl. Unfortunately, whenever my mother saw my *pawpaw*, as I called her, consoling me, she would scream at her and threaten to kick her out of the house, which she did several times. As I got older I was careful not to let my mother see me run to my *pawpaw* whenever I was upset. Except for the servants and my father, not many people were aware of my mother's unkind behavior towards me.

I attended a private Catholic school, but was excruciatingly shy because I felt different from the other girls. I was Eurasian, neither European nor Chinese, and even in the land of my birth I never felt that I belonged. It was only years later when I was able to truly find my identity in who I was rather than what I was. As a child, I was still too naïve to know the difference.

It was not until I was about eight years old when my grandmother and the rest of the family spoke to my mother again. Unfortunately, by then my mother's feelings for them had turned quite bitter and she did not encourage their participation in our lives. Since my mother's preoccupation with her social schedule did not leave her much time to spend with me, and my father was so taken by her and under her control, I learned early on to entertain myself and enjoy my own company.

I found my escape in books, content to fantasize and let my imagination travel to countries I hoped one day to see. Every night, before going to bed, I would stand at my bedroom window in our new house on the beach, and gaze at the ships sailing through the Straits of Singapore. I dreamt that one day I too would be sailing away on one of them to a distant land far away from my mother.

When I turned twelve, I was sometimes allowed to join in my parents' parties. My father considered it very important that I learned to be comfortable in the company of adults, and to be able to do so with grace and proper manners. Subsequently, I was trained from a young age to feel at ease with everyone, including professionals, diplomats, and even royalty. Over the years, many of my parents' friends became my "aunts" and "uncles," as my real ones were never invited to our house. I learned a lot about life and business listening to the adults talk, and being around such interesting and successful people was the basis of an invaluable rite of passage for me. Ironically, the only person in whose presence I felt uncomfortable was my own mother. I spent a lot of time hiding in my room so that she would not have to see me, nor I her. I was terrified of her, never knowing when she would turn on me with unfounded rage and recriminations.

As teenagers, my best friend Ei-Ling and I spent almost all our free time together. We went to the movies, shopped, played tennis, or hung out at the American Club with friends. Ei-Ling's father was President of the Chinese Chamber of Commerce and also a successful businessman, and since our parents were friends, my mother approved of our friendship. My mother was very selective with whom I socialized, wanting to be sure that they were from the "right" families. As I grew older, I became more and more embarrassed by my mother's behavior, especially the way she treated people whom she considered unworthy of her time or company. It seemed that as my father's professional and financial success increased, so did my mother's pretentiousness and arrogance

Whenever my parents discussed sending me away to boarding school in England or Switzerland, I would quietly listen to those conversations with my heart dancing and my mind filled with the dream of being free from my mother. My wish finally came true at the age of fifteen, when my parents decided to send me to a finishing school in Switzerland. My father said I would be travelling to Europe on an Italian liner, the *Asia*. I would then take the train from Genoa to Zurich, where I would be met by someone from the school.

That was the happiest day of my young life. I was thrilled to finally leave home and travel, but I was sad to leave my *pawpaw*. Neither my mother nor my grandmother liked that I called a servant *pawpaw*, which was Cantonese for "grandmother," but I refused to call her *amah*, which meant servant. It was the only thing they could not make me do.

When I saw the "Asia" on the day my parents and my nanny took me to the harbor, I couldn't wait for everyone to go home and for the beautiful white ship to start sailing. I did cry, however, when I said goodbye to my nanny. She held me in her arms, with tears streaming down her face, crying uncontrollably. She made me promise to be a good girl. I vowed that I would come back one day and take care of her. When I left for Switzerland, I did not realize that my *pawpaw* would be relieved of her job, and that I would never see her again. My separation from her left a void in my life that has never been filled. She taught me love, humility and kindness, which has helped guide me through life; she was the one who instilled in me the importance of appreciating what I have and feeling compassion for those less fortunate than me.

I was even sad to say goodbye to my mother, who was giving me last-minute orders, but I knew she was relieved to see me go. She had never said "I love you" to me, and I think I was hoping maybe she would that day, but it didn't happen. My father, on the other hand, seemed genuinely sad that I was leaving, probably wondering if I were too young to be sent so far from home.

As the departure bell rang and the three most important people in my life walked down the gangplank, I too wondered if perhaps I was too young to leave home and go alone into the unknown world outside of Singapore. But as the ship started to move from shore, I waved goodbye to my parents, my nanny, and Singapore. I had to be ready to start my new life on my own.

I was assigned a dining table with three expat bachelors who were going on home leaves.

Hans was slightly built, with baby blue eyes and sandy blond hair. He was from Aarhus in Denmark, and seemed quite fascinated with me being half Chinese and half Dane.

"You could pass for Danish," he said, after finding out my father was from Bornholm, "There are many Danes with dark hair and olive skin!"

"That's what my father told me, but I think most of them are from Greenland!" I laughed, and he thought that was funny, and liked to call me the little Eskimo after that.

Malcolm from Scotland, was more serious. From our conversations, I gathered he had worked in Hong Kong for many years and was worried he might not be reassigned back to the Far East. He was tall and thin, with very pale skin and dark hair. Of the three men, I felt the most comfortable with him as he did not flirt with me as much as the other two.

"I need to keep an eye on you," he told me when we introduced ourselves to each other. "You are too young and too pretty to be on your own!"

Alan was the more assertive and the oldest of the three, and also the best looking. I sensed that he was ready to settle down and was looking for an Asian wife, mistakenly thinking I might be a candidate for the job. He actually asked me to marry him before the journey ended, which I thought somewhat presumptuous.

They always invited me to join them in the lounge after dinner, where I would dance with all three of them as well as some of the ship's officers. I told anyone who asked that I was seventeen, and I was able to get away with that because I was quite matured for my age. I loved all the attention I was getting, a new experience for me], after years of being told by my mother that I was ugly.

On the first night at sea, my eyes were drawn like a magnet to a man who walked into the lounge. I was instantly awestruck. He was the most handsome man I had ever seen in my life: an imposingly tall, well-built Italian, with jet-black hair and eyes the color of a deep blue tempestuous sea. His crisp white uniform and officer's cap showcased a magnificent body, and he moved with purpose and the gait of authority. He was the ship's purser, and he looked like a movie star. When he looked at me, I felt as though I were a goddess he worshipped, the first man to ever make me feel that way. I fell in love for the first time in my life, and I have no doubt that I must have acted like a silly, giddy schoolgirl. I had never been kissed before, and I so wanted to be kissed for the first time by him. I danced with him every night for three weeks. His name was Virgilio.

The night before the ship docked at Genoa – our final destination and Virgilio's hometown – Virgilio escorted me back to my cabin after the band stopped playing and the lounge closed. Before we got to my cabin, he led me outside onto the deck. When we reached the railings, he told me to look at the ocean and remember that moment for the rest of my life. Taking my hand in his, he told me that he was going to marry me one day when I was ready.

"You are my Bird of Paradise," he whispered, in the most beautifully accented English I had ever heard in my life. "You are the girl I have been waiting for all my life."

I thought I was going to faint, and when he put my face in his hands I was ready, but he only kissed me on the forehead. That was as far as he went, but for me, it was the seed of many fantasies for the next few years.

Professor Buser Tochterinstitut was in Teufen, about an hour's drive away from Zurich. It was essentially a finishing school for girls from the ages of fifteen, with an emphasis on languages, literature, etiquette, and international protocol. There were a few girls from aristocratic European families, a Greek shipping magnate's daughter, a Ford heiress, daughters of CEOs, and generally girls from very wealthy backgrounds. I think my family would have been considered poor in comparison to most of those there.

My roommate was Claudia, who was from Austria. She was the only child of the chairman of one of Europe's major electronic companies, and extremely spoiled. She was blonde and beautiful, but demanding and rude. She was one of those beauties who became less beautiful as you got to know them. To the envy of many of us though, she had designer clothes sent to her at the beginning of every season from a major couture house in Paris. We would drool over the selections, which she would nonchalantly divide into keepers or send backs, all the while complaining.

The oldest girl at school was Monique, who was twenty-two. Her father was a dictator from one of the African countries, who sent her away because he did not like the man she was in love with. Instead of a seasonal shipment of *haute couture* clothes like Claudia received, a Rolls Royce and chaperone would pick Monique up at the start of each season, and a private plane would fly her from Zurich to Paris for a shopping spree. She was a tall, stunning girl who moved with fluid grace, the only black girl at school, and my first black friend. She was soft spoken, and had a dignified air about her which I admired. She spoke fluent French, but like me, was having problems with the German grammar. She told me all about the man she wanted to marry, worried that her father would throw him in prison or worse. She always looked sad and, of course, I thought I understood how she felt since I too dreamed of marrying Virgilio one day.

There were only about seventy girls at the Institut, and we were divided into five houses. Each house had its own supervisor and maid, and we all ate our meals at the main house, which was also where most of our classes were held. The school hired three chefs, so that we would be familiar with French, Italian, German, as well as Swiss cuisine. During the opera and symphony season, we would be driven to Zurich for performances, with instructions to wear black with pearls, which we called our social uniform. Then throughout the ski season we would be bussed to different ski resorts around Switzerland.

The only man at school, besides the cooks and gardeners, was the tennis instructor, Herr Faber, who was also the fencing teacher and ski instructor. He was short, stocky, and almost bald, with overly tanned and weather-beaten skin. He strutted around like a peacock, with an exaggerated stomach-in chest-out gait. We were sure that he was hired by the school because he would never be a temptation to any of us girls. He seemed to enjoy barking directions at us on the tennis court or ski slopes, and many of the girls would roll their eyes behind his back. He was quite unattractive and annoying, but I don't think he realized that, as he would flirt with us when no one was watching and make suggestive innuendoes.

By the time I left Switzerland after two years, I was able to converse comfortably in German and French, and I knew the names of every haute cuisine European dish! Teufen, in the canton of Appenzell, is one of the most beautiful areas in Switzerland, but I was desperately homesick for tropical Singapore. I missed my *pawpaw*, Singaporean food, and most of all, the freedom outside of a very restricted boarding school.

After a one-month vacation in America with my parents, I returned to Singapore for one year to finish my twelfth grade at the American School so that I would be prepared to attend college. When I got home, I often checked the *Straits Times* shipping section to see whenever the *Asia* would be coming to Singapore. I wanted so badly to see Virgilio again, but I was also too afraid of what might happen is I did. Finally, after graduation, I decided it was my last chance to see him before I left for the United States to attend college.

On the day the *Asia* sailed into Singapore Harbor, I brazenly lied to my mother that I was having tea with my best friend Ei-Ling at the Goodwood Park Hotel. To cover me, I made her swear to hang around the shopping district on Orchard Road for the whole afternoon by herself.

At precisely one hour after the ship docked, I took a taxi and went straight to the harbor. When I got to the ship, it did not take me long to find him. There he was, standing tall and erect, talking to an elderly couple in the main lobby. He was in his formal white uniform, and he still looked magnificent.

I hung back so that he would not see me, though I suspected he would not have recognized me. I was no longer the impressionable fifteen-year-old who thought wearing candy-pink lipstick was so grown up. I was now all made up, dressed in a stylishly Westernized *cheongsam* I had designed and had tailor-made for the occasion, and my hair was coiffed in the latest style. I knew I was at the age when men were starting to look at me, in part probably wondering where I came from, as I looked neither Chinese nor European.

I was seventeen years old, and perhaps more worldly, but I still had a romantic schoolgirl crush on this man about whom I knew nothing. I had no idea what I was going to say, but I think I was hoping he would take me in his arms and kiss me, at the very least. I had gone out on some dates after returning to Singapore, but found all the young men immature and boring compared to Virgilio. However, my parents would kill me if they knew what I was doing. Suddenly, I panicked and felt stupid and ashamed. I quickly left the ship and took a taxi home. That was the end of my first love, but the whole experience matured me a little emotionally as a woman. I had tasted the experience of a "love affair", real or not, and Virgilio would become the gauge I used for my future relations with men, good or bad. Such is the lesson and consequence of first love.

The other person I looked for was my *pawpaw*. I asked my mother about her one day because I wanted to see her.

"How would I know!" My mother replied caustically, as if I had bothered her by even asking.

Exasperated by my questionings, she finally yelled at me: "She's a servant! I didn't need her anymore after you left," she continued, without any regard to my feelings. "She actually had the nerve to come by one day to ask for money. I gave her ten dollars and told her not to bother me again!"

Even seeing my expression of shock, she went on to casually mention that she was probably living on Sago Lane, where old servants go to die. I was appalled by my mother's lack of compassion, and heartbroken, wondering if my old nanny was dead or alive. I was determined to go and look for her, and with only an old photograph in hand, I walked up and down the street in the old section of Chinatown, going door to door, showing her photograph and asking if anyone knew her. I did not even know her name, as I had always called her *pawpaw*.

Finally, an old servant renting bed space at one of the "death houses", as they were called, told me that she thought it was someone who had once lived there. She said the person in the photograph had gone out one day and never returned, and they assumed she died on the streets. I broke down and cried in the taxi all the way home. I never told anyone for years about what happened, and the rawness of that pain will never leave my heart. I blame my mother for her lonely and tragic death, and I have never forgiven her for what she allowed to happen to my *pawpaw*.

In the fall, I left Singapore again, this time for Hood College in Frederick, Maryland. My father loved America, and thought that it was the ideal country where his daughter with a bi-racial background would be accepted and have a sense of belonging. Besides, my father argued, the winters in Maryland were very mild. Unfortunately, my first winter at Hood was anything but. That year, Maryland experienced the worst blizzard in seventy-five years, and I was snowed in at Coblenz Hall for three days.

I was invited to spend my first Christmas in America with a college friend, Mary, and her family in Rochester, Michigan. They lived in a lovely, old colonial house, beautifully decorated for the holidays, with fireplaces in almost every room. Her parents were gracious hosts, and they set the bar for my cultural introduction to American home life. That winter in Michigan reminded me of the two very cold and damp Christmases I had spent with my father's sister in Copenhagen. Aunt Ruth was like my *pawpaw*, always showering me with love and encouragement. She taught me a lot, not just about Danish customs and food, but also about life in general. I trusted her so much I had even told her about my childish interlude with Virgilio. I loved her for not laughing. Instead, she told me wisely, "Every experience is a lesson. You are so young, Esther, why settle for one dish when you can have smorgasbord!"

After two years at Hood, I begged my parents to let me transfer to the Corcoran School of Art in Washington, D.C. to complete my degree in Liberal Arts. I did not know it then, but the move to D.C. would mark the real beginning of my life as an adult. For it was there that I met my Libyan.

CHAPTER 3

WASHINGTON, D.C.

It was in January when I moved into the International Student House in Washington, D.C. It was off Connecticut Avenue, on Eighteenth and R Street, about two blocks from Dupont Circle. It was a beautiful old English Tudor building on a quiet side street, which housed about thirty students from all over the world. After living two years in Frederick, it was exciting to be in a city again. I was looking forward to everything the nation's capital had to offer, and knew that I would thrive in the diversity of cultures, reminiscent of Singapore.

The International Student House, affectionately called the I-House, or just the House, was coincidentally right across from the Singapore Embassy. Later, after I had met Ambassador Monteiro, we would wave to each other in the mornings, as my bedroom was directly across from his office. It made me feel secure knowing that the Singapore Ambassador to the United States was checking in on me daily...

I was told that my roommates were from El Salvador and Iran, but they were not there when I arrived. The spacious corner suite we shared overlooked the courtyard on one side and the street on the other. The reception area on the main floor was off a wide marble staircase leading to a huge ballroom on the second floor, complete with an oversized

fireplace and a large minstrel gallery. I was informed by
a student receptionist when I arrived, that a dance was
held there every Friday night and a tea party every Sunday
afternoon.

After the long flight from Singapore via San Francisco, I
hastily unpacked. Even though I was exhausted, I wanted to
walk around and explore my new neighborhood before tea.
It was a cold day, but the sun was strong and soon warmed the
brisk mid-afternoon air. I had visited D.C. several times when
I was at Hood and was, therefore, somewhat familiar with the
city. I found a little Greek café off Connecticut Avenue and
bought a gyro, taking it to eat on a bench in Dupont Circle.

It was fun watching the people sitting around the foun-
tain and relaxing on benches. There were hippies, foreigners, and people watchers like myself, a veritable hodgepodge
of ages, cultures and sub-cultures. It was a new scene for me,
and I drank it all in with pleasure. After finishing my lunch,
I decided to go back to unpack, freshen up for tea and
hopefully make some new friends.

I had designed many of my new outfits myself, which I
had made by my favorite tailor in Singapore, and I was keen
to start wearing them. For my first event, I picked a simple
black and red raw silk dress that I matched with patent-
leather black heels and the opera-length strand of Mikimoto
pearls my parents had given me for my eighteenth birthday.

When I walked downstairs to the ballroom, it was already
crowded with faces and accents from many different countries. The sound of laughter mixed with classical music in
the background, giving the grand room a delicious air of
revelry. I immediately felt at ease and excited to be there.

I looked around before making my way over to a table where an elaborate silver Samovar tea service was set up, accompanied by silver trays of biscuits and pastries. After getting a cup of tea and settling for an interesting looking pastry, I picked an empty chair by the window where I could observe everyone in the room. Some of the students were dressed in their national costumes, therefore easily identifiable, and the atmosphere was lively. Fascinated, I got lost in trying to guess what each person was like, where they were from and what they were doing in the capital of the United States. In the middle of my day dreaming, I was interrupted by a familiar accent.

"Hello!" A dignified-looking Indian man dressed in a suit came up to me with his hand outstretched. He was dark, ruggedly handsome, with bright grey eyes that looked right into mine.

"My name is Raj," he drawled in a deep, low voice.

He spoke with a distinctively Americanized Indian accent and was obviously very charming and personable. I shook his hand, introducing myself,

"Hello Raj, nice to meet you. My name is Esther Kofod, and I'm from Singapore!"

"Singapore, eh?" he confirmed, nodding his head, "I hear it's a beautiful country!"

It was refreshing for me to talk with someone who had even heard of Singapore. When I was in Frederick most people thought Singapore was in China. One of the janitors even asked if we used furniture there, as he had heard people in China sat on floors, obviously confusing China with Japan.

Raj asked me a lot of questions about myself, and told me all about the I-House and some of the people who lived there. It was an enlightening introduction to my new home by someone who seemed to know everyone and everything. Over the course of the next few months, Raj became my friend and sometimes protector, even though he didn't live there, as he had graduated and was working at the World Bank.

While we were conversing, several other people came by to introduce themselves until I found myself in the middle of a large group. They all seemed interested in a new-comer, and everyone was very friendly. I instinctively knew that I had found my niche at the International Student House.

"I understand that there is usually a chess game here on Sundays?" I asked Folke, a burly, blond Swede with eyes the color of the stormy Baltic Sea and an unruly beard. His accent reminded me of my Aunt Ruth and Denmark. I found out later that he was quite a favorite with the girls, who were attracted to his rugged good looks. He was the only guy there that afternoon who looked unkempt, like a hippie, and I was a little wary of the way he kept staring at me.

"Oh yes," he answered. "It should be starting soon. Do you play?"

"I used to," I said. "But not very well!"

"Too bad I don't. I'd love to play with you…" I ignored his innuendo.

"Well," cautioned Folke, "there's a guy here from Russia who's very good. No one has beaten him. He comes here every Sunday to play, and he always wins. The rumor is that he is an amateur champion."

"Maybe I'd better start with the worst player!" I joked.

"That's me!" volunteered Raj jovially. "Come, let's go play a game together."

I followed Raj to an area by the large stained-glass windows overlooking the street, where a few tables were laid out for chess, most of them already occupied. I quickly surmised that it was a popular game at the House. After a few moves, I realized that I could easily beat Raj; when I did, he was a good sport about it. I went on to play another game with a Ceylonese diplomat, who proved a little more challenging.

As I looked around at the other tables, I realized that I was the only girl playing chess. By the time the tea was put away, I had made friends with many of the people who lived in the House, as well as some who didn't.

Before leaving, I had also met my roommates, both of whom seemed very nice. Leticia was an attractive, talkative girl from El Salvador who was studying International Law at American University, and Armineh was the daughter of an orthopedic surgeon from Teheran, who was going to study medicine at George Washington University.

I went back to the Great Room for tea every Sunday, mostly to play chess, and sometimes for the dances on Friday nights. The International House soon became a large part of my social life as well as my home away from home. I was happy there, growing close to a dynamic group of intelligent and venturesome friends. We would go out for dinners and parties all over the city, usually ending up in someone's room, smoking cigarettes, drinking cheap wine, and talking about every subject under the sun, which somehow always led to intense political debates and arguments.

No matter how vocal anyone got, the nights always ended in laughter, with hugs and kisses all around as we stumbled, exhausted, to our respective rooms in the early dawn. Being alcohol intolerant, I was always the only sober one in the group and would tease the others the next day about how silly they had behaved the night before.

It was the chess games, however, that became my obsession.

"Do you know," Raj told me one day, "you're the only girl playing chess here?"

"I know…"

"I think all the boys want to learn to play chess now so they can play with you." He was always teasing me.

Whenever I played, a crowd would congregate around me, just as they did around "The Russian" who, I was told, was unbeatable. He and I never talked, but we would smile at each other whenever our eyes met. One time he gestured for me to play him, but I politely shook my head and rolled my eyes.

I noticed one day that a very interesting and attractive man was often watching me play chess. He was of above average height, with a sturdy well-proportioned body, and light skinned, with slightly wavy black hair framing features so chiseled they reminded me of an ancient Roman sculpture. What I noticed most were his luscious lips, which seemed to be ever on the verge of a smile, with an expression hinting of a man who had seen pain, but also much pleasure. However, it was his lingering dark eyes

36

and detached attitude I found most captivating. He never spoke to me, yet he didn't break eye contact when our eyes met. I would quickly disengage so that he wouldn't think I was interested. I got the impression that he very much wanted to speak to me, but was too proud or maybe not sure if he should. He seemed to only talk to a few of the other men there, even though many of the girls vied for his attention.

I suspected he was either from southern Europe or the Middle East, somewhere in the Mediterranean. He was always well dressed, usually in suits and ties. Most of the foreign men there were naturally chivalrous and solicitous of the girls, always flirting and heaping compliments, all in fun and generally quite harmless. This one, however, was very aloof. I was unsure whether he thought himself too good, or not good enough, to challenge me in chess, as he seemed to show a great interest in my games. I surmised that he was a student who lived at the house, and not a visitor, even though he seldom had his meals there. I decided to wait and see if he would make the first move. He was the first man I felt any attraction to since Virgilio, and I was curious about him.

One Sunday, while I was playing chess, the Russian came over and silently watched. After the game was over he congratulated me on my win and introduced himself as Ivan.

"You're a very good player," he said, smiling at me with an expression I could not quite decipher.

Looking up at him, I wondered if he were mocking me.

"I'm serious!" He laughed when he saw the skeptical look on my face.

"I'd very much like to play with you sometime."

"Really?" I felt honored. "That would be very nice for me, but I'm afraid it wouldn't be much fun for you."

I was intrigued and flattered, but did not want to be made a fool of.

"Look, the best way to learn is always to play someone better than you, no? I'm usually here during the week after four. Why don't you come by sometime and we can play without so many people around."

"Okay, I will!" The Russian took my hand and made a big show of kissing it before walking away. Everyone around started laughing and teasing me.

"Better watch out for him, Esther," Raj teased. "I think I'd better chaperone you!"

The lessons started, and Ivan proved himself to be a serious and excellent teacher. During our chess sessions, he told me that he was married, had two children, and that his family was in Moscow. He was working on his PhD in education at American University and planned to go back to Moscow after he graduated. As was rumored, he had won several minor chess amateur championship games in his country.

I learned a lot from him and soon we became friends as well as regular chess partners. Although he was far superior to me, I became in time, and with his coaching, what he would say was his most formidable opponent at the House. Whenever Ivan and I played on Sundays, people would gather around to watch. Sometimes our games would last for two hours, but I would always be beaten in the end.

One Sunday, while Ivan and I were engrossed in an intense game, I realized to my surprise that I was holding my own against him quite well. Then, he made a move that gave me an excellent opportunity to trap his queen. After several minutes of careful contemplation, I made what I thought was possibly a brilliant move.

"I wouldn't do that if I were you!" Someone behind me ventured, confidently but almost inaudibly.

I ignored him, but knew who it was without looking up. It was the handsome stranger who never talked to me, but always seemed to be around.

A few minutes later, Ivan was trapped.

I was elated! I had won my first game against him. Ivan conceded like a proud father, and our spectators started clapping. It was the first and only time I won a game against Ivan. I suspected that he lost only because he felt sorry for me and purposely let his guard down, but I was happy nevertheless, and blushed with pride.

I looked around to find him, but my handsome stranger was gone. I wondered if he had felt embarrassed for the mistaken assessment of my move. I hoped not.

Through a mutual friend, I met Steve, an international attorney from California. He was amusing to be around because he was funny and told great stories. He also took me to the best restaurants in town, since we shared the same passion for good food. The last woman he had dated was "Miss Peru," which I told him I found a little intimidating. He then said something to me I never forgot, "Esther, there are beautiful women on every street corner. What you have is rare, so don't compare yourself to them."

I did not understand nor ask him what he meant by "rare" as I was never comfortable with compliments, but I felt badly when I saw his handsome, boyish face look hurt that I should think him so shallow. I've never forgotten what he said and, thanks to him, I never compared myself to another woman again.

Steve was the only man I dated who accepted me unconditionally, but my feelings for him were more like those for a friend. Washington D.C. in the seventies was like a candy store for young single women. Many of the men were exciting and interesting, but there always seemed to be a shortage of eligible women. I did not want to date anyone exclusively because I think I was making up for the years I did not date at Hood. The guys I met there were either too immature or too dull.

Another man I dated was Peter, a lobbyist for the Ford Motor Company. He was a little wild, but he was respectful of my feelings, even when he didn't understand or agree. One night, he drove his brand new custom built Mustang over 100 miles an hour speeding down Massachusetts Avenue, presumably to impress me. I was so angry that I told him I would never talk to him if he did that again. He would tell me that I was the most difficult girl he had ever dated, and he didn't understand why he kept coming back to me, since I wouldn't even have sex with him. Dating him was a little bit of a struggle at times, as he was not as understanding or as accommodating of the culture I came from as Steve.

It was a job juggling dates, much less having to go to classes every day. My social life was so busy that school became a duty. Luckily I was majoring in art and not something that required extensive studying.

Like a big brother, Raj tried to remind me to be careful, constantly warning me not to go anywhere by myself. "D.C.

is a dangerous city," he kept telling me, "Don't go anywhere by yourself at night. Call me if you have to go somewhere by yourself, okay?"

But of course I didn't. One night, as I was walking to a girlfriend's apartment for dinner, only one block away from the House, I had a feeling that I was being followed. When I turned around, a young black boy, who couldn't have been more than sixteen, grabbed me by my coat and tried to force me behind some bushes.

All I could think about was that I would rather die than be raped, so I fought him back like a wild animal, going for his eyes. When he reached into his jacket, and I saw a flash of metal in his pocket, I was sure I was going to die.

Screaming as loudly as I could and fighting for my life, I saw a group of four people across the road pretending they didn't see or hear me. They obviously did not want to get involved. Whether it was their presence or my attempt at trying to gouge out his eyes, my attacker fled.

I ran as fast as I could back to the House, banging on the glass door for help. The few students loitering around the reception desk thought I was kidding until they saw I was crying. They quickly ran to open the door for me, and after breathlessly gasping out what happened, three of the men ran out into the street to look for my attacker, without any luck.

A police report was filed, and a few days later a detective came by the House to ask me if the man in a photo he showed me was the same one who attacked me. It was. The officer told me that the seventeen-year-old boy had stabbed a ninety-two-year old man to death at a bus stop and stolen his ring and a few dollars. The police found the ring in the boy's possession when he was apprehended.

That next night, I related to Steve the events of the past few days while we were having dinner at an Italian restaurant near the House. When we left the restaurant after dinner, he drew me into the alcove of a shop doorway, shielding me from the sidewalk. I was wondering what he was doing when I saw him take something out of his jacket. It was a handgun. He had apparently been carrying one around without my knowledge.

"Esther, please take this, and next time just shoot."

"I promise I will defend you in court if anything happens, sweetheart."

He tried to convince me to take his gun, but I refused. The thought of carrying a gun around in my bag was too alien and frightening. I resolved to be more careful in the future and never venture out on my own again at night.

My resolution wasn't enough to keep me out of harm's way. I had another bad experience, this time at 3 p.m. in broad daylight. I was stopped by two men who were trying to drag me into a car while I was walking home from school, a block from Dupont Circle. The worst part was that as they were forcing me into a car, a police car slowly drove by without stopping. I cannot imagine how the officer in the patrol car could have thought we were friends kidding around.

After I managed to break loose and run into the Iraqi Interest Section building nearby, the same cop came in asking me if I was alright. I was so angry I told him to go to hell, and instead let one of the consular members drive me back to the House.

D.C. was a great city for a young girl in those days, but it was also dangerous. After the assassination of Martin Luther King in April 1968, there was a lot of anger and hatred, and often those feelings were badly channeled. One morning, my Swedish girlfriend arrived in class with blood all over her face.

"What happened, Ula?" We were all aghast, and rushed to help her.

"A man came up to me and asked for a kiss," she was shaking so bad she could hardly talk.

"When I told him to go away, he pushed me to the ground and started slapping me. He said I was prejudiced…"

I cannot explain why, but that probably frightened me more than being forced into a car. I quickly learned to find ways of protecting myself. I was never alone after dark, and even when walking alone on the city streets in the day, I tried to walk with other people. Luckily, living with a houseful of men, I was never at a loss for escorts when necessary.

As I was walking past the game room one afternoon, a Ping-Pong ball flew out, bouncing near my foot. I picked it up, just as the man who had been watching me play chess every Sunday came out to retrieve it. He was without a jacket, his tie was loosened, and his shirt-sleeves were rolled up. I inwardly gasped at how handsome he looked. I hoped my eyes did not betray me.

As I handed the ball to him, he thanked me and introduced himself. He said his name was Kamal Ben Ramadan and added that he knew mine. "You're Esther, the girl who plays chess and beats all the boys," he said with a cheeky smile.

I nodded and smiled back at him, at a loss for words and blushing. I quickly moved on. For some inexplicable reason, my heart was beating a little faster, and my head felt a little lighter.

After that encounter, I started to see more of him. He was the only man around who made my heart skip a beat. Most of the other guys at the House were like brothers, and I had decided when I moved in not to date anyone who lived there.

I began to notice that whenever I came home from a date, Kamal seemed to be around the reception desk, regardless of the time, with other students or alone. He never stayed to say anything to me, but when he saw me coming he would usually just walk away.

Peter apparently noticed it too, because he asked if Kamal was bothering me.

"No! Of course not! Why?" I asked, pretending I didn't know what he was talking about.

"Honey, every time I've brought you home, he's there, looking at me like I've done something wrong. I'm tempted to ask him what the hell his problem is."

Peter took me to some of the best parties in town, where I met celebrities like Helen Hayes, Chief Justice Warren Burger, ambassadors and senators. It was fun, but Peter was starting to get too pushy. After that night I decided to stop going out with him. Part of it was his attitude towards Kamal. It was difficult for a man like Peter to understand that someone like Kamal or Raj would be protective of a girl they considered their friend, especially someone like me from a more traditional background.

There was a group of us who always went out together at least once or twice a week and, before long, Kamal joined our group. I learned that he was from a town in Libya called

Khums, and though I had traveled extensively, I had never met a Libyan before. In fact, I had not even heard of Libya before I met him. He started to relax a bit more while he was around me, and before long we became friends.

There were only two girls in our circle of close friends, Nadia and I, so we got a lot of attention from the guys in our group, who all teased us mercilessly. Nadia, a beautiful Jordanian, was quiet and ladylike until she got drawn into a controversial subject. She would then charge like a lioness. Then of course, there was Raj, who was always everywhere and knew everyone. Martin, who was from Vancouver, was the most vocal, lively, and easy-going in the group. He was always the one to initiate doing anything, anytime, and any-where. Folke, who was from Stockholm, was the most flirta-tious and cynical, always mocking me about being so uptight about sex because I wouldn't do it with him! He seemed to assume all the girls were after him. And Josh, who was Jewish, always ended up getting into hot political debates about the Arab/Israeli situation with Martin and Nadia.

Adel was a gifted Palestinian artist and poet who was study-ing art at the Corcoran. He had also studied in Rome and the Sorbonne in Paris. Serious and hardworking, Adel was the philosopher of the group and usually the mediator and voice of reason. I think he really must have liked me, because when I left D.C. he gave me two of his beautiful water colors. And there was Venancio, the best dancer I had ever danced with. I could have danced with him all night and sometimes did. He was from Angola, black as night, charismatic, sophisticated, and the most charming of the whole group.

It didn't take long for Kamal to naturally and fluidly blend into the group, or for him to be accepted. I don't think he had danced much before, but he was a fast learner and he moved with soul. When we danced, he made me feel like I was the only one in the room. He told me while we were dancing one time that I danced like Pan.

"Peter Pan?" I asked, puzzled.

"No, like a tree," he answered, laughing at me.

It still didn't sound good until I found out he meant like a willow tree swaying in the wind. That was my first compliment from Kamal.

He told me all about his family in Libya, and how much he missed them. He had four sisters and three brothers and, from the way he talked about them, they were all very close.

"My sisters all live at home. My parents had four boys before they had a girl. You would like them, Esther, and I know they would love you!"

I envied anyone who had a sibling, much less seven loving ones. His eyes softened whenever he spoke of his parents, and I could tell how much he loved and respected them.

"You are so fortunate to have such a loving family. I always wished I had a sister or a brother." I wistfully added.

From everything he told me, I didn't think he would have understood how different my mother was from his.

Everyone was forced to get on the dance floor on Friday nights at the International House, the good, the bad and the atrocious. The worst dancer was an Afghani, a gigantic man who didn't seem to understand a word of English, who would dance with any girl he could. He would grab his victim and stomp, march, and throw her around the dance floor. We suspected he had never been around women in his life, except for the women in his immediate family, of course. All the girls would quickly go in the opposite direction when they saw him coming towards them. He once practically threw me across the dance floor, but luckily someone stopped me from falling.

Even when he was not dancing with me, Kamal always stood close by on the sidelines watching. Except for Nadia, he never asked anyone else to dance.

My time in Washington was the most carefree and exciting period I had ever known because for the first time in my life I had the freedom to be me.

Kamal invited me out several times, but I always asked if I could bring Nadia with me. I think it was because I did not trust us to be alone together. Nadia understood, and agreed to accompany me on those dinners. Kamal was very amiable about it; he thought it was nice that she was looking out for me. Whenever he invited me out, he would naturally assume that Nadia would be joining us. But, after a few weeks the situation changed.

I came home one night from dinner with Steve, and just as he was giving me a quick goodnight peck on the lips, I noticed Kamal sitting at the reception desk. Steve saw him too, seemed a little annoyed, and made a comment about always seeing Kamal hanging around.

"He's just looking out for Nadia and me." I said defensively, hoping Steve wouldn't go up to him and say something rude.

After he left, I went into the House, feeling somewhat unsettled by Steve's reaction, especially since he was right.

Kamal was still sitting at the desk when I stepped into the reception hall but he did not look up at me.

"Hi, Kamal!" I ventured hesitantly, for some reason feeling guilty.

He didn't answer or even bother to look up, so I walked on towards the stairs, wondering why he was being so rude.

"Esther!" he called after me, "I want to talk to you!"

The commanding tone of his voice surprised me because it sounded almost angry. I didn't understand why, since I was not his girlfriend, and had never even gone out on a date alone with him.

I turned around, but stood still, forcing him to get up and come to me.

"What's wrong?" I asked, somewhat puzzled, but suspecting it had to do with Steve.

He gestured for me to follow him into the empty dining room next to where we were standing and held out a chair for me to sit down. He positioned himself on another chair across the table from me and stared at me for what seemed like a long time, enough for me to start uneasily shifting in my seat.

He finally broke the awkward silence with a loud sigh, as I nervously waited.

"For two months now, I have seen you going out with different men, including me. I have to ask you something. Are you serious with any one of them?"

I had been strictly raised not to lie, to give direct answers. Though what he was asking me was not his business, the fact that he dared to ask deserved an answer. I was starting to suspect what he was getting at.

"No, not at all, I'm just friends with them. Why are you asking me this?" I was annoyed.

48

I was having the time of my life dating and, though I could have had my pick of any of the guys I wanted, I was not ready to be tied down to anyone. The only way I had been able to handle dating five different men was not getting romantically involved. I had been successful in keeping them from trying to seduce me; in some ways it was easy because they perceived me as naïve and inexperienced—which I was—and they didn't want to scare me off.

"Is there anything going on between you and any of them?"

I knew exactly what he meant.

"Of course not!" I was appalled that he should think that, and even had the nerve to ask it so blatantly.

"Not even your lawyer boyfriend?"

He was pushing me, and I was beginning to think he was getting a little too personal, but somehow I was not angry. I was beginning to actually like it. He was jealous!

I did not consider Steve my "boyfriend," regardless of what he or anyone else may have thought. I enjoyed his company and was flattered that he was so attentive and patient, but I did not feel the passion, the heart pumping and the light headedness that I had felt only once before in my life – and wanted again. I didn't want to settle for less… It was obvious that Kamal was jealous, and for some reason it felt good to me…it made my heart beat faster!

"No! Why are you asking me these questions?" I wanted him to tell me exactly what was on his mind.

He looked straight into my eyes for a long time before answering.

"I am not sharing you with anyone. You have to decide whether you want to go out with me or with them. I don't want the girl I have chosen to be dating other men. Is that so difficult to understand?"

He said all this in a very calm, matter-of-fact voice, never taking his eyes off me. This was a side of Kamal that I suspected existed, but never experienced. I found his passion very exciting, and I think I was beginning to understand why.

"I'll think about it," I answered demurely, my heart and my head pounding, hoping he couldn't hear them.

It suddenly dawned on me that the reason I never took any of the other men seriously was because I had a very strong attraction for this man. I could have had almost any man around, but here I was, gravitating towards someone who came from a country I had never even heard of until recently, a Muslim, and someone who was obviously quite controlling. Still, he exuded self-confidence, gentleness, charm, and now, a directness that was very appealing.

"Good night." I said softly, not trusting myself to say anything more as I got up to go my room. Luckily, he didn't say another word.

After I got into bed that night, all I could think of was him and the way he looked at me, the sound of his voice and most of all, how fast my heart was beating.

I couldn't sleep that night and went to get my atlas. I quietly slipped into the bathroom to look up Libya on the map. I had been to Egypt and Lebanon, but knew nothing about Libya. While my roommates slept, I studied the map of Libya, looking for Khums. I had so many questions I now wanted to ask.

Over the next couple of weeks, I started dating less and noticed that Kamal was hanging around the House even more. Before I knew it, he was taking Nadia and me out to dinner almost every night.

"Why all the dinners out?" I asked.

"Because I have to fatten you up," he answered, explaining that because I was skinny, without much "meat" on my body, I would not fetch much of a dowry in Libya! He had a great sense of humor and loved to tease me, which always made me laugh.

Kamal finally asked me on a first date. Alone.

"Do you trust me enough now to go out with me by yourself?"

"Yes," I answered, "I do."

"Good," he said with a laugh. "I'm going broke, feeding two hungry girls!"

I had no idea what I was getting into, and really didn't care. I had never felt the way I felt with any man before, and I liked it...very much.

CHAPTER 4

THE JOURNEY BEGINS

My life changed the day I agreed to go out with Kamal alone. It was as though something inside me had always known I would no longer have control of myself and my feelings once I gave in to him.

On our first date, he waited for me by the reception desk, all dressed up in an elegant suit and tie, looking a little nervous but excited. I wore a simple fuchsia Thai silk dress I had designed myself and a fuchsia cashmere coat I had bought in Hong Kong to go with it. I set it all off with a pair of elaborate gold dangling earrings I had bought in Beirut.

"You're beautiful," Kamal whispered as he was helping me with my coat. "You look like an Arab princess tonight."

Always embarrassed with receiving compliments, I shyly smiled at him.

We went to the Calvert Café, a very nice Lebanese restaurant run by a lady known as Mama Ayesha. As soon as he walked in, Kamal was warmly welcomed by the maître d' who immediately seated us. Soon after, Mama Ayesha herself came to greet us, fondly hugging and kissing Kamal. When he introduced me, she reached out to kiss me on both cheeks and turned to say something to Kamal, all the while holding my hand. She kept looking at me, beaming; I wondered what they were talking about. I could see that Kamal looked embarrassed, so after she left I asked him what she had said.

"I don't think I should translate it." He smiled at me.

"Please…." I persisted.

"I cannot refuse those eyes anything," he whispered.

Looking deep into my eyes, Kamal reached for my hand and brought it to his lips, slowly kissing it softly. That was the first time he kissed me.

"She said you're beautiful, and that you must be very special, because you're the first girl I've ever brought here." He said it with a broad smile, knowing that it would please me to hear that.

Kamal ordered a variety of dishes from the menu, and we enjoyed our first dinner alone. On my way to college at Hood, I had spent one month in Lebanon with Sameera, whom I had met on the *Asia,* and had become quite fond of Lebanese cuisine, which delighted Kamal. He wanted to be sure I tried everything. He kept feeding me from his plate, which I found very sensual.

After dessert and Arabic coffee, we were both so full that we decided to walk back to the House instead of taking a cab. We had so much to talk about that it didn't matter that it was a long walk. Before I realized it, we'd ended up by the Reflecting Pool, between the Lincoln and Washington Memorials.

In a secluded spot, under the shadow of a majestic flowering cherry blossom tree, Kamal very gently and very slowly took me in his arms and kissed me—passionately but patiently, savoring every second. I wanted to live in that moment forever.

"I've been waiting to do that for months," he whispered into my hair, breathing in my scent.

It felt so good, and right, like something I had been waiting for all my life.

We walked home without another word, holding hands, both of us realizing that something extraordinary had just happened. After that kiss, I had no more desire to be with any other man except him.

Kamal had a great sense of humor, and was indulgent. He seemed agreeable to doing whatever I wanted. He was charming, engaging, and well read. His knowledge of history and understanding of international current affairs were remarkable. He was deeply passionate about politics, and through him I became more interested in and understood more about the volatile situation in the Middle East.

We became inseparable after our first date. He was an extremely romantic and attentive suitor, completely unabashed about his feelings for me. Every day he brought me a gift: flowers, stuffed animals, accessories, sometimes a poem he had written specially for me. A few times he surprised me with pastries to "fatten" me up, as he liked to say. He also loved to buy me different perfumes, but his favorite on me was *Miss Dior*. Everything he gave me was special, because I knew he put thought into everything he did.

Instead of calling, Kamal would often go on the street and throw pennies at my window so he could see me and talk to me that way, in person. Before long, the flowerbed below my window was littered with pennies. Our friends soon started calling him the Libyan Romeo, which did not bother him in the least.

The first and only fight we had in D.C. started when a friend told me she had seen Kamal having lunch with a girl at the University. When I asked Kamal who it was, he got upset that someone would tell me about something "so silly".

"All I want to know is who she is." I insisted.

"She's not important, Esther. She's just someone I know at GW."

"So what's her name?"

"What's more important is who would tell you about it, knowing it might hurt your feelings."

"If you know it might hurt my feelings, then you shouldn't have lunch with a girl without telling me!" I was getting exasperated with him withholding a simple answer from me. "I want to hear it from you, not someone else!"

It would have ended if he had just told me who it was, but he wouldn't, so I refused to talk to him.

After the first day of silence, he wrote me a letter apologizing for the way he had behaved, and told me who it was and the circumstances of the lunch. I was still upset, so I ignored him. On the second day, he sent me a dozen red roses, but I was too proud to give in, even though I missed him. On the third day, he paid an old violinist he found at Dupont Circle to play music under my window. I finally had to beg Kamal to ask him to stop playing because of the scene it was creating on the sidewalk. Before acquiescing, he made me say in front of all our friends who had gathered around him, laughing, that I forgave him, and I did.

Because he was so handsome and charming, women gravitated to Kamal, but he never again gave me cause to be jealous. On the contrary, he would always make a point of reassuring me, like a mantra: "God has not created a woman better than you. You are his gift to me, you are my Stora."

Stora. He gave me this name as we were walking back from dinner in Georgetown. He asked me to look up at the sky, at the single star brightly shining alone.

56

"You are that star, the only star in my sky," he told me very seriously, pointing with his arm and finger stretched towards the sky.

"You are, and always will be my Stora..."

Our next few months together were like a dream. It was easy to fall in love with him, and I was in love for the first time in my life. It was nothing like my infatuation with Virgilio, only a silly girl's fantasy. With Kamal, it was wonderful waking up every morning knowing I was going to be with him that day and going to bed thinking over the day we had shared. Because he knew how much I loved to dance, he would take me dancing every Saturday night, usually with a group of friends. We would then all end up in the wee hours at *Nino's,* our favorite late-night Italian restaurant. On weekends we would go to museums, art galleries, watch the latest foreign films, or sometimes go on trips outside of Washington. There was always so much happening in the Capitol that we had to allot ourselves time to study.

Kamal was taking courses at Georgetown, but he was planning to go to Florida State University in the fall to start work on another master's and then a doctorate in political science.

"Stora, please go with me to Florida..." He kept begging me every day.

I had not decided what I was going to do or where I was going to go after graduation, but following Kamal to Florida was out of the question. My cultural upbringing was too ingrained in me to run off with him, and the thought of my mother finding out was quite terrifying. I was also not yet ready to return to Singapore, as expected by my parents. I thought about applying to Pan American, which was one of the most prestigious airlines in the world. Flying around for a year or two seemed like a fun thing to do, and maybe it would get the travelling bug out of my system before settling down. On an impulse, I sent in a stewardess application to Pan American World Airways without telling anyone, including Kamal. I had a feeling he would not have approved, and I didn't want to be discouraged.

To my surprise, I heard back from them quickly; they would be conducting interviews in D.C. in two weeks and invited me to come for one. I still didn't tell Kamal, in case I was rejected, and it became a non-issue.

When I went to the Pan Am interview at the Willard Hotel near the White House, there were about two hundred girls there, and I was so disillusioned that I almost left because I knew there were only four positions available. When my turn came, I was interviewed by several different people, weighed, measured, and asked many questions. I was there a lot longer than I had expected. After almost three hours of testing, I was sent to an empty room and told to wait. Within fifteen minutes, a tall, distinguished-looking black man, immaculately dressed in the Pan American uniform, came into the room. After introducing himself, we talked for a little while. Without warning, he suddenly offered me an outstretched hand and said,

"Welcome Aboard!"

I wasn't sure what he meant at first, but he proceeded to congratulate me and told me that I had been accepted to join Pan American. He said that after my training in Miami I would be based in Honolulu and that because of the five languages I spoke, I would be on the coveted round-the-world route.

I was totally taken by surprise, not just by getting my first job, but by the speed with which it happened. I was in such a confused and elated state after leaving that I decided to go somewhere for tea and do some serious thinking. I had just been accepted for a dream job, and if it weren't for Kamal I would have been ecstatic. Instead, I felt conflicted, not sure what to do or where to go.

I went to *Crystal City*, which was close to the House, and found a seat in the far back corner of the long room. My friends and I had spent many happy hours in this place, and I was already starting to miss it. I knew that very soon this carefree life in Washington was going to come to an end. No more Embassy parties, dancing at the *Junkanoo*, boisterous Greek belly-dancing dinners at *Astor*, and late-night debates. The hundreds of pennies that Kamal threw at my window to "call" me would be buried deep into the flowerbed below, and my whirlwind courtship with a handsome Libyan would become a beautiful memory.

For some reason, I thought of my friend, Faribuz. Tall, skinny and very elegant, Fari, as he liked to be called, came from an aristocratic family in Teheran, and was very conscious of his appearance and manners, which were flawless. We suspected he was gay, but no one cared because he was so nice and great fun to be around. Two nights before, he had asked if I would like to go with him to a dinner party at the Persian Embassy for the Shah of Iran.

"Of course I would! But why me?" I asked suspiciously, even though I was happily surprised.

"Because you're beautiful, the best dresser I know, and my classiest friend! I don't want to be embarrassed in front of the Shah and everyone at the embassy." He explained it as a matter of fact.

"Thank you, I would love to, and I will wear my prettiest dress for you!"

That was such a compliment, coming from him, and I wanted to meet the Shah and his beautiful wife, Queen Farah Diba. I was quite excited actually, until I told Kamal about it.

His response was swift.

"Absolutely not!"

I thought I was telling him, not asking him!

"It is an insult to me for Faribuz to invite you!" He was clearly upset, but I was not used to being told what to do by any man except my father.

It was the first real argument Kamal and I ever had. After explaining his cultural sensitivities to me I understood, even though I still wanted to go.

In the end I gave in and told Faribuz I couldn't go with him to the dinner and why.

"Oh, I see – he's jealous!" Fari stated simply, grinning.

What I gleaned from that incident was my own understanding and respect of cultural restrictions from growing up in a multi-cultural society. I accepted Kamal's explanation because I understood and respected his culture, his values and principles, but I seriously questioned in my heart whether they were something I could live with forever...

As I sat in a dark corner of the restaurant by myself sipping tea, I knew I was coming to a crossroad. If I joined Pam Am, I might never see Kamal again, but then maybe what we had was just for now, in this exciting city that brought us together. Even if we were to get serious, I didn't really know what Libya was like. I had been to Lebanon and Egypt, but I knew enough from what Kamal had told me that Libya was not the same. Of course in his opinion it was better, but in the opinion of my other Arab friends it was a very conservative society where women were second-class citizens.

I decided that the best thing to do was accept the position with Pan Am and see what happened. In any case, Kamal would be leaving for Florida, and I would be graduating from George Washington in a couple of months. I was not ready to go back to Singapore, so Honolulu would be the perfect choice. My mind made up, I resolved to tell Kamal and my parents soon. I tried not to think of the distance between Honolulu and Tallahassee.

That night, Kamal and I went to a quiet little French bistro in Georgetown for dinner, and he told me that he had talked to one of his brothers about me. He said that his brother was worried that he was falling in love with me, but Kamal told him it was too late. I was somewhat surprised that he had told someone in his family about me. I had not mentioned him to my parents because I knew they would probably disapprove of me dating a Muslim and an Arab. I decided to wait another day to tell him about Pan Am.

I summoned the courage to tell him about it the next day, when we were having lunch between classes at our favorite little Chinese restaurant on M Street. After listening without saying a word, I could see that he was very upset. I was somewhat surprised at his reaction and felt guilty, so I explained my reasons as best I could.

When I stopped talking, he didn't say a word. He just looked at me for a very long time, until he finally reached for my hand across the table and kissed it before he started, the way he always did when he had something special to tell me.

"Stora," Kamal loved calling me that, "I am not just another one of your admirers, and I am not playing games. If you don't know by now how much I am in love with you,

61

then you don't feel the same way I do." He was speaking softly, his voice breaking.

I was at a loss for words. I was overjoyed to hear what he said, because I believed what he was telling me, and I felt the same for him. I just didn't know what I was supposed to do. Though it was not a formal proposal, it was a suggestion of sorts. He had told me many times that he loved me and had once even proposed to me on the M Street Bridge on the first night of spring, but I had not taken him seriously.

He had a few years left before he finished his doctorate, and I knew he was planning to return to Libya. He was very excited that King Idris was gone and was sure Gaddafi would turn Libya into a progressive and democratic country. He admired Gaddafi so much he even carried a photo of him in his wallet, which I found strange.

"Why do you have a photo of Gaddafi?" I asked him. I could not imagine me carrying a picture of Lee Kuan Yew or Richard Nixon in my wallet.

He explained that, even after oil was discovered in Libya, most Libyans did not get to enjoy the new wealth.

"Only a few people around the king profited from the oil money but now, with Gaddafi gone, all Libyans will be educated and have more opportunities. He will change Libya, and make it one of the strongest and most successful countries in the Arab world." I could see the pride and hope Kamal had in his new leader, and I found his enthusiasm infectious and his passion exciting.

"I cannot offer you marriage now, *Habibti*, my love, but I will be able to very soon. I was waiting to talk to my parents when I go back for a visit, and then I will have to get permission from the government. Please, *Rohay*, my soul, wait for me to get everything in order. I beg you..."

He looked at me with tears filling his eyes, trying to read what was in mine. My head was trying to process what he was saying, while trying to keep my heart from pumping out of my chest. I was elated, because at that moment I realized how much I was in love with him. The thought of losing him now was almost unbearable.

Since I wasn't saying anything, he continued, "If you live in Honolulu, I will never see you again, and I will lose you forever."

"I have a few weeks to decide what I'm going to do," I whispered, weakly. "Let's just both wait and see."

We walked out of the restaurant into the balmy May night, our hands tightly clasped, afraid to let go, each lost in our own thoughts.

From that day on, Kamal could not bear to let me out of his sight, as if I would board a Pan Am flight and fly away from him forever. I was waiting for paperwork from Pan Am, and knew that I had to decide what I was going to do by the end of the month. Kamal was leaving for Florida in August; my options were Pan Am, Singapore, or find a job in D.C. The thought of staying in D.C. without Kamal was depressing. I had gotten so used to having him around— and I really did not want to be single and alone in the city that had become ours, while feeling I belonged to someone else.

I knew I had to tell my parents about the offer from Pan Am now and see what they thought. I called them one night, and, after I had said hello to my mother, my dad got on the phone, and I proceeded to tell him about the deal I had been offered by Pan Am.

He listened until I finished. After a pause that seemed to last forever, he said, "Esther, I want you to do what makes you happy, but think about this very carefully before making a decision."

I could hear him telling my mother what I had told him, and immediately she was back on the phone.

"Are you crazy, Esther? We didn't send you to finishing school and private schools to clean vomit!"

What she said startled me, more than being yelled at. I had never thought about having to clean vomit. All I thought about was having fun travelling the world. But cleaning up vomit? I was paranoid about even using public bathrooms!

The first thing I did the next morning was call Pan Am to tell them that I was declining their offer. Kamal was elated. I am sure he thought I had given up my opportunity for him. I didn't disabuse him because, in my heart, I knew I had chosen him from the beginning. What my mother said was only a good excuse for me to opt out. At that moment, I was reminded of the famous lines by Robert Frost, which I felt was a premonition of my life with Kamal: "Two roads diverged in a wood, and I, I took the one less travelled by."

In August Kamal moved to Tallahassee to begin his second master's degree. He had received his first in economics at the University of Alexandria. On our last night together before he left, he took me to the Calvert Cafe for dinner. Neither of us spoke or ate much. I could feel Kamal's eyes burning into every part of me, savoring each moment to carry with him for the seemingly infinite time before we would be together again. I was so sad that I think for the first time that night I understood the true meaning of love...that it can sometimes also be devastating.

Over Arabic coffee, which Mama Ayesha said she had made herself especially for us, Kamal took my hands and brought them to his lips, kissing them, and swearing it would not be long before we would be together again.

"Stora, wherever you are, just call my name and I'll be there..." I smiled at him, appreciating his reference to Michael Jackson's newly released song. I loved the way he would quote poems and songs to me.

He looked so sad I didn't know what to say, so we just shared the pain in silence together. I was scared that life would somehow find a way of separating us forever, and that I would never see him again.

He was the one to break the silence. "I promise you, *Habibti*, I will always be there for you until there is no more air left in my body."

He took a small box out of his jacket and handed it to me. Nestled inside, on its velvet cushion, was a small diamond ring. I was speechless.

"I know it's so small you need a microscope to see it, but please wear this until I can afford to buy you a bigger one!"

He smiled at me with eyes clouded by tears and anticipation, waiting for me to say something.

"It's beautiful." I was very touched, and keen to break the excruciating intensity of the moment.

"But you're right, I need a microscope!"

Our laughter broke the melancholy mood of what might be our last night together.

"Seriously, my Stora, will you promise to wear it and wait for me?"

Nodding, I held out my hand to let him slip the fragile but precious promise ring onto my finger.

"Never forget, my love, that you are my eyes, my heart, and my soul. I will always love you, until the day I die and beyond..."

Shortly after Kamal left for Tallahassee, I returned to Singapore. I quickly found a job working for Argus, an international advertising agency owned by a family friend. I received a letter almost every day from Kamal, who called me at least once a week. His letters were beautiful, and so filled with love they became my daily sustenance. My job was demanding and exhilarating, and my days so busy that I did not have much time to miss him in the beginning. I knew he was also overwhelmed with starting school and settling into a new apartment. His letters and calls cushioned our separation. My social life revolved around dinners and lunches with girlfriends and occasionally going with my parents to parties. I mentioned Kamal to my parents, but I did not tell them that my feelings for him were serious.

I began my job at Argus as a copywriter and designer, but after two months, when the Creative Director in the company received a better job offer in Australia, my boss Sonny offered me his position. I worked on local as well as international accounts including Slazenger, Carnation and Ronson, and managed to turn out some very successful ad campaigns. I loved what I did, and completely immersed myself in my work.

My nights began to feel longer and lonelier after the initial period of settling down. I knew Kamal was feeling the same. Unfortunately, my parents did not understand why I was not going out more with my friends to parties and night-clubs. To appease them, I would occasionally be sociable, but always returned home early and more depressed. Kamal said he would be going to Libya over the Christmas holidays to tell his family about me. I threw myself into my work, often stay-ing late to escape my mother's questioning. I had no doubt she would make my life miserable if she knew I was in love with an Arab and a Muslim, but I felt that somehow I had to find the right moment to tell her and my father.

After dinner on the terrace one balmy evening, I sum-moned the courage.

"Mummy, Dad, I have something to tell you," I bravely but very nervously opened the conversation.

"Remember the friend I told you about? Kamal? From Libya?"

My mother was an impatient woman, so I decided to get straight to the point.

"Yes, I do…" answered my father, somewhat suspiciously, as if he suspected what was coming.

My mother definitely knew. She was instantly alert, and I could see her eyes starting to smolder.

"What about him?" She asked sharply, disdainfully. I was beginning to realize that my mother was a racist and a snob.

I looked at her defiantly, not something I often did.

"I am in love with him…"

There was absolute silence for what seemed like a very long time. Even the crickets, lizards and bugs seemed to stop their nightly tropical noises.

"I want to marry him!" I lurched ahead, my heart defying the silence.

"Are you crazy?" My mother looked disgusted, while my father looked slightly troubled.

"I will never allow my daughter to marry an Arab and a Muslim! Do you understand me? Never!"

She spat her words at me, while my father absently stared at the garden beyond the terrace. I wondered if he too was thinking, as I did, of my mother's hypocrisy.

"Lian," he finally said, almost inaudibly, "The only thing that matters is our daughter's happiness…"

"No, Ernst, she has no idea what she's getting into. She can have almost any man she wants in Singapore, and she wants to marry a Muslim from God knows where? I forbid it!"

As far as she was concerned, the conversation was over and never to be resumed. When I related the conversation to Kamal, downplaying it a little, he tried to be very positive.

"Don't worry, Stora. When they see how much I love you, they will accept me."

I had no heart to tell him that my mother took every opportunity, after my revelation, to scorn me for what she referred to as my stupidity.

Christmas went by quietly, and in January I had plans to go to London for six weeks, to work with a major advertising agency on a Singapore Airlines campaign targeting Europe. It was such an honor, as I was the only woman chosen from Singapore. I could not believe how much I had been able to accomplish in less than a year. I was excited, and looking forward to working with my British counterparts in a major international advertising promotion. I loved what I did, and I knew I was good at it, but I didn't know if I wanted to spend the rest of my life in Singapore under the ever watchful eyes of a controlling mother. I also realized that I was not professionally ambitious enough to sacrifice losing Kamal's love. All I had ever wanted to do was be a wife and a mother. It was something ingrained and bred in me by my family and cultural and social upbringing.

When I left from Singapore that day to fly to London, I wished I could go on from London to Florida to see Kamal, but knew I would never dare. If I had, and if my mother ever found out she would never forgive me. She constantly reminded me that only cheap women pursued men, as if I were one!

I was embarking on one of the most exciting projects I had ever been involved with, professionally, and I was making top money by Singapore standards, but I was desperately missing Kamal. I did not know how much longer I could bear being separated from him.

I arrived in London on a cold dreary morning at the end of January and spent my first day settling into my small one-bedroom flat and exploring the neighborhood. The next morning I took the tube to Knightsbridge, nearest the agency offices. The damp cold and gray skies reminded me why I had chosen to go to school in the United States versus England as most of my friends in Singapore had done.

The offices were in an older building, with a newly renovated and elegantly decorated interior. For the next few weeks, all I did was work until very late every day, picking up something to eat for dinner on my way home. I spent my weekends shopping and wandering around the different areas of London by myself. Kamal would call around 6 a.m.

every morning to wake me up, after he had been working in the library until it closed at midnight. His love for me kept me warm and I knew I would wait for him as long as it took. By now, there was no doubt in my mind that I wanted to marry him.

In my sixth and last week in London, I came home one night later than usual. As I was climbing the steps to my flat, I caught a glimpse of someone sitting on the top flight of the stairs. Frightened, I turned around to quickly go back downstairs. I could sense someone getting up and coming after me.

"Stora! It is okay, my love. It's me, Kamal!"

CHAPTER 5

FLORIDA

We were married under state law on a crisp November morning in 1973 at the courthouse in downtown Tallahassee by Judge McClure. That same night, we were married under Muslim law in an Islamic ceremony at the Country Club, officiated by Mohammed, a Saudi prince who was also studying at the University.

Fawzia, Mohammed's wife—who was also a good friend of mine—helped me get ready for the wedding. She was a beautiful woman who carried herself like a true princess, which she was. In spite of her status, she was unpretentious and supportive of my marriage to Kamal, unlike some of the other Arab women. In the days before the wedding, Fawzia went over the main points of the Islamic ceremony with me. She assured me that there was not such a big gap between the fundamental basis of a Christian and an Islamic marriage, except, of course, that a Muslim man was allowed four wives. However, she and my other Muslim friends were quick to stress that that was no longer approved of, and rarely practiced anymore by the younger generation of educated Muslim men.

Several of our friends arranged for a dinner party to follow the ceremony. My girlfriend, Joy, collected hundreds of roses from her garden to scatter around the cake table, and decorate the large banquet room where the ceremony and party was to be held.

In anticipation of our marriage, Kamal had bought me a stunning Moroccan white and silver embroidered formal satin dress when he was in Libya, to wear as my wedding gown. It fitted me perfectly, and after shopping with Fawzia for a veil and white satin pumps, I was ready to get properly and stylishly married.

Neither Kamal nor I had any family present, but we had so much love and support from our friends that it did not get in the way of our happiness. We just hoped that in time both our families, in particular our mothers, would come to accept that we loved each other and allow us to shape our destiny as we so desired. My father had tried to convince me to spend a month in Libya before getting married, but of course that would not have been feasible, given that Kamal's mother was not happy with him marrying a Christian.

Kamal was sure his family would accept me once we married, and after months of waiting for permission from the Libyan government he finally received a special edict signed by Gaddafi allowing the marriage to proceed. He insisted that he would have married me with or without the edict. Without one, he would have lost his Libyan scholarship, which paid for his education and living expenses, as well as a generous allowance. He would also have been unable to work for the government upon his return to Libya.

One of the benefits of the new regime was their scholarship program, which sent out the cream of the crop to be educated abroad, mostly in Europe and the United States. However, the students were not allowed to marry foreigners, and it was only through a lot of paperwork and insider connections that made obtaining an edict possible. The whole process took almost six months. During that time, without my knowledge, I was also apparently investigated to insure that I was not an agent working for the American government. While we were waiting for the permission to come through, I worked at the advertising department of the local newspaper. Kamal was so happy the day the edict arrived that he told me to immediately start planning our wedding.

The wedding reception was put together within a couple of weeks, for around one hundred guests. In addition to the Libyan students and some of our other Arab friends, many of Kamal's professors and our American friends attended. Several long tables were covered with scrumptious Arabic dishes and delectable pastries which Fawzia had specially flown in from Lebanon. An Egyptian lady sang and belly-danced in our honor, eventually joined by almost every guest present. It was a jubilant beginning, which we both prayed was an indication of the path that our lives together would be leading us. The ceremony itself was simple, conducted in both Arabic and English. As part of it, Kamal bestowed on me an Arabic name that he had chosen. The name was "Hiba", meaning gift from God. He said that I was his desire from the first moment he saw me, and that God granted him his gift when he married me. From that day on, Esther Kofod no longer existed. I became Hiba Ben Ramadan. I felt absolutely no sense of loss for who I was, happily embracing my new name and the beginning of my new life with Kamal as his wife.

Two days after our wedding, we left on our round-the-world honeymoon, which was a gift from Kamal's father and brothers. Kamal kept reassuring me that now we were married, his mother would accept me as her daughter. We went on a one-month trip, which included London, Tokyo and Honolulu, with one week in Singapore being the longest stopover.

Much to my relief, my parents were welcoming and gracious. They hosted a large party in our honor at their showcase mansion, a sit-down Chinese dinner for about one hundred of what my mother considered her "closest" friends. The guest list included the British High Commissioner, Sir Sam Fall and his Swedish wife Margarethe, two cabinet ministers, the Chairman of the Chinese Chamber of Commerce, the island's leading American and Singaporean businessmen, and several ambassadors, including the Egyptian ambassador and his wife Dahlia. The only friend of mine invited was Ei-Ling.

I am sure the guest list was carefully selected to impress Kamal. My mother was an exceptional hostess, and when she wanted she could be the most charming and vivacious of women. She was a people collector, and she perfected the art of making all her chosen ones feel very special. I am sure that, in turn, every person who was there that night also considered themselves my mother's close personal friend.

Sir Sam and Lady Fall had gone on several vacations with my parents. Given her status, Lady Fall, or Margarethe as she preferred to be called, was a refreshingly unpretentious and friendly woman. She would sometimes be seen shopping at the local wet markets in her flip flops while her Rolls Royce and uniformed Gurkha chauffeur waited outside. I later found out that she had cajoled my mother into accepting her Muslim son-in-law, just as they had when their son married a Malay girl who was a Muslim. Sir Sam had been

British Ambassador to several Arab countries, so he and Kamal spent a lot of time discussing politics.

One of the guests, Datin Lee, heiress to the Tiger Balm fortune, was very taken by Kamal and made him laugh at her jokes and antics all night. She was always the life of any party she attended, and also one of my favorite "aunts." After dinner, she insisted that Sir Sam dance the "Funky Chicken" with her, which he did, much to everyone's delight. An unabashed flirt, she also made Kamal dance with her, despite his obvious embarrassment.

The week went by quickly, and we had a wonderful time exploring Singapore together. We even managed to fly up to Penang in Malaysia for a day so I could visit my grandmother's grave and pay my respects together with my new husband. I was relieved that my father seemed to like Kamal. I knew, however, that my mother still had reservations.

After our honeymoon we returned to Tallahassee, where Kamal started work on his doctorate in political science. He did not want me to return to the *Democrat*, the local newspaper, because he did not want his wife to work, so I began my role as a housewife. Unfortunately, I had never cooked and barely knew how to clean a house, so I had a lot of learning to do. I bought many cookbooks, and Kamal became my guinea pig. Due to my desperation for good food and the lack of many decent restaurants in Tallahassee, I was forced to be a fast learner. My mother was shocked that her daughter had to cook and clean, constantly insinuating that I should have married someone who could afford to hire a maid. She simply could not understand how I could be content doing what she considered to be menial work.

"All your friends have servants except you," she consistently pointed out, as if I cared. "My friends would laugh at you," she'd add, "if they saw you washing and cleaning like a servant!"

What my mother did not understand was that I was truly happy for the first time in my life, taking care of my husband in our little apartment. Growing up with a mother who controlled everything I thought, said and did, being with Kamal seemed liberating. He loved everything I said and did.

With my copywriting background I was able to help Kamal edit his numerous papers, and for breaks we would play cards or chess in the evenings. He taught me an Italian card game called *Scuppah*, which we frequently played together. He also taught me Arabic and how to sing a couple of funny ditties in Arabic, including a silly Kent commercial jingle extolling Kent as the cigarette my lover smokes!

"Kent, Kent, Kent, cigarette, Habibi. Kent, Kent, Kent, bedaccan, Habibi!"

Most of all, Kamal loved reading and translating Arabic poetry to me. I learned to appreciate the beauty of the Arabic language and the many different ways of saying certain words. Often before going to bed, he would recite verses from the works of Khalil Gibran and Omar Khayyam, and explained to me what they meant. Since we played chess together, there was even a poem on chess that he was particularly fond of reciting. He also introduced me to his favorite Egyptian singer, Um Khaltum, the Edith Piaf in the Arab world of music. He told me how she would sometimes sing for up to eight hours straight, and he translated many of her songs to me.

I learned to love the romanticism and passion of the Arabic language, but most of all, I loved my husband's adoration of me. He always told me that I melted him, and loved calling me *ayuni*, his eyes, and *rohay*, his soul.

Our apartment was always open to Libyan students as well as our American friends, and in time I learned to cook food that was somewhat edible. Luckily most of the Libyan students were rather good cooks, so I was introduced to many Libyan dishes, the most popular of which was *umba-coupka*, a macaroni and lamb stew seasoned with tomato paste and wonderful spices.

Our home became a home away from home for all the Libyan students who were attending FSU. They looked up to Kamal as their *capo* or leader, and he took the honor seriously. They asked his advice, and went to him with all their problems. A few of the younger ones would come and ask me for advice on love and dating, and a couple of them even called me Mom, even though there was hardly any age difference between us.

Whenever Kamal had some time off for a short vacation, we would drive to Washington, D.C., to visit our old friends and to indulge ourselves with shopping, going to ethnic restaurants and popular nightclubs to listen to good music—all of which were not available in Tallahassee.

One night, on our way home, we stopped at a diner outside of Valdosta, Georgia, for coffee and a snack. Since we were the only ones there, we decided to sit at the counter. There were two ladies behind the counter, and I noticed that after we gave our orders they kept looking at us and whispering to each other. Finally, just before we finished our coffee and pie, one of them came over with a piece of paper in her hand and asked for our autographs.

I was bewildered. When I asked them why they would want our autographs, one of the women said they knew who we were. I laughed and asked just who that was... She smugly replied that she knew we were stars on *Hawaii Five-0*.

We laughed, assuring them that we were not, but they did not believe us, insisting I was the girl with the long hair in the opening scene, running on the beach.

Finally Kamal said, "Okay, we give up!"

He took his pen and scrawled something on the two papers, passing them to me when he finished. I signed mine "Hiba" and gave them back to the ladies.

I felt guilty, but Kamal was having a good time playing it up, and the girls were thrilled. When we left, he handed the older one his gold Schaffer pen as a gift. We laughed about it on the way home, as we were wondering who they thought he was. He was sure they thought he was Steve McGarrett, but I told him I am sure they thought he was Zulu!

A few months after we married I found out that I was pregnant. We were ready to start a family, and had been praying for a baby, so I knew Kamal would be excited. That evening, I laid out three places for dinner that night, and when Kamal looked at the table he asked who was coming.

"I'm not sure, *Baba* or Daddy, or whatever you want to be called..." I answered nonchalantly, using the Arabic word for father, and turning away as if to leave the room.

He ran after me and grabbed me in his arms. I had never seen such joy and excitement on that handsome face.

"Are you sure?" he asked, tears filling his eyes.

"I'm sure, *Habibi.*"

He took me in his arms and held me for a long time. When he let me go, I saw tears streaming down his cheeks and was once again reminded of why I loved him so much.

Kamal was a very masculine man, sometimes chauvinistic, but he had the softest heart and the strongest passion, especially for me and his family. He always made me feel loved like I had never imagined possible, and because of that I had never been happier in my life. I knew without a doubt now that I had chosen the right man to be the father of my child.

We were both overjoyed, and spent a lot of time thinking of names. I suggested that he look for boys' names and I look for girls'. For a girl, I wanted a name that was pronounceable everywhere we went, considering our diverse backgrounds. I finally came up with the perfect name for a girl. The name was Layla.

My doctor suggested we take Lamaze classes, which we did once a week during the latter months. Kamal was a disciplined student and would work in the library every night until 6 p.m. On the nights of our Lamaze classes I would pick him up at the library and we would have a quick dinner in the car until it was time to go into class. He made a lot of jokes about doing Lamaze with me, hoping none of the Libyan students would see us eating dinner in the car, or worse, realize where he was going. It wasn't something a Libyan husband would do.

"If my family could see me now they would laugh at me," he would say, shaking his head and chuckling.

My pregnancy was a joyful time in both our lives. We spent hours talking about our baby, and we didn't care if it were a boy or a girl, just as long as it was healthy. We went for walks every night after dinner and Kamal made sure that all my food cravings were satisfied. Strangely enough, what I wanted most was lobster, cherries and Fudgesicles. Late one night, I developed a strong craving for Fudgesicles, so Kamal drove around for miles to find a store that was still open. He proudly came back with his prize at 2 a.m. only to find me snoring away peacefully. We both had a good laugh about it the next day, but after that he always made sure our freezer was well stocked with Fudgesicles.

On a lovely autumn morning, I gave birth to a baby girl who we named Layla. Kamal had stayed by my side the whole night comforting me until Layla was born. As soon as she was born, he quickly told me that she had ten perfect fingers and that she was the most beautiful baby girl God had ever created. He could not have been a prouder father.

Two days later, I returned home from the hospital to find our apartment filled with red and pink roses and balloons, and a big pot of Libyan lamb *sharba* (soup) ready on the stove. We had no family around, but overnight, my husband became cook, housekeeper, and diaper changer.

I had a very dear friend, Anne, who stayed with me during the day when Kamal had to go to the University. For two weeks, Anne helped me recuperate by doing almost everything for me. She was like a sister, lovingly taking care of Layla and me. I had never cared for a small baby before and she looked so fragile that I was afraid of hurting her. With no family around, I don't know what I would have done without Anne, and to this day I think of her with love and gratitude whenever I remember those two weeks we shared fussing and fretting over a little six-pound baby girl together.

The next two years Kamal and I spent in Florida were blissful years, watching our daughter grow and Kamal working towards receiving his doctorate. He was an adoring father, surprisingly patient and doting of "the most beautiful girl in the world"— his favorite phrase for her, after the song of the same name. Except for attending classes and studying in the library, Kamal spent all his free time with Layla and me.

For the first seven months, Layla suffered from colic. I would spend all day trying to make her comfortable by walking her around or rocking her. By the time Kamal got home, I would be exhausted, but he would immediately and tenderly take his daughter into his arms and spend the rest of the evening trying to soothe her. We discovered that the only remedy was to drive her around. The effects of a moving car would immediately lull her to sleep, and subsequently there were many 3 a.m. drives her father and I took around our quiet neighborhood.

My parents were delighted with their new granddaughter, and when my Aunt Ruth came to visit, we all went to Disney World in Orlando. Layla had just turned one year old, but we all swore she was so clever that she took everything in. Her favorite ride was *It's a Small World*; we did it so many times that we all felt sick and had the tune ringing in our heads for months!

Amir, Kamal's eldest brother, also came to visit us in Tallahassee shortly after Layla was born. He was doing a lot of business in the United States, exporting technical equipment to Libya, so he spent a week with us on his way to New York. He was the first Ben Ramadan family member I'd met, and I found him warm and charming. He was attentive to me and his new niece, for whom he brought a gift of ten all-white dresses from Harrods in London, including a cashmere outfit with matching bonnet and mittens. I am sure he spent a small fortune. He was slim, with a good-looking boy-ish face that reminded me of the American actor Richard Dreyfuss. He stayed at the Killearn Country Club Inn, which was very close to the apartment complex where we lived.

Amir was always elegantly attired in a suit and tie, even in the hot Florida sun, and stylish, with his gold Philippe Patek watch, his gold Dunhill lighter, and his custom-made Savile Row suits and Bruno Magli shoes. He smoked Rothman's Silk Cut cigarettes incessantly, alternating with a constant replenishing of tea or coffee. He was the type of man who made smoking look sensual.

While he was in Tallahassee, Amir gave us several thou-sand dollars as a wedding gift, and offered to buy us any-thing we needed. He treated Kamal more like a son than his brother. Kamal explained that it was quite common in Libya for the eldest son to assume that role. Before he left, Amir assured me that the family was looking forward to meeting Layla and me and that they all sent their love.

"Everyone is waiting for you to come to Libya, Hiba. They're all very excited to meet you and see Layla," said Amir, as we dropped him off at the airport.

"See," said Kamal, "I told you everything will be alright."

"Of course it is!" Amir brushed off Kamal, "She's a Ben Ramadan now!"

Kamal was just as happy and relieved as I was. I couldn't wait to be part of his large and loving family, something I had never known but always wished for since I was a little girl. I also wanted to be sure that, unlike me, Layla would have a sibling.

Kamal finished writing his dissertation about a year after Layla was born. While he was busy getting ready to defend his dissertation, I started the process of getting ready for our move to Libya. I was both nervous and excited. On the same day that Kamal defended his dissertation, I found out that I was pregnant again, and our celebration that night was two-fold. All the Libyan students came over, bringing with them three huge pots of *umbacoupka*, a large Libyan salad, and a big sheet cake from Publix. They were all sad that we were going to be leaving soon, but each one promised that as soon as they graduated and went back to Libya they would visit us in Tripoli. Our years in Tallahassee had been happy, but I was looking forward to begin a new life with my husband in the country he loved so much.

After a lot of shopping and packing, we sent everything ahead of us to Tripoli. Kamal decided that we would take a vacation before going back to Libya, so we left Tallahassee in December to spend Christmas and Chinese New Year with my parents in Singapore. In February of 1976, we left Singapore to begin our new life in Libya.

CHAPTER 6

LIBYA

As I descended the steps of the Libyan airliner, the intense brilliance of the winter midday sun almost caused me to lose my balance. Straining through the filtered veil of light, all I could see was a kaleidoscope of colors. The rhythm of unfamiliar sounds in the distance floated up, reminding me of previous arrivals in new places. Nothing felt like home, either in the United States or Singapore, and yet this was my new home, my newly adopted country.

Though I had anticipated this moment with excitement for over two years, I now found myself fighting a rising wave of anxiety. I believed in him, shared his values and respected his principles, and I was also undeniably, hopelessly in love for the first time in my life. He was also the first person in my life to love me unconditionally, who did everything to give me pleasure and joy. I would have gone with him anywhere.

After years of waiting, we were finally here as a family, with our precious daughter and another baby on the way, to be born in Libya. Just the month before, Kamal had gained the distinction of being the third Libyan to attain a doctorate in political science. It was a stepping stone for him to now be an active participant in Libyan politics and the development of his homeland.

I turned to my husband for reassurance; though his arm was still guiding me, he was absorbed in searching for a familiar face amidst the sea of humanity on the tarmac. His handsome Arab features glowed with excitement, and I knew how overjoyed he was to be home, on the soil of his ancestors. This was the moment he had been waiting for ever since I had known him. This was the beginning of his life-long dream. I had not fully understood the significance of it until now. Looking at him in that midday sunlight, I could not help but share in his joy and know that I had made the right choice in marrying him and becoming a part of his mission to change Libya.

I shifted my daughter Layla in my arms, to ease the strain on my protruding stomach. I was only four months pregnant, but was already showing substantially. Having slept the entire four-hour trip from London, my fifteen-month-old daughter was startled by her new surroundings. I gently showered her with kisses and tried to reassure her with quiet baby talk. Layla pretended to understand and was temporarily satisfied with my explanations. I nestled my face in her soft brown hair and breathed in her comforting sweet smell. Holding my firstborn in my arms, and carrying another in me, I offered a silent prayer that Libya would accept us.

As soon as we entered the airport terminal, Kamal was engulfed in his brother Amir's arms. It was reassuring to see him, a familiar face in an unfamiliar country. He kissed his brother several times on each cheek, before turning to Layla and me with the same affectionate greeting.

"*Ahlan Musahlan*! Welcome to Libya, Hiba!"

He was an effervescent man whose small build and gentle, baby-faced features belied his toughness, part of what made him a successful businessman. I couldn't help but notice that the expression in his eyes always seemed sad and preoccupied, even when he was not. Though prematurely balding, he was still good looking, with the charisma that helped him to get everything done his way. As he was in Tallahassee, he was very smartly dressed and maintained the same air of always being in a rush. Being the oldest and most favored son, Amir naturally assumed the dominant role of the Ben Ramadan family. It was also apparent how much he relished it. I would learn in the years to come that though he was very generous, he was just as demanding in return.

I was curious about how Amir's wife, Noor, would receive me. Kamal told me that she came from a large and respected family, and that she and Amir had hoped to arrange a union between Kamal and one of her relatives. Whenever I asked Kamal why he did not choose to marry a Libyan, or even an Arab, his answer was always the same. Unlike his own mother and sisters, he felt that many of the Arab women he met were materialistic, only interested in jewelry and shopping. I would argue this point with him by stressing that such pursuits were not exclusive to Arab women, and I hoped he did not think I was much different. I finally realized that it was just his way of reassuring me that he would never regret marrying "the foreigner", as he would sometimes jokingly refer to me.

"Anyway, it's too late," he would say, pretending to look defeated. "You own the key to my heart."

Even so, I wanted to be sure he had no misgivings about marrying a non-Libyan, but he was unwavering in his declaration that he would never have any regrets about marrying me. I believed him, but I also knew that marrying a foreigner—especially an American—was frowned upon by the Libyan government in those early days of the revolutionary period. I had, of course, been thoroughly investigated by the Libyans after Kamal applied for an edict from Gaddafi, and apparently also by the State Department in D.C. after we were married.

The other man with Amir was Kamal's second brother, Ali, whom I immediately took a liking to. He was a physically imposing man with soft, kind eyes and a radiant smile. A high ranking general, he wore the green decorated uniform of the Libyan Army. Ali struggled in English to warmly welcome me, then swooped Layla into his arms and covered her with kisses.

I was touched by the brothers' welcome, and my earlier anxiety was quickly diminishing. I prayed that his parents were as welcoming. I could see that Layla was going to thrive with so much family around, and for that I was grateful. Growing up an only child, I was happy that Layla would soon have a little brother or sister.

After the luggage was delivered by an airport official, Kamal and I were ushered outside to a silver Mercedes and a white Peugeot parked directly in front of the airport. They were being guarded by a young, eager-looking soldier, who immediately stood at attention when he saw Ali approaching. He saluted the men, but never even acknowledged me. With his head bowed, he quickly opened the back door of the Mercedes, and mumbled something, gesturing for me to get into the back as Kamal got into the front with Amir. The soldier then got into the white Peugeot, and with Ali driving, they followed our car out of the airport towards Tripoli.

Kamal and Amir were jovially conversing from the front seats of the car, both obviously happy to be reunited.

Occasionally one of them would turn and apologize for speaking in Arabic, giving me the gist of what they were saying. Even though I couldn't understand everything, I was grateful to feel included. Kamal had been working and waiting for this moment all through the years he spent in America, and I was taking pleasure in his happiness.

I wished I had taken the time to learn more Arabic, but it was difficult to find time to do anything with a new baby. However, Kamal had taught me enough to get by, and with some hand gesturing I could make myself understood if someone had the patience to "listen". I looked forward to becoming fluent enough to at least converse comfortably with his family.

Content to be in my arms and oblivious to everything else, Layla started to doze again from the rhythm of the moving car. Turning my attention away from my daughter and my husband, I looked outside as we sped towards the city. The road leading from the airport into Tripoli was grey and dusty, with an occasional olive or palm tree dotting the sides. From inside the comfort and luxury of the car, I was struck by the stillness of the air outside and the barrenness of the terrain. Even the few buildings I saw looked bleak. They were mostly white or gray and sometimes crudely constructed. Suddenly I realized with a shock what was missing. There were very few trees, and no grass.

I remembered the first time I had seen snow, when I was fifteen. I had looked out of my bedroom window early one morning when I was at Professor Buser's Tochterinstitut in Teufen, and everything was covered in white. After the first minutes of surprise and enchantment had worn off, I rushed outside to brush off an area of snow so I could see the grass underneath. I felt comfort in knowing that it was still there, and that in the spring it would regrow and be green again.

I knew this was different. It was going to be the same in spring and summer. I felt a little twinge of homesickness for the familiar greenness of Singapore and Florida, and resolved to plant a lot of trees and flowers in my new garden.

I also began to notice how few people were on the streets. Some of them were very dark, and some were dressed in costumes I did not recognize as Libyan.

"Kamal, are these people Libyans?" I pointed to them. "No, Hiba," Amir replied for him. "They're mostly foreign workers from surrounding countries, like Egypt, Ethiopia, Sudan, and Chad."

Amir spoke English well, but with a distinct Libyan accent. He had lived in Texas for two years while earning a MBA.

"They do the jobs no Libyans would do, especially manual work."

"After the oil," he continued, "Libyans think they're too good to do manual work, so the government pays them to sit in offices to do nothing, as long as they don't cause any trouble."

"They need to start thinking differently," added Kamal, "or else one day we'll be totally dependent on outside help."

Amir shrugged, "As long as there's oil, they think they can buy anything—including people."

I detected a hint of sarcasm in his voice but I reminded myself that it had only been six years since the revolution, and that it would take more time to rebuild a stronger and better nation.

"Real change requires patience," said Kamal, as if he could read my thoughts.

I was relieved when the conversation switched back to Arabic. I had been around Kamal and his friends long enough to know that political discussions could go on for hours. Right now, my only interest was meeting the rest of the family and seeing where we were going to live. I looked back and saw Ali's car still behind us.

The scenery did not change much until we arrived in the city. There were many more buildings, but they were quite indistinguishable, and the tallest building I saw was only four stories high. The roads were full of litter and mostly quiet. I could not help but think how beneficial it would be to establish an urban planning committee.

"What are you thinking, Hiba?" inquired Amir, smiling at me through the rear view mirror.

I appreciated his perceptiveness; it was one of the characteristics that made him so successful.

"I was thinking how quiet it is, even in the city."

"Ah, everyone's home, either eating or sleeping. You know, we have our big meal around two in the afternoon, then we rest until about five o'clock. Most people go back to work after that for a little while, but not everyone."

I looked forward to taking a nap every afternoon, especially now that I was pregnant.

Amir turned the Mercedes into Ben Ashor, a street wider than any I had seen till then. It was in a residential area centrally located in the city, where all the large houses were mostly hidden by high concrete walls. A short driveway led to two sets of massive steel doors, each at least ten feet wide. Amir stopped the car and honked. Immediately, one set of doors opened.

"Welcome to your new house!" said Amir with pride. "It is a gift from my father and me."

I was surprised because Kamal had told me we would be living in one of his father's houses until we built or bought our own. I had been looking forward to building a house that would be our very own, preferably on the Mediterranean, but I was glad to be so central. The house was large, probably twice the size of my parent's home in Singapore. Kamal and Amir estimated that it was around twenty thousand square feet. It had three stories, with the garage on the ground floor, which also included the servants' bedrooms, a living room and the main kitchen.

Amir parked the Mercedes in the cavernous garage, which held three other cars, with room to spare for at least two more. Ali pulled in right behind us, driving the Peugeot into one of the empty spots.

The small, wizened man who had opened the gate came to open Kamal's door, bowing his welcome with great deference and obvious familiarity. His wide smile displayed a set of brown teeth, stained by years of strong tea and unfiltered cigarettes. He was dressed in a flowing white *jalabeya* and a white skullcap.

"This is Abdo," explained Kamal, introducing Abdo as he helped me out of the car. "He's from Egypt, and has worked for Amir for years."

"I sent him over to prepare the house for your arrival. I'm going to let him stay here with you for a while," Amir added. "He can guard the house and take care of the garden."

Amir motioned for Abdo to take care of the larger suit-cases while Kamal helped me with Layla and my hand luggage, which was mostly filled with food and toys for her.

We exited the garage through a side door into a large, formal garden hidden from the street by twelve-feet-high concrete walls. The garden was lush with orange and lemon trees loaded with fruits. On the lower terrace, a long arbor flanked by grape vines seemed to go on forever. I felt as if I were in the vineyards of an Italian villa. Immediately to our right, a wide expanse of marble steps led upwards toward a palatial home. At the top of the stairway, a covered marble veranda extended the length of the entire front of the house.

It was there that the rest of Kamal's family stood gathered, waiting to welcome us.

As soon as I looked up, a loud shrill filled the air. The women were ululating. I felt gooseflesh prickling my skin and found the entire scene surreal, and moving. Layla thought it was fun and started clapping, trying to imitate them, and jumping up and down. I was ecstatic. I realized in that moment that they were sincerely welcoming us with love and joy.

Kamal leaned down to swoop Layla up into his arms, laughing at his daughter's delight.

"See, *Habibti*," he said, turning to look at me with a smile, "You're a part of the family now."

He beamed with a mixture of pride and relief. Kamal had not ever been sure how I would be received by his family. His mother's particularly strong reaction against it had troubled him the most. I knew this was the sign he was hoping for, even though he had always told me that they would love me after they met me.

As soon as we ascended the steps we were surrounded by the entire family, everyone anxious to show their welcome by showering us with hugs and kisses. Though I did not understand everything they were saying, I felt the sincere warmth of the welcome. Layla was passed from one relative to the other, each one vying with the other to hold her longer. This kind of love was what Kamal had told me about for years. He had not exaggerated.

My mother-in-law took my hand and pointed to the bottom of the marbled stairway.

"*Shufi! Shufi!*" She was gesturing me to look at the scene below. She appeared excited, and with pride looked to see my reaction.

I looked down and saw Abdo leading an immaculately white fat sheep from the garage.

"Look, look, Layla! It's Baa-baa black sheep!" I said happily, drawing my daughter's attention to the sheep.

She turned to look and, when she saw the sheep, tried to wriggle down from her aunt's arms to go play with it.

Looking up at us and smiling, Abdo pulled a knife from the pocket of his *jalabeya* and swiftly slit the sheep's throat. Blood gushed from the poor animal's neck as it crumbled to the ground.

I screamed in shock and, frightened by my reaction, though not really knowing what was happening, Layla started to cry.

Ibrahim, Kamal's father, quickly came and enveloped me and Layla in his arms, to soothe me and calm his granddaughter.

"*Malesh*, Hiba, *Malesh*," he said, softly, but with a mischievous twinkle in his eyes as he held us both in his arms. He tried explaining, with a little Arabic, Italian and English all mixed in. He was so gentle and so understanding. I think that was the moment I fell in love with my father-in-law.

Kamal translated for his father, "When a new woman comes into the family, they slaughter a sheep to welcome her. It's okay, *Habibti*, they are doing this to honor you."

I nodded to my in-laws that I was okay before turning back to my husband.

"I just wished you'd warned me, *Hamar!*" I hissed softly at him so no one else would hear.

"Donkey" was the pet name we would call each other when one was mad at the other. In all the years we were together, Kamal never once cursed or used bad language with me. It was an unspoken rule that donkey was only to be used in fun, never in anger.

"Sorry...I forgot," he apologized, looking appropriately chastised.

Kamal turned to the astonished family to explain my reaction. They responded with laughter, nodding their heads towards me in understanding. Then, as though it would make me feel better, Kamal told me that Amir's cook would immediately start preparing the lamb for our celebratory dinner later that night.

A large foyer welcomed us into the house, its floors shimmering with beautiful imported Italian marble. An immense sparkling chandelier hung in the middle of the room, centered over a big, round, and ornate Italian gold-gilded table. A double staircase with heavy mahogany banisters led to the top story, which Amir told me was a private family living area and bedrooms. Several sets of doors led from the main foyer into rooms crowded with heavy oversized furniture.

I could feel everyone's eyes on me, so I tried to look happy with my new house, knowing they had gone through a lot of trouble and expense to please us. At the same time, I could not help but wish I could have decorated the house myself in a simpler style.

Amir was obviously in charge of orchestrating the day and, in time as I would learn, almost everything concerning the family. Almost childlike with pride, he pranced around giving instructions and orders to his wife, sisters, and the maid who hovered around.

"You go eat first, Hiba," Amir said, gently leading me towards one of the doorways.

"You can see the rest of the house later..."

Rogaya led the women into a salon bare of furniture. Instead, mattresses with colorful coverings and large soft pillows lined the room with exquisite Persian carpets over the marble floors. A chandelier cast a dim light on walls lined with reproductions of revered Italian artists and tapestries of someone's skillful and dexterous imagination.

In the center of the room sat two three-foot round silver trays full of an assortment of beautifully presented foods. In the middle of each tray was a large hand-painted bowl of couscous, covered with stewed vegetables and lamb. Plates of different dishes surrounded the center bowl: a Libyan salad of diced tomatoes, cucumbers, onions, and hot peppers with a dressing of olive oil and lemon juice, *Kufta* – ground lamb meatballs spiced with cumin, coriander, garlic, and onions on a bed of pomme frites, stuffed grape leaves, and freshly baked baguettes. The only condiments were *harissa*, a paste made from tomatoes and hot chili, and bundles of scallions. The tray held a silver tablespoon and a cloth napkin for each place setting.

Following the women's lead, I seated myself cross-legged on the floor around the tray with Layla seated on my lap. Everyone was speaking in Arabic, and I was sure it was somehow referring to me. However, they were smiling and seemed happy to have me there, so I felt confident that whatever they were saying was good.

The only person whom I felt a little unsure about was Noor, Amir's wife. I knew that Noor spoke some English because she and Amir had lived in Texas. However, she had made no attempt to speak to me beyond the initial welcome. I assumed she was assessing me before committing herself, probably wondering why Kamal had picked me for his wife over a Libyan.

I glanced around the two circles of women, trying to follow their cues while attempting to put faces with names I had heard of for almost four years.

My mother-in-law, Rogaya, was a gracious lady in her early fifties with beautiful, glowing skin the shade of sun-kissed olive oil. Henna markings decorated her hands and face – in the patterns of her tribe. Her voice was very soft and sing-song-like, and though she spoke no English, every move she made bespoke of her gentle nature. Our inability to verbally communicate was compensated by animated gestures; our exchanges were followed by her lovely smile that seemed to radiate from her heart. For her new daughter-in-law's first meal, she wore a lovely traditional Libyan costume, or *Urrday*, in a richly subdued peach color, with gold jewelry on her neck, wrists, ears and fingers. Her hair was covered in a lovely matching silk scarf, which framed what could only be described as an angelic face. I could not imagine this woman as anything but sweetness incarnate. She was what I had always wished my own mother had been.

Next to her sat Noor, Amir's wife. Tall and broad-shouldered, she gave the impression of one who was used to controlling every situation, much like her husband. Her long black hair framed a face with stunning, classic features and rich olive skin. Like Rogaya, she too wore an *Urrday*, but one more colorful, and adorned with even more gold and jewels. I sensed her to be a strong and self-assured woman who did not hesitate to give her opinion.

Lamia, Ali's wife, was a schoolteacher, one of the few acceptable working roles for women in Libya. She was a striking pretty woman, but I was more drawn to her infectious smile and cheerful disposition. She was petite and unassuming, dressed in a simple western styled silk dress. Her longish, wavy, soft brown hair was gathered into a chignon and she wore little jewelry in comparison to her sister-in-law. Though she did not speak any English, she gestured animatedly in an attempt to translate the on-going conversation. I liked her from that first day, and my early assessment of her never changed in the years to come. She was gracious and hospitable, and was always there to help me when I needed it. In all the years I knew her, I never once heard her disparage anyone. I soon saw her as the role model for the younger women in the family with her work ethic, kindness and role of peacemaker. She was also the only woman in the family who drove, got things done quickly and efficiently, and was liked and respected by everyone. She taught me a great deal, and became my guide in the nuances of culture and social interaction in Libya.

The four sisters—Yasmine, Rania, Maia, and Nahla—sat together next to each other around another tray. They were all beautiful girls, well mannered, and soft-spoken like their mother.

The eldest was Yasmine, also a schoolteacher. Tall like her father, she was fair with a dusting of golden freckles across the bridge of her nose and her hair was the color of tea. She spoke a little English, and seemed the most anxious to try to communicate with me.

Rania, the second sister, emanated sensuality. Darker and more exotic-looking, she seemed comfortable with her beauty and accomplished in the art of presenting her best. To me, she was the one who most resembled Kamal, only a more beautiful and feminine version. Her knowledge of English was better than the others, and she acted as the main interpreter for much of the conversation. She was self-assured and quite opinionated in a matter-of-fact way, which I admired. She and Noor vied to be the center of everyone's attention, and I could sometimes detect the impatience on the older woman's face with her headstrong and outspoken younger sister-in-law. It was obvious that neither of them ever bothered to hide their feelings.

The third sister was Maia. She tried to blend into the background and avoid being noticed, but her nature made it difficult to do. Unlike the others, her hair was almost blonde, framing shimmering hazel-colored eyes, which took in every movement I made. Seemingly shy and quiet, she was eager to learn about everything. In time, I found her to be the most inquisitive and adventurous – the traits that I loved about her and which helped bring us closer together. Her name meant flower in Arabic, and suited her perfectly.

Nahla, the youngest, was gentle and composed. She had soft, pretty features and carried herself with grace, like her mother. She was the one everyone would boss around, yet she would do whatever was asked of her with a smile. She was the baby, but she was not spoiled, and in fact had the most accommodating and sweetest disposition of all the siblings.

The four sisters were everything Kamal had described and more. I looked forward to knowing them better and having them as a part of our lives. I had a feeling, though, that they were just as anxious to learn English as I was to learn Arabic. It was obvious that they adored Kamal and fought to hover over their niece, smothering her with kisses. They were loving aunts, and I could see that, being the baby of the family, Layla was going to be thoroughly spoiled.

The other children, daughters of Lamia and Noor, sat beside their aunts and openly stared at me, occasionally giggling at any attempts I made to communicate in my limited Arabic vocabulary. They were sweet little girls, and extremely well behaved, hanging on to every word and gesture of their new aunt. I could tell that they were anxious to get their hands on their baby cousin as soon as they were allowed.

"*Bismillah,*" Rogaya said, blessing the meal. She turned to me smiling and gesturing to the food, she said, "*Kuli, Kuli.*"

In time I learned that this literally translated to "help yourself," the Libyan version of "Bon Appetite."

The women took up their spoons and started to dip into the bowl and platters. I hesitated for a moment when I realized there were no individual plates, but quickly imitated them. The food was delicious, better than any of the Libyan food I had had before in the States, though I was a little

100

leery of the lamb after seeing what had transpired earlier. Rogaya kept putting food into her granddaughter's mouth and babbling to her. Layla giggled and glowed in the light of all the attention she was receiving.

I was aware of the scrutiny of the women as I ate, as if I were being studied closely to see how adaptable I was to their social and cultural circumstances. I hoped I passed, because everyone had been so gracious. I had grown up in a multi-racial, cultural and religious society, so I was naturally raised to be adaptable. My first meal in Libya was filled with love, laughter, lots of questions, and very creative gesturing. It was the perfect celebratory meal, even without my husband, who was in another room eating with the men.

After the meal, Nabila, the Tunisian maid, took away the trays from the room. After she finished clearing the room, she brought in another smaller tray, which contained a small coal-fired brazier, a small metal water-filled teapot, a can of black tea, and clear shot glasses. She set it down in front of Rogaya.

"You know Libyan tea?" Noor asked me skeptically.

I nodded proudly. "Yes, Kamal has made it for me many times before."

I could see that Rogaya was intently taking it all in. She was an observant lady, and I doubt if much got past her. She was undoubtedly the matriarch of the family.

"*Chai!*" She smiled at me, pointing to the tea. She grabbed a handful of the loose tea, put it into the pot of water, added some sugar, and set it on the brazier to boil. The mixture boiled for about ten to fifteen minutes while the women lounged on the pillow-strewn mattresses and continued to talk. I would occasionally recognize a word or a phrase as they spoke. Noor would sometimes translate questions from the other women, and I am sure, editing what she might have considered unnecessary. I tried using my hands to convey answers when she had difficulty, or when I wanted to express my own feelings, much to the amusement of the ladies and the children.

I noticed the amount of gold my new female family members wore: row upon row of gold bracelets, thick ornate neck chains, rings, and dangling earrings. In contrast, I wore only a wedding band, a diamond engagement ring, and a strand of pearls. Seeing me admire their jewelry, Noor told me that I needed to tell Kamal to buy me more gold, because it was a reflection of a husband's love as well as her dowry—or what I thought she meant specifically, her worth.

Nabila came back in carrying trays of fruits and pastries, passing them around to everyone before setting it down on the carpet. I could see her sneaking looks at me, probably wondering whether I'd be accepted by the family and how it was going to be working for me. Apparently she came with the house, and Noor had already told me that she spoke no English, punctuating it with a flick of her thumb from under her top teeth. I had seen some of Kamal's friends in Tallahassee do it before, so I assumed now that it must be a Libyan way of expressing and finalizing an absolute zero.

My mother-in-law was seated cross-legged on the floor in front of the brazier, checking the progress of the boiling leaves. When she seemed satisfied that the tea was ready, she picked up the teapot and began an artful process of decanting the tea. Over and over, she poured the strong, almost black liquid between the teapot and a large handled cup. I watched fascinated, as Rogaya lifted the pot higher and higher each time over the receiving cup. A thick layer of froth formed in the tea as more air was mixed with each pour. Finally, after repeating it numerous times, Rogaya poured the foamy dark liquid into small shot glasses and passed the tray around the room.

She gave me the first glass, smiling and nodding her head at me, almost daring me to try the potent brew. I winced slightly at my first taste of real Libyan tea. It was much stronger and sweeter than any I had tasted before.

"*Bahi, bahi?*" Rogaya kept asking me, while her daughters were looking at me giggling.

"Is it good?" Noor translated. "She wants to know if you like it."

I smiled and nodded, while indicating that it was quite strong and sweet. The women explained that the first round was usually the strongest. I decided that I had better learn to enjoy the tea, no matter how strong it was. Kamal had told me that it was the main staple of hospitality and social-ization. I never drank coffee, and the only tea I had ever enjoyed was Chinese tea, which was lighter and more subtle, and never served with sugar. I especially never liked iced tea, and in fact found it nauseating, not good when one is living in the South. I was determined to learn to enjoy Libyan tea. Eventually I would, and became quite addicted to it.

Rogaya continued to make pot after pot of tea, adding to each pot a different ingredient for flavor—mint, fresh whole almonds, and fresh attars - scented geranium leaves. The entire meal and tea ceremony lasted about two hours. The atmosphere quieted down after the huge meal, with everyone languidly lying around on comfortable mattresses on the floor, which I learned was called a *mindar*. Layla, exhausted, finally dozed off on my lap, and I was starting to wonder when I would see Kamal again, when he and Amir entered the room.

Amir sat down on one of the cushions and gestured to his wife, apparently asking her to do something. She reluctantly got up from her comfortable position and left the room. When she came back a few minutes later, she placed what looked like a large jewelry box on my lap without a word. I felt every eye in the room watching me.

"I hope you will like our present," Amir said. I could see that he was anxious for me to open his gift.

When I did, I was overwhelmed. It was a complete set of emeralds and diamond necklace, bracelet, and earrings. It was quite elaborate and obviously very expensive. I thanked Amir and Noor profusely for their extremely generous gift. I could see that even Kamal was impressed by the exquisite present.

My father-in-law came into the room at that point and handed his wife another velvet box. The dear, sweet lady struggled up from the floor and came over to hand me the box, kissing me repeatedly on both cheeks. When I opened the box I was struck by the magnitude of the piece. It was an enormous gold pendant, about three inches round, heavily studded with diamonds into an intricate calligraphic design.

I was overwhelmed by these gifts, and seeing the joy and pride on their faces, I got up and hugged them all, expressing my heartfelt appreciation.

"Come on, Hiba," my husband said, breaking into the emotional weight of the moment.

"Let's go and see our new house!" I could tell he was so proud and honored by what his family had done for us.

I could also see the looks of anticipation on everyone's faces as we left the room, but I already knew what to expect, after having already seen a few of the rooms.

It was the largest, most ostentatious and impractical house I could have imagined. Heavy velvet drapery, flowery jewel-toned Persian carpets and ornate gold-gilded Italian furnishings filled every room. In the large central living room, rows of overstuffed velvet armchairs and sofas lined the walls, interspersed with modern glass side tables and Italian marble top coffee tables.

I had envisioned living in a modest villa by the sea, furnished in contemporary Italian and Chinese antiques, with highlights of my Singaporean culture dominating the ambiance. I could see now that it would not be happening for a very long time. It was so obvious that Amir and Ibrahim had poured a lot of their heart and money into this extravagant gift for us, so I could never let them know how disappointed I felt. One day I would have the house I had dreamed of, but for now I would simply enjoy this gift from my new family and be grateful for all their generosity.

I had to remind myself that what mattered most was that we were starting a new life; my husband's dream of coming home and helping build his country had begun. I finally had a real family, and they were everything I had longed for.

CHAPTER 7

TRIPOLI

I didn't fully comprehend what a large family Kamal had come from until after our arrival in Libya, and apparently it was important to meet all of them as quickly as possible. The level of hospitality and generosity that greeted us at every home we visited was unparalleled to anything I had experienced in the United States, or even Singapore.

We were invited to homes of relatives for lunches and dinners almost every day during our first few weeks, either in Tripoli or Khums. Regardless of their financial circumstances, every house we went to slaughtered a lamb in our honor, served us their best foods and gave Layla and me lovely gifts, often in the form of jewelry. They were not only celebrating our marriage and the birth of Layla, but also the occasion of Kamal having received a doctorate degree, a first in the Ben Ramadan clan. We stayed about a week at Kamal's parent's home in Khums while we visited his aunts and uncles who lived in the surrounding areas. During that frenzied period of introductions, two extraordinary experiences were etched in my memory.

One of the first families that we paid our respects to in Khums was Ibrahim's brother, Khalid, who lived with his two wives and all their children on a large farm on the outskirts of the town. Growing up in Singapore, I was familiar with the laws of Islam as well as the custom of secondary wives and concubines among wealthy Chinese men. Still, Kamal's sisters were concerned that I would not be comfortable, and tried to prepare me for the visit. They made it clear that they themselves would never accept such a situation.

When we arrived at the sprawling compound, I saw that there were three separate small buildings consisting of a main house and two houses, one for each wife. Khalid, the two wives, and all their children ran out to greet us as we drove through the gate. The adults proceeded to go to the main house, where we all sat down on *mindars* for refreshments before lunch. Perhaps it was because of my limited Arabic, but it crossed my mind that they seemed like a happy threesome. As Kamal translated the conversation, I noticed that the women looked at me unabashedly, often remarking to Kamal that I was pretty and courteous.

"If you only knew!" he told them. I nodded my head at them to show that I agreed with him. They found this greatly amusing.

Everything about the women seemed so equal that they almost looked alike; the only difference was one was younger than the other. Seeing them dressed up in their finery, each of them contentedly sitting on either side of their husband, I saw in practice what Kamal had told me about the Koran saying that wives had to be treated equally. Those ladies could have been sisters who loved each other and liked wearing similar clothing and jewelry. They had even cooked a wonderful meal together, and as I sat on the floor with them and their children to eat, I could feel that they were truly contented women who found satisfaction and meaning in their lives, in their own way. Before leaving his uncle's farm, each of his wives presented me with identical gold bangles.

On the way back to Khums, I asked Kamal his thoughts on marrying more than one wife.

"First of all the wife has to agree," he stated very matter-of-factly. "Then, the man must treat them both absolutely equally, to the point that the weave on the two handkerchiefs he gives them are equal and identical."

"However," he continued, "that is almost impossible. In this day and age I would never accept that for my daughter or for my sisters."

I was very pleased with his answer but could not resist letting him know how I felt.

"That's good, *Habibi*, because I would never allow you to have a second wife. So don't ever think about it."

"Don't worry...you are more than enough for one man to handle."

"Besides, *Rohay*," he continued, his voice softening, "how am I going to find someone better than you?"

A few days later Kamal and I traveled south to visit his aunt Khadija, Ibrahim's eldest sister. She lived deep in the desert in a small village where there was no electricity. Ibrahim told Kamal that we did not have to go if I didn't want to, but I insisted that we go, which pleased my father-in-law.

Khadija had not left the village since her arranged marriage about fifty years ago, and had never met a foreigner, not even another Arab. She was a fragile but graceful Bedouin lady in her sixties, welcoming us with kisses and a charming smile. I could tell, however, that she must have led a difficult life, living under harsh conditions. She had lived without electricity or even running water until a few years ago. They essentially lived off the land, except for an occasional trip by the men to the nearest town for supplies. Her face was spellbinding, heavily decorated with henna in the pattern of her tribe, and yet through it her delicate features and luminous hazel eyes still managed to stand out. I could tell she must have once been a beauty, because she was still striking, even though her skin was wrinkled and toughened by the desert sun.

As I sat on the floor of her simple house eating lamb and couscous, she gazed at me, smiling and nodding her head in approval. She kept picking choice pieces of meat, feeding me with a hand also covered in the same elaborate henna design. There were no spoons, so we all ate with our hands. I knew that they were not wealthy, and for them to slaughter a lamb that day for us was special. Instead, she and her family kept telling us what an honor it was for them to have us in their home.

As we were leaving, his aunt talked at length with Kamal, all the while holding on tightly to my hand, as if she did not want to let me go. As we kissed goodbye, she slipped a well-worn gold bracelet from her wrist and handed it to me. I tried to refuse it—touched that she wanted me to have what belonged to her—but Kamal said that I would be insulting her if I did not accept it. I finally accepted her gracious gift, thanked her profusely, and kissed her goodbye. I knew that I would probably never see her again, since she never left her village, and even Kamal had only met her twice in his life. I felt honored as the newest member of the family to have been able to pay my respects to this inspiring lady. I asked Kamal on the drive back to Tripoli what she had said about me.

"She told me to take care of you because you were so far from home and have no family here."

He told me this pensively, like he had never thought of it in such stark terms before. He reached for my hand, turned to me, and said, "She also said how lucky I was to have found someone like you."

I thought about what the older lady said, marveling at how someone so cut off from the world could have such sensitivity for another woman so different from herself. She touched my heart, and reminded me of another woman, my *pawpaw*. I have often thought of this simple Bedouin lady and wished that I had been able to listen to her story over Libyan tea.

A week after our arrival in Libya, Kamal and I drove to the airport to pick up Kamaria, our new nanny from Singapore. Farah had lost her husband in a fishing boat accident in the Straits of Malacca several years before, and since her own children were grown, she was enthusiastic about living and working in Libya. She had been highly recommended by a friend of mine in Singapore, who said that she was also an excellent cook, specializing in Singaporean cuisine. We had only spoken with her on the phone once before meeting her in person in Singapore over Christmas. Both Kamal and I liked her immediately, and knew she would be the perfect match for our family. The pay Kamaria received from us was excellent compared to what she was making in Singapore, and she would be able to save her entire pay as we would be responsible for all her living costs.

When we picked up Kamaria at the airport, she was in excellent spirits despite the long trip from Singapore and a six-hour layover in Rome. She was dressed in her Malay *sarong* and *baju* (a tunic like top over a sarong), carrying in her hand luggage a bag of Malay and Chinese spices, herbs, and even some special foods, which Kamal and I had warned her might not be available in Libya.

My Malay was a little rusty, since I had not used it in years, and Kamaria's English was limited, but her ever-pleasant smile, gentle nature and enthusiasm was all we needed. I knew that within a short time and some practice, I would have no problem conversing in Malay again.

Though Kamaria was only in her early forties, the sadness in her eyes and the difficult life she had led made her look older. I was determined to make her feel like a part of our family and make her life with us pleasant and rewarding. She was a short, rather plumpish woman, with golden brown skin and almost Polynesian-like features. She was pleasant to look at but not particularly beautiful, yet the energy she projected made her presence known and felt by all.

Kamaria had her own room between the children's rooms, which she said was the most beautiful room she had ever slept in. She loved the modern Italian furnishings and having her own bathroom. After a tour of the house and unpacking, I told her to relax for the rest of the day, but she insisted on feeding and bathing Layla before putting her to bed. My little girl took to her without hesitation, and from their interaction I could tell that Kamaria loved children.

The next morning, Kamaria was the first to wake up, and by the time we got out of bed, she had picked oranges from the garden, squeezed a whole pitcher of fresh juice for breakfast, and cooked our breakfast. She had never plucked oranges from trees before, and was so excited by the experience that I suspected we would be having fresh juice every morning. By the end of the day she had established a routine. From her first day on, we would wake up each morning to the smell of breakfast cooking, followed by aromas hinting at the delectable treats to come later in the day. She made excellent Malaysian curries and Malay *kueh* desserts, which we often served to our guests.

It was Kamaria's job to take care of the family area on the top floor, which included all our bedrooms, baths, a family living room and a kitchenette. Nabila, our Tunisian maid, did all the Libyan and Arabic cooking, and was responsible for clearing up after meals and making sure that the rest of the house remained in pristine condition. Abdo took care of the garden, washed the cars and guarded the house as well as whatever else we needed him to do. It was usually also his job to go every morning and evening to the nearby bakery for fresh bread, and the dairy shop for fresh milk.

When we were expecting a lot of guests, Kamaria would help Nabila with the cooking. Libyan food is largely based on tomatoes and pasta, an influence of Italian cuisine. The combination of Italian and traditional Arabic ingredients and spices gives Libyan cuisine a unique and exceptional taste. I loved the food, and over the next few months I learned to make many dishes myself, thanks to the coaching of every woman in the family. Noor was an excellent cook, and had taught Nabila how to cook many Libyan dishes; luckily for us she sometimes also cooked wonderful Tunisian and Egyptian dishes. The main meal almost always included the obligatory lamb dish with couscous, pasta or rice, accompanied by a few side dishes and salad. The evening meal was usually simpler, except during Ramadan. It was my responsibility to get all the ingredients for the meals as well as shopping for the house, which took up most of my morning. We had people over almost every day for both the main meal as well as for supper, and it was a rare occasion when we did not have guests when Kamal was home.

I soon discovered how important it was to have a good supply of bottled water and at least one bathtub filled on each floor. It was necessary to be prepared for days when there was no water, which happened quite often. Due to the poor electrical infrastructure in the country, frequent power outages was another problem, so we would always keep plenty of candles and kerosene lamps around. Even when we had electricity, the chandeliers and light bulbs functioned at a minimum, radiating dim, flickering light.

Shopping was the biggest challenge I faced, especially shopping for food. It became my main preoccupation. Almost everything was imported and seasonal and despite the lush groves and orchards near the coastal areas, it was often difficult finding laborers to pick the fruits, olives and dates, even in season. Most Libyans would not consider doing manual labor after the discovery of oil, so workers had to be imported.

The biggest lesson I learned early on was the importance of making friends with the shopkeepers. When certain items became scarce, they would start hiding them for favored customers and then sell them at higher prices. More often than not, one would be so grateful to even have the item that price was not an issue.

"To honor our Libyan guests," Kamal instructed me early on, "you must only serve *kharuf watani*, freshly slaughtered local lamb. Never buy frozen or foreign."

That was easier said than done in the city, because it meant a special trip to a particular butcher every day, and hoping it was available. If not, I would have to drive around town until I found *kharuf watani*, which was what everyone else was looking for, if they could afford to. It was easier to have fresh lamb everyday living on a farm, like in Khums, where they slaughtered their own sheep.

To present a perfect meal, I learned to shop at several different places around the city in order to find everything I needed. Adam, Amir's Ethiopian driver, spoke a little English, and in the first few weeks showed me where to find all the specialty shops Noor frequented. Chicken and beef were mostly imported and inexpensive compared to local lamb. I could buy a whole filet for only $15, since lamb was preferred over beef by Libyans. Only vegetables in season were offered, and items I had taken for granted in the States were often difficult to find. Layla was particularly fond of bananas and strawberries, but neither was readily available.

There were bakeries everywhere. Sometimes there would be a shortage of milk, but never *khobsa*, or baguettes. They were as fresh and delicious as any found in Paris or Rome and the cheapest luxury.

Driving was another challenge. After learning my way around, I began to drive myself rather than depend on Kamal or Adam. We had shipped a Chevrolet Monte Carlo with us from the United States, but I didn't like driving it because it was too difficult to park and attracted too much attention. Kamal finally decided to buy me a tiny Fiat 500, which was inconspicuous. Unlike in Saudi Arabia, women in Libya were allowed to drive, though there were still some men who had a difficult time accepting it.

In Tripoli everyone was in a rush to get somewhere and everyone had their own traffic rules. Honks were used unsparingly and tempers flared easily. Tailgating and minor accidents were taken for granted, and road rage was the acceptable norm. Most people were not bothered by dents and scratches, which cost too much to fix; besides, it was almost impossible to find someone to do the work. It was one reason broken-down cars were simply abandoned on the roadside.

Whenever I felt adventurous I would go to the Souk al-Hout, the largest indoor wet market in the center of Tripoli. It was less expensive there than the grocery stores where the shopkeepers spoke English, and was generally a one-stop shop for a typical Libyan meal. However, one had to bargain. Growing up in Singapore I was quite accomplished in the art of haggling, but doing it in Arabic was more challenging. I once paid $15 for a pint of strawberries out of season because I got five and fifteen confused. I didn't want the shopkeeper to get angry with me after making the sale for having pretended to understand him! However, when certain fruits were out of season or when milk was unavailable, it could not be found anywhere, not even at the souk.

One day during my last month of pregnancy, I decided that I needed to go to the Souk al-Hout. It was a very hot morning during Ramadan, the holy month of fasting from sunrise to sunset, but I needed to buy ingredients for what I planned to be an exceptional *Iftar*, the breaking-fast meal at sunset. Kamal had invited Ahmed Shahati, head of the Libyan Foreign Liaison Office, and his boss, Ali Treki, the foreign minister, to meet some of his friends who had also graduated with doctorate degrees from the States.

I was not obligated to fast, given that I was pregnant, but out of respect I never ate or drank in front of anyone. By afternoon most people looked rather parched and listless. The breaking of the fast always began with dates and buttermilk, usually followed by the traditional Libyan *sharba* lamb soup, a lamb entree, stuffed grape leaves, *kuftas*, salads, fruits, and later in the evening *mahallabiya*, a rice pudding sprinkled with cinnamon and grated coconut and studded with raisins. I decided to go to the souk to spare myself driving all over town in the unrelenting summer heat.

It took me a longer time than usual to find a parking place, as the traffic was especially bad. I finally found a spot close to one of the entrances, which would allow me to take my purchases to the car each time they got too heavy to carry. After finishing with my last purchase, I made my way slowly to my car. To my astonishment, the car was gone. In its place was another.

I was sure that was where I had parked, and started to panic because I didn't know what to do – except to find a policeman. Oh God, I thought, I don't even know the Arabic word for lost...I'll just use the word *Imshi* for go away! *Car go away*? I hoped it made sense!

There was a lot of honking and people shouting further down the street, so I decided to see if perhaps I could find a policeman there. There was no policeman, but in the middle of the road sat my little Fiat, with everyone around shouting and cursing.

Unbelievably, it turned out that someone who had trouble finding a parking place decided to move my car out of the way, simply because he could. He had literally pushed it down the road and went back to park his own car! I saw the

117

guy as he was getting back into the car in my space, and he was actually grinning proudly. Though I can smile now, in the mid-summer desert heat that day I lost my temper and cursed him out in Arabic. Everyone around laughed, including him.

Gagaresh was an area of Tripoli known to some as the American section because many expats working for oil companies lived there. Imported items from Europe and the United States were more readily available in the stores in that section of town, and many of the shopkeepers spoke English. However, the prices on imported American products was highly inflated, about three times what they cost in the States. Luxury items were not only exorbitantly priced, but the selection was scarce. I also noticed during my shopping excursions there that most of the goods, including medicine, were past their expiration dates.

I was so desperate for diapers once because we were going on an overseas trip that I paid $45 for a box of twelve. I had looked all over town, but there was apparently a shortage. I finally went to a shop in Gagaresh where I knew the shopkeeper, who told me to wait while he went to the back room; out he came with the coveted box of diapers. He swore to me that it was his last box and that I could have it for the equivalent of $45. I had no choice.

In another grocery shop in Gagaresh one day, I witnessed a weather-beaten, middle-aged oil-rigger very loudly asking the storekeeper if he had any beer. Everyone within earshot laughed, but the man was serious and was growing somewhat belligerent. I thought he either must be really stupid for not knowing the law, or trying to make a point about not being able to buy alcohol. Instead, he finally left the store with a box of bottled baby food. The conclusion of this heated scene seemed odd to me. When the storekeeper Mohammed saw my puzzled expression, he explained that hardcore drinkers out on the oil fields used baby food to manufacture some kind of beer!

Alcohol was banned in Libya, and possession meant a prison sentence (or, it was rumored, some people got tarred and feathered). It was not the first time that I felt embarrassed at the lack of respect and irreverence, especially when it was an American, and since the Libyan economy provided so well for them.

Pork was another banned item, but discovery of it did not entail the same punishment as alcohol. At a tea party one afternoon, an elegant Italian lady casually told me that every time she came back to Libya after a trip to Italy, she would smuggle in a ham by rigging it to hang between her legs, under a long flowing skirt. During one of these comical smuggling episodes, an unusually strong wind was blowing as she disembarked from the plane. The back of her skirt flew up, but she said she was too embarrassed to turn around to see who had seen the ham hanging between her legs!

Gagaresh was one of my favorite residential areas in Tripoli because it was near the sea. My father-in-law owned a small Italian-style house there, which he rented out, and which was one block from the Mediterranean. Because it sat up high from the road, the panorama of glistening water from the house was so beautiful that I dreamed of renovating it and living there one day.

One morning, as I was driving on the road leading to Bab Al-Azizya, the military compound, I spotted a truckload of bananas. It was quite a sight, as we had not seen bananas in months. Sitting in the back seat with Kamaria, Layla also saw them and got excited.

"Nana! Mummy, nana! Lala want nana!" my banana-deprived baby wailed.

I followed the truck to see where it was going. After a couple of miles, it finally turned into the large compound of military-styled barracks. I parked, watching as the bananas were unloaded into a large storage space close to the road.

"Don't worry, sweetheart, Mummy will get you some bananas."

I got out of my car and asked one of the soldiers carrying the bananas, "*Gadash? How much?*"

He ignored me, so I tried again, repeating the words slowly.

"*Imshi! Imshi!* Go away!" The soldier yelled at me, slashing his arm through the air for me to leave.

Mortified, I turned around to walk back to the car, only to see Layla jumping up and down in the back seat, desperate for her bananas. There was only one way to accomplish it. Kamal had taught me a few phases for emergencies, and as far as I was concerned, this was one. I turned around and approached the soldier again.

"Listen!" I said sternly to the soldier in my poor Arabic.

"My name is Hiba Ben Ramadan, and I am the sister-in-law of General Ben Ramadan and the wife of Dr. Kamal Ben Ramadan. I want to buy bananas. Do you understand?"

I despised myself for name-dropping, but I was told that it always worked because everyone was paranoid – and often it was the only way to get anything done. If necessary, I would probably have begged for the damned bananas.

The soldier stopped and looked at me, unsure whether to believe me or not. He could get into serious trouble if he insulted a member of the general's family. On the other hand, he was probably unaccustomed to being spoken to like this by a woman, much less a foreigner.

He asked several questions, none of which I understood as I was quite scared by then.

"*Ana lah atakhalem Arabiya.* I do not speak Arabic." It was the one phrase I knew very well.

"Telephone General Ben Ramadan," I told him, using my hand like a telephone.

The soldier impatiently motioned for me to wait as soon as he heard the word general repeated, and walked to the building next door.

Oh, God, I thought, *I'll probably get arrested.* I was afraid I had gone too far.

I considered running back to the car and quickly driving away, when I saw the soldier returning with another man who looked like his superior.

"Madame Ben Ramadan?" he asked politely in English.

"Yes," I replied, uneasily.

"Are you related to General Ben Ramadan?"

"Yes, I am. He is my husband's brother."

"*Fada, fada,* please, please." He pointed to the truck. "Take all the bananas you want."

"*Shukran.* Thank you." I could not believe what was happening. It worked!

I grabbed a large bunch with shaking hands and fled back to the safety of my car.

Later that evening I told Kamal the story of how I was able to get bananas for Layla.

My husband was not amused.

"You asked a soldier for bananas?" He looked incredulous.

"I didn't ask him to give me bananas, Kamal. I offered to buy them."

"It doesn't matter! You should not be talking to him at all!"

"Why?" I asked, defensively. "I always talk to strange men at the markets!"

"That is different! You don't need to ask soldiers for favors. Never again!" The conversation was over.

It was the first time Kamal had ever been angry with me, but I was somewhat relieved that he was more upset with me for talking to a soldier than for my actions.

The next day, when Kamal told his brother what happened, Ali laughed.

"*Mabrouk*, Hiba," he said, congratulating me.

"You are learning the Libyan way. But next time you want bananas, ask me first!"

Our house on Ben Ashor soon became a social hub for family, friends, politicians, and visiting professors and businessmen. I made sure that we always had plenty of extra food because it was acceptable for a guest to bring someone along, or for friends and relatives to show up unexpectedly. Sometimes Kamal would be invited out for dinners, but I would only go if I knew the hostess or if she spoke English.

As it was customary for the men to eat separately from the women, I missed eating many of my meals without Kamal. The only male guests I would sit and eat with were Libyans I knew during our time in the States, or with foreigners. It was one of the biggest adjustments I had to make, but in time I got used to the custom. I regretted missing out on conversations, which I knew would have been more interesting in the men's section. Knowing how I felt though, Kamal would always tell me what they were talking about after everyone left.

The first few months in Libya were hectic—adjusting to a new life, taking care of my family, all the while trying to run a busy household. However, it was also exciting meeting so many unique and culturally significant people, and in many ways I felt Libyan history was being made. I liked the Libyans I met, especially their humor and their candor, but most notably, the warmth and kindness with which they welcomed me into their world. And of course I loved my new family, who had accepted me as their own. Rogaya called me her fifth daughter, and Lamia and Noor included me in their social lives. They introduced me to other Libyan women, which opened up a whole new outlook for me into Libyan society. I became very close to Lamia, Ali's wife, and always felt that spending time with her brought me closer to understanding Libya and the Libyan way of life. She was a very good teacher and had a kind and gentle demeanor I found calming and reassuring in my new life.

Weddings and children's birthday parties were the main social events, occasions for the women to dress up and socialize. Shortly after arriving in Libya, Noor invited me to a birthday party for one of her relatives' three-year old daughter. I was looking forward to it, especially knowing that Layla would enjoy meeting other children. When Noor's chauffeured limousine door opened, the look on her face told me something was terribly wrong.

"You're wearing that?" She pointed at me, her expression incredulous, as if I were half-naked.

I didn't understand what she meant. I was wearing my best maternity dress, beige linen I accented with my Mikimoto pearl necklace and matching three-strand bracelet Kamal had bought me as a gift after Layla was born.

I thought I looked rather smart, until I realized she had on a ball gown and was dripping in diamonds. Self-consciously, I got into the car, feeling grossly under dressed.

When we arrived I saw that I was the only one there apart from the maids who were not in formal gowns and covered with jewelry. I understood then what she meant; surely, she was embarrassed to walk in with me. It was four o'clock in the afternoon, and I tried to explain to Noor later that women in the States don't dress up that way for children's parties, and definitely not in the afternoon.

"This is Libya, not America," she reminded me.

I thought about it later, and realized she was absolutely right, but I still wished she had prepared me for it. I decided from that moment on to never compare again, as there would be many things about Libya I would miss if I were back home. Still, I could never make myself wear a formal dress to an afternoon party for kids. Instead, I loaded up on all the jewelry I owned, as I didn't want the other women to think that my husband didn't love me!

Because of the separation of men and women, there were only a few occasions for women to get really dressed up, except for weddings and parties. However, I found out later that not all birthday parties for children were like that. Many of the other birthday parties I went to were not as dressy. Even though Kamal told me repeatedly that one of the things he loved about me was my simplicity, and my reluctance to show off, I tried my best to get more dressed up, and fit in better, by piling on all the jewelry I owned and wearing my best dresses! But no ball gowns...

One of the birthday parties I attended proved interesting in a way I had not anticipated. Soon after I arrived I was introduced to a woman accompanied by two of her little boys around Layla's age. She was a handsome woman with strong features marred by unyielding eyes and an unsmiling mouth. She was Safiya Gaddafi, Muammar Gaddafi's wife.

I made no attempt to speak with her after our introduction, because I really didn't know what to say except to ask why her husband was terrorizing Libyans, and why she let him. I noticed that she sat mostly by herself that afternoon, looking as if she was doing the hostess a favor by virtue of her presence. I didn't see her engaging in any extended conversation, and I am sure some of the women were uncomfortable having her around, even though everyone treated her graciously and respectfully.

I discovered over the years that Safiya Gaddafi did not have much of a presence in Libya, and was very private, whether by choice or not. The gossip was that she was really a nurse of Bosnian and Hungarian descent, and had met Gaddafi when he was in the hospital for an appendectomy. She was considered by many Libyans to be a foreigner, even though she was officially declared to be from the Barasa tribe in eastern Libya.

At times I felt lonely not having someone to talk to who understood some of the feelings and anxiety I was experiencing. Kamal was gone a lot, and other than his family,

I had no friends of my own I enjoyed spending time with. All that changed one day, when Kamal said he had invited a couple he wanted me to meet to dinner. Their names were Mary and Ahmed Sharif; they had just moved to Libya from the States. Kamal was wary of me socializing with other Americans, but I assumed that he must have liked Ahmed enough to invite them to our house. All he knew was that the couple had met in Iowa when they were both studying at the university, and that they had no children.

Ahmed was from Misrata, and was teaching Civil Engineering at the University in Tripoli. He was an easy-going, handsome man with an infectious smile. His thick jet black-hair and mustache complemented a big mole on one side of his face. Mary was a down-to-earth mid-westerner from Dubuque, Iowa, who worked for the Occidental Oil Company in Tripoli. She was a beautiful woman with short curly blond hair and sparkling blue eyes radiating with warmth and sincerity.

I had not known what to expect that evening, but Mary and I bonded from the moment we met. I had instructed Kamaria to cook a special Malaysian chicken curry dinner, and the four of us sat at the dining table for hours eating and laughing. Mary loved food and she had a weird sense of humor, just like me. She was well educated, witty, and a fun conversationalist, but most of all she had that special quality of openness and candor, which attracts me to certain people I want to befriend.

From that night on, Mary and I became almost insepa-rable. Having no children of their own, Mary and Ahmed became like family to me and my children. Since I had a cook, and they loved her cooking, they would eat with us almost every day. We would sometimes just sit around talking for hours, drinking freshly squeezed juices or rose syrup water, and indulging in seasonal fruits and delicious Arabic pastries from my favorite bakery downtown. We loved to laugh and we laughed together through many funny and sometimes difficult moments. Whenever Kamal's family saw me, they would always ask how my parents were and then would ask about Mary, as if we were related.

One thing I really wanted to do was simply be able to walk around the neighborhood, but Kamal warned me not to go out and wander around. I decided to do it anyway one day when he was away in Paris on a business trip. I noticed that a brand new supermarket had opened about half a mile from our house, so one afternoon I decided to take Layla there to get an ice cream. It was extremely hot that day, and I wanted to do something fun with my little girl.

On our way back with our ice cream, without any warning, the wind started blowing powerfully—and with it the sand. The force of the sand startled me; it actually hurt as the sand hit our faces and even went through our clothing to our bodies.

I swept Layla into my arms and quickened my pace. Layla was scared and crying by now. I covered her with my body as much as I could. I had never been in a *gibli*, or sandstorm before, and not knowing what to expect, I was terrified. We managed to get home, but naturally I did not dare tell Kamal what happened. Luckily for me, Layla, who was known as a tittle-tattle after telling everyone Kamaria had false teeth, had forgotten about the incident by the time her father got home.

A few years later, after my second child was born, I was still determined to do fun things for my children, with or without Kamal's permission. When I found out there was one cinema in Tripoli that showed English movies, I asked Kamal if I could take the kids one afternoon, but he was adamant that women did not go to movies in Libya, and even he would not go with me.

"This is Libya, Hiba, not America. Women don't go to movies here."

"Why not? If someone like you, educated in America, married to an American, is not willing to let his wife do it, then how do you expect anyone else to?"

"Be patient, Hiba, these things take time." I was beginning to see the pattern he used to end these uncomfortable discussions.

Regardless, on Kamal's next overseas trip, I decided to take the children and Kamaria to see an English movie. My two-year-old son had never been to a cinema before, and I thought it would be fun to take him and Layla to one. I timed it so we would get there after the show started and everyone was seated, in the middle of the day on a Wednesday. I bought our tickets for the balcony, which was a little more expensive and totally empty. We sat in the first row upstairs.

To see my little boy's eyes widen in amazement at the big screen was worth defying my husband's wishes. Tarek hung on the brass rail, so happy, totally mesmerized by the big screen. Then, when a huge truck came on the screen, he started jumping up and down shouting, "Fuck, fuck".... I tried everything to quiet him down, but he was so excited that I could not stop him. When the men on the lower level started looking up and laughing, I knew it was time for us to go.

There were two very unhappy children on the ride home, and a not very understanding husband to whom I felt obligated later to relate the experience. It was the first and last time I ever went to the movies in Libya.

I was not so lucky the second time I decided to take another walk by myself. After finding out the chances of a *gibli* occurring was improbable since it was cooler, I decided to take Layla to the store for ice-cream once again. Halfway there, a young boy on a bicycle rode up to us and exposed himself. While trying to protect my daughter from seeing what he was doing, I also managed to scream at him and push his bicycle away. When he realized that I was not going to quietly let him get away with his disgusting act, he laughed at me and rode off.

Almost immediately, I saw a police car close by and frantically signaled it to stop. I tried to explain what happened. Though it was difficult to explain, I think he understood but basically told me to forget it. His attitude bothered me because I got the impression that he probably thought I deserved what happened for walking around without a man. I finally insisted that he drive me to Kamal's office at the Arab Development Institute, which was not far away. When he realized that my husband was Libyan and a "Dr."—which I intentionally stressed—he started to pay more attention and respect.

Where did the boy go, he asked? After I pointed in the direction, he signaled for Layla and me to get in the back of the small police car and started driving in that direction. A few blocks down, I saw the bicyclist. The policeman shouted at him to stop, and got out of the car to question him.

To my horror, he proceeded to bring him back to the car and made him sit in the front seat. I understood enough

Arabic to hear the boy denying everything, but the policeman ignored him and loaded his bicycle onto the roof of
the police car.

When we got to the building where Kamal worked, Layla
and I sat in the car waiting while the policeman grabbed
the boy and took him upstairs to Kamal's office. After a few
minutes, Kamal came running out. The policeman followed,
dragging the boy with him.

Clearly distressed, Kamal asked me what happened.
After telling him my version, I could see he was extremely
angry, and immediately turned around and slapped the boy
in front of the policeman. He then told him that if he ever
even looked at me or his daughter again, he would hang
him from the nearest lamp post.

I knew that Kamal was only trying to scare him, but I was
starting to feel sorry for the boy—who couldn't have been
more than sixteen. By now, the police realized that Kamal
was not only Libyan, but possibly politically well connected,
and started to put on a big show for his benefit. Kamal told
me later that he threatened to arrest and put the boy away
in Solitary for the rest of his life!

After getting over his own anger, Kamal told the police to
let him go, swearing that if he ever came near me or his family again he would do what he said. By now the poor boy was
in tears and begging, and I could tell Kamal was also starting to feel sorry for him. Finally, after a lot of yelling and
another slap from the policeman, the boy hastily rode off on
his bicycle.

That evening, Kamal told me that I was never to walk
around the neighborhood again.

"A lot of these men aren't used to seeing women outside of their immediate family," he explained. "Some of these sick ones, like the one today, go crazy when they see a pretty lady walking around. They'll treat you like a *sharmuta*—a whore—because they are ignorant, uneducated and idiots!" I had never seen Kamal so angry.

"I let him go today because he was young and because he was mentally retarded."

His anger frightened me, but I knew he was only upset at what could have happened to Layla and me.

"Hiba, if you're not careful you could put me in a situation where I may have to kill someone to protect your honor and my name. I cannot allow any man to disrespect my wife. Do you see the position you put me in?"

Seeing I was just as upset, he softened his tone and took me in his arms.

"Just be patient, my love," he said gently, nuzzling his lips in my hair. "One day Libya will change, and be a kinder society to women. Believe me, Hiba, I want that so much too, for the sake of my children and all Libyans."

For my daughter and the women of Libya, I hoped and prayed the change would happen in our lifetime.

CHAPTER 8

THE BUBBLE ROOM

As I walked into the American Embassy that spring morning, I glanced surreptitiously at the rooftop of the building across the road. Libyan Secret Service men were perched there like vultures, just as Kamal had warned, watching and filming every person entering the Embassy.

I was riddled with guilt for not telling my husband what I was doing. I was sure he would tell me not to go—so I hadn't asked, by rationalizing that the welfare of my unborn child justified my defiance. By my doctor's calculations back in Florida, the baby was due in June. It was already April, and I had not seen a doctor since leaving the States in December. Four months.

The embassy was housed in an old Italianate terracotta stucco villa in the city center, surrounded by modern buildings that already looked tired and aged due to neglect. The reception room was packed with Libyans and foreigners, all frantically vying for an official's attention. I idly wondered if any of the men there were also secret police.

It was hot and stuffy inside, despite several window air conditioners struggling to suffuse cool air into the close quarters. The scores of all our hot bodies pressed closely together defeated their tireless efforts.

I wiped the perspiration from my forehead and took deep breaths to overcome a creeping tide of claustrophobia, both from the surroundings as well as from the heaviness of my advanced pregnancy. I heaved a determined sigh and got to the back of one of three long lines.

It was obvious that most of the people were there to get visas to the United States. For some reason, I felt safe simply knowing that I was diplomatically on American soil. I just hoped I wasn't doing anything wrong by being there, and that Kamal wouldn't be too angry with me.

After standing in line for a while, I felt a soft touch on my arm and turned to see an attractive black woman with an overly friendly smile. Despite the heat, she looked impeccably crisp in a smart white linen suit with matching white pumps.

"May I help you, Madame?" the woman asked.

She was an American! My spirits lifted immediately. It was nice to hear an American voice.

"Oh, yes, please!" I replied with relief. "My name's Hiba Ben Ramadan. I'm American; I'm here to register."

"So nice to meet you, Mrs Ben Ramadan! My name's Lynn Pendleton. I'm the liaison for consular affairs."

Her accent hinted at Ivy League. She extended a bony, well-manicured hand, which I happily accepted and shook. Her smile widened, and I wondered if she already knew who I was. Using her other hand, Miss Pendleton lightly laid it on my shoulder.

"Please follow me," she said in a low voice, drawing me out of the line.

I was quite taken aback by this show of favoritism, and while relishing in it, I was also a little self-conscious. Her manner exuded such grace and hospitality that it made me feel more like an honored guest in her home. I noticed the questioning expressions of some people in the crowd as I was whisked away, but I didn't care. Often, because of my olive complexion, I would be mistaken for an Arab, so they were probably thinking I was in trouble.

I followed Miss Pendleton down a long narrow hallway into a room at the end. It was a small room, about twelve by twelve feet, but the walls were very unusual. They were completely covered in a metallic quilt-like fabric, including the ceiling. The temperature in the room was much cooler than the other rooms, almost cold. A low wooden round table stood in the middle, surrounded by four comfortable looking club chairs. The only other thing in the room was a large crystal ashtray on the table, overflowing with cigarette butts.

I sensed Miss Pendleton was watching my reactions very closely. With a gracious smile, she motioned for me to take a seat, simultaneously removing the ashtray.

"I'll be right back," she said reassuringly, as she made a move to leave the room. I settled into one of the chairs, marveling at how quiet the room was. It was nice to just sit and relax after standing in line for so long in the oppressive reception room. Miss Pendleton returned in about ten minutes with someone.

"Mrs Ben Ramadan, there's somebody here I'd like you to meet."

Before I could answer, a large man, wearing thick glasses, with sandy-colored hair and a bushy mustache walked into the room. He wore khaki trousers and a navy blue sports jacket over an open-neck white shirt. I suspected he was

responsible for a lot of those cigarette butts in the ashtray.
He too had a very big and friendly smile, eagerly extending
a beefy hand followed by a firm handshake. He was average-
looking, and if I had not known he was American, he could
have passed for a fair-complexioned Libyan like my father-
in-law. Despite his thinning hair, I suspected that he was
only in his early forties.

"Mrs Ben Ramadan! I'm James Moore. Delighted to meet
you!" His exuberance seemed genuine.

"Very nice to meet you, too," I nodded, feeling somewhat
confused and overwhelmed by this special treatment.

"Well, I've got to get back to work," Miss Pendleton interrupted with a demure smile, laying one hand on my arm. "If
there's ever anything I can do to help you, anything at all,
please let me know!"

"Thank you, Miss Pendleton. It was nice meeting you," I
mumbled—still uneasy by the curious exchange.

She left discreetly, closing the door carefully behind her.
The room was so sound-proofed I could not even hear her
heels clicking down the corridor.

I was now left alone with James Moore. I felt a little
uncomfortable, realizing that Kamal would not be pleased
to know that I had been alone in a room with a strange man.
I knew enough about Libyan customs by now to know that I
was in a compromised situation politically as well as culturally.
Once again, I was torn between what I was and how I was supposed to behave. For now I was just glad to be in the company
of an American-speaking person, yet I had a suspicious feeling there was something behind all this hospitality.

Mr Moore turned out to be a pleasant and engaging
conversationalist. He told me he had been working in the

Middle East for many years, and let on that he was a collector of Arabic art and artefacts. He asked if I spoke any Arabic, and inquired about my family back home. I had the feeling he already knew the answers, because he was asking all the right questions. However, I was enjoying the conversation so much that I really didn't care.

Reluctantly, I decided to change the subject, and take the opportunity to gear it to the real purpose of my visit.

"Mr Moore, I..."

"Please, call me Jim."

"I'd like to have my baby delivered at the American Oil Clinic, but apparently only employees of oil companies are allowed. However, my husband and I are willing to pay whatever it costs." Kamal had said nothing of the sort.

"Is there any way the embassy can help me?" I sounded like I was begging, but for my baby's sake I could afford to be a little shameless.

"Consider it done!" He replied, without hesitation.

"In fact," he continued, "I'll make sure that Dr Watson, Head of Obstetrics, will personally take your case. You'll also have the best suite there!"

I couldn't believe it was that easy. I was so relieved I wanted to hug him. I had been trying to get Kamal to make an appointment for me there ever since I arrived in Libya. Both he and Amir had assured me that it would not be a problem; however, I still had not seen a doctor, and was already in my seventh month. I was becoming annoyed with Kamal for not being more concerned. I knew he was very busy, but I felt that under the circumstances I deserved more attention. That was when I decided to take matters into my own hands.

Nabila, our Tunisian maid, had just given birth to a baby girl the week before at the main hospital, and when I went to visit her I was horrified. There were two women to a bed, with pillows at opposite ends. The bed linens stank, and the bathroom floors were wet and dirty. Kamal said it was because there were not enough hospitals and that they were unable to hire competent doctors and nurses. Generally, Libyans would not do menial jobs, so most of the workers had to be brought in from countries like Egypt, Tunisia, Chad or Sudan. Many of the nurses at that time came from Pakistan and Egypt.

The nurses at the Oil Clinic, however, were all from the U.S. and Britain, and were better qualified. I had heard that the rooms were pristine and well furnished, and I was determined to go there or go home. I had no doubt that Kamal's family could make the necessary arrangements, but I felt the delay was due to their reluctance to ask favors from foreigners. However, I was desperate, and was ready to ask anyone who could help.

"Thank you so much, Mr Moore." I gushed, with relief and gratitude, trying not to sound too desperate, but I was thrilled! Kamal would not consider letting me go back to Florida to have the baby, and I was terrified of having my baby at the hospital I had seen (which was considered to be one of the newest and best in Tripoli).

"Mrs Ben Ramadan, if you would please give me your telephone number, I'll have someone from the hospital call you with details."

Without hesitation, and without thinking, I quickly wrote down my number with the pen and notepad Mr Moore had removed from his jacket pocket and happily handed it back.

"I'll take care of this right away, Mrs Ben Ramadan. I promise you'll be hearing from someone by tomorrow, at the very latest."

I thanked him and started to get up to go, but Moore cleared his throat and subtly gestured for me to stay.

Looking me straight in the eye, with a more serious tone in his voice, he said, almost apologetically, "Mrs Ben Ramadan, I'd very much like to meet your husband, Dr Ben Ramadan. Do you think it would be all right for me to call him?"

Surprised at what he was asking, I was at a momentary loss for a reply. I also realized that, of course, now that I had given him our home number he could call anytime. I was starting to feel a little worried.

"Well…I'll have to ask him. I think our phones are bugged, and …"

I wondered if this man realized that a call from the American Embassy would put Kamal in a precarious position. There were eyes and ears everywhere, and Kamal could easily be accused of working with the Americans.

"Mrs Ben Ramadan, I absolutely understand your hesitation," he interrupted, in a sympathetic tone.

"But I want to assure you I have no intentions of putting your husband – or you," he paused and looked at me seriously, "in a compromising position. All I ask is if you would just please tell him that I would like very much to meet him."

"All right," I replied, uncertainly, and with some hesitation. "I'll tell him."

I was perplexed by this request, but I also wanted to try to be accommodating and not appear ungrateful. Despite everything, the hospital booking remained foremost in my mind.

"Mrs Ben Ramadan, I think there's something I should tell you," continued this big American with a gentle smile. "Nothing said in this room can be heard by anyone, anywhere, which is why we brought you in here. I want you to feel comfortable to say anything you want," he said, pausing for a second. "Do you understand what I'm trying to tell you?'

I nodded, his implication slowing sinking in. I thought quickly about the secret police monitoring who was coming and going, into and out of the embassy. However, I was an American citizen, and didn't see why I would get into trouble. In fact, I had not even registered my presence with the embassy, which was the required and perhaps sensible thing for all Americans who reside abroad to do.

Mr Moore let his words sink in before continuing.

"This room is totally isolated from any kind of sound or visual devise. We call it the Bubble Room."

It finally dawned on me that he was CIA!

How the hell was I ever going to explain this to Kamal? I suddenly felt very nervous – and wanted to get out of that Bubble Room as quickly as possible.

"Mr Moore, I'll tell my husband what you said. However, please understand that our phones are tapped, and I don't want him compromised in any way because of me."

I could feel the panic rising in my chest.

"I assure you, Mrs Ben Ramadan, that all I want to do is offer Dr Ben Ramadan any assistance in expediting any of his research or visa needs."

In fact, he was correct about Kamal needing a visa soon. Kamal had told me recently that he would be going back and forth a lot to the States representing the Libyan Ministry of Foreign Affairs with talks at the State Department in Washington. However, I also knew that all his travel arrangements were made through the Ministry and not by him.

"All right, I'll tell him." I got up out of my chair. "Thank you so much for helping me with the hospital."

I was indeed still very grateful for that, but I was starting to feel that it would come with too high a price.

"Before you go, Mrs Ben Ramadan, there's something else I need to suggest to you."

I was feeling so guilty by now—though I wasn't exactly sure why—and braced myself for what he was about to say. *Perhaps I should just fly back to Florida to have my baby there.*

"I strongly urge you not to acquire a US passport for your baby here in Libya. Wait until you return to the United States, and only use the children's Libyan passports to travel in and out of Libya."

I was confused, and he noticed, because he quickly proceeded to tell me what I had not previously been aware of.

Apparently Libya, unlike the United States, did not recognize dual citizenship. A child born to a Libyan father was considered Libyan, just as that child would be considered an American born to an American parent anywhere abroad. Technically, my children are Americans, but the Libyan government considered them Libyans, as long as they were in Libya. If a child was found to have an American passport in Libya, the parents could conceivably be charged with treason or, at best, be at the mercy of Libyan authorities.

Moore also told me that in case of a divorce, or if Kamal died, he, or the children's grandparents would

141

become legal guardians, and I would not be allowed to take them out of the country. To top it off, he told me that as a wife I was not allowed to leave the country without my husband's written permission. My ears were starting to burn with the newfound knowledge of all these rather ominous laws.

This was a lot of information for me to take in, along with the implications of it all, and I was growing increasingly upset that my husband had not been forthright with me. I didn't like being kept in the dark, especially about issues that concerned my children or me. I hoped he had not done it on purpose. I brushed the thought aside, sure that he didn't.

I hurriedly thanked Mr Moore again, and I could see he did not realize (or at least pretended not to realize) the effects of all the information he had just dumped on me. As we shook hands goodbye, Miss Pendleton miraculously materialized, offering to show me out. By now, the welcoming smiles were starting to wear thin.

I was feeling thoroughly guilty and remorseful, even though I had not done anything wrong. But as I left the embassy, I made a point of avoiding looking at the building across the road.

On the slow drive home, it occurred to me how much control Kamal really had over my life, if he so chose to exercise it. Thankfully though, I felt confident that neither he nor his family would ever do anything to hurt me or my children.

By the time I returned home I felt calmer, and was prepared to tell Kamal about what had happened. As usual, we had guests for dinner, so I did not get a chance to talk to him about what happened until everyone had left and we were preparing for bed.

"I went to the American Embassy today," I bravely but casually declared, trying to set the pace of the conversation.

"What for?" he asked, a bit bewildered.

"To try and find a doctor and a hospital, which you and Amir have been promising to do. I couldn't wait anymore."

He started to look defensive, so I cut him off.

"Anyways," I continued, "it's all set. I've made arrangements to have the baby at the Oil Clinic and I'll start seeing a doctor next week. His name's Watson. I think he's Canadian."

Kamal didn't say anything, but I could see he was not as thrilled about it as I was.

"Ali said he could get you into the military hospital, which is very good. You'll be very well taken care of there."

"No, Kamal, I really want this. I want to be where they can speak English."

I had only been in Libya for a few months, and my range of the dialect was limited to conversing with my family members and shopkeepers. There were very few times in my marriage that I had been demanding, but I was adamant about this; Kamal knew me well enough to know that it was a losing battle for him.

"Okay," he conceded. "Next time just let me know when you're going to do something like this." He was not finished. "This is not America. You cannot do whatever you want or go wherever you want, and now they'll be wondering what you were doing at the embassy."

"Kamal, I met someone at the embassy today, and you need to know what happened."

I braced myself and told him everything, ignoring his facial expressions in case I lost courage and omitted something important.

When I finished, he simply said, "I'm not interested in talking with them, but you can go ahead and make the arrangements with the hospital if you want."

"Why didn't you tell me any of those things about exit visas and custody of children and all that stuff?"

"Why would I? It doesn't concern us!"

I wasn't satisfied with the answer, but I felt that the conversation was over, and I wanted it to be over, too. So I turned my back and pretended to sleep. After a minute, I felt his arms around me.

He quietly whispered, "*Habibti,* don't worry about that nonsense. I love you, and you have to trust me. I would never do anything to hurt you or the children, I swear. Just please don't go to the embassy again without telling me first, okay?"

The tone of his voice troubled me. "Is there something more? Something I should know?"

"There are people here who would love to make trouble for me, so you must be very careful about who you see and what you do. They're watching you, too, and would find any reason to accuse us of doing something wrong."

"So, are you telling me I can't be seen with Americans?"

"It would be better not to, especially the ones working in the embassy."

I suddenly began to feel walled-in, cut off from the world I had known. I finally realized how much life had changed for us since arriving in Libya. I loved my husband and my

Libyan family, but for the first time I understood that there was someone far greater than all of us who dominated our lives. His pictures were everywhere, his voice on the TV and radio constantly, and all our conversations were centered on him and his actions. And in all those conversations, something was missing; something we talked around. The missing element was personal freedom, fueled by the omnipresence of Gaddafi, who seemed to have his ears and eyes everywhere.

After my visit to the embassy, Kamal told me that Ali said I was being followed by a man driving a black Peugeot. After that revelation, I started to take notice. From afar, all I could discern was his dark sunglasses. Once on a hot morning, I even saw him sitting under a tree across the road. I had no doubt that he knew I was aware of his presence.

On my way to my Italian hairdresser one day, I noticed that the black car was right behind mine. For the heck of it I decided it was time to say hi, so I stuck my hand out the window and waved to him. Kamal did not think that was funny when I told him. It seemed to me that just because of Kamal's position and me being an American I was suspected of being something or other. I was not afraid because I obviously had nothing to hide, but innocence was irrelevant in those days.

Kamal said that Gaddafi gave pointless jobs to people like the guy following me because they were not smart enough to do much else, and spying on people gave them purpose and self-importance. Kamal considered them to be thugs, but probably better paid and compensated than he or his peers.

"Are you worried about something, Kamal?" Though I could see and feel his frustration every day, this was the first

145

time he had expressed any concerns to me. He would usually brush them off, saying things would get better.

"Yes, *Habibti*, I am. The situation is not like I imagined it would be, but I'm just hoping it'll change and get better." He hesitated for a moment before continuing. "I see and hear many things that disturb me, and I'm trying my best to change people's minds. But it seems like most people are operating on fear. No one dares to trust anyone or do anything different, for fear of losing their jobs, or worse."

I was trying to absorb what he was saying, and wondered if he had already been encountering roadblocks professionally, but I didn't want to push him for more answers. I sensed that night, for the first time since arriving, that the political situation was much worse than Kamal had suspected.

Libya was at that time still a fairly young country, and as Kamal kept trying to explain, going through growing pains. He was involved in the process, and I know he had hopes for Libya toward which he was working tirelessly. With oil, Libya had a chance to prosper and thrive. He was convinced that he and his peers, who had the opportunity of gaining a higher education abroad, could help shape this into a reality.

There was so much to be done, but even with the oil money and an educated population, change was happening too slowly. Gaddafi had been in power for almost eight years, but there was little to show for it. For now, I had to focus on my family. All I really wanted was to have my baby delivered safely. That prospect was looking better, and I was looking forward to my first appointment. I just hoped the price was not going to be too high.

CHAPTER 9

TAREK

Shortly after my visit to the embassy I was contacted by the hospital administrator and made my first doctor's appointment. It was April, and by now, with the due date only two months away, I was getting larger and feeling more uncomfortable. So, I was definitely looking forward to this long-overdue checkup.

After having been told how my mother-in-law delivered her own child, I felt a little embarrassed to be complaining, but I did nevertheless. The women in my family, especially Rogaya, were even more sympathetic than I'd expected. My sweet mother-in-law tried to look at situations concerning me through my eyes, and always stood up for me. She and Ibrahim were like the parents I never had but always wished for.

On the day of the appointment, Kamal drove me to the hospital, which was on the outskirts of the city. I felt a weight lifting from my shoulders, and I could see that Kamal was relieved as well.

"I know it's going to be a boy," he kept saying. "But of course it doesn't matter, as long as it's healthy," he would quickly add in response to my expression.

"By the way, *Habibti*, I just want you to know that we won't be doing Lamaze this time," he said, glancing over at me to make sure I was all right with it.

"That's fine."

"Just don't tell me I have seven more to go!"

He laughed, remembering how upset I was when I was in labor with Layla and he jokingly made the comment, "Eight more to go," referring to beating the number of children his mother had by one.

I, too, secretly wished for a boy this time. I felt Libya was not fair to girls and that it might be a long time before women would be able to enjoy equality with men.

I tried to memorize the way to the hospital, knowing that sometimes I might have to drive there myself. After about twenty minutes, the hospital came into view at the end of a long and dusty road. It was like a mirage in the middle of the desert, a neat and attractive, sprawling American-style ranch house.

When we entered, I felt a renewed sense of security wash over me. Everything was going to be all right. The clinic looked professional and clean. The nurses were in tidy-looking white uniforms with matching white caps, and the marble floors looked polished, as did the walls. I glanced at Kamal and saw that he shared my relief.

We had once taken Layla to the children's ward at Fatah Hospital when she had an alarmingly high temperature in the middle of the night. I was absolutely appalled by what I saw there. First of all, they had to put us in a makeshift room because all the other rooms were filled, and we refused to share. When we walked into the room, I saw discarded bloody bandages on the floor, which I had to ask to be removed.

The Egyptian nurse on duty was friendly, but only just. Whatever I requested seemed like an imposition. There was no soap by the washbasin, and when I asked for some she nonchalantly replied that they were out. Out of soap in a hospital? I was incredulous!

She shrugged and snickered, "What can I do?"

I started to grow fearful, seeing that Layla's health was being compromised by this type of incompetence. Kamal and I held her for the entire four hours we were there because the sheets looked used. I received a lot of exasperated looks but I didn't care. Neither did Kamal, who was also becoming very upset by what he saw.

Gaddafi's regime had spent so much money on modern hospitals, but the quality of administration and labor was atrocious. New buildings started looking old within a few years. Employees were not properly trained and supervised, and the upkeep of places such as this hospital was left mostly to foreign workers who were just interested in collecting a paycheck. The general attitude was that since it was not their country, they really didn't care.

It seemed like the quality of people hired were usually those who had a difficult time getting jobs in their own countries – understandably because of their attitudes and lack of qualifications. They were paid very well in Libya, but living conditions were not as favorable for foreigners. Our Egyptian nurse was probably only friendly because of the presence of a Libyan. After being examined by a Pakistani doctor, who prescribed antibiotics for Layla, Kamal and I waited for the nurse to bring the medicine to us, anxious to get Layla out of there. When she finally came back with it, Kamal looked at the bottle and I could see his face darken.

"What is this?" he asked the nurse, in disgust.

"This medicine says adults only, and my daughter is not even two! What is wrong with you people?"

He was shouting by now in Arabic, and she made the mistake of arguing with him. Kamal got so upset that he threw the bottle on the bed. I knew enough Arabic to know that he was cursing. He took Layla from my arms and stormed out of the room, with me following, flabbergasted by the whole experience.

"This is ridiculous," he said, when we got to the car. "They can't even be bothered to read the directions of medicine that they give out – especially to a baby. We can't even hire decent people with all the money we pay them!"

Dr Charles Watson was much older than I expected, probably in his seventies. He was a retired Canadian gynecologist from Vancouver. He had lovely bedside manners and was grandfatherly, but I also noticed he had hand tremors.

He showed us around the hospital, which was impeccable and orderly – and almost empty, a good sign for me. I was thoroughly satisfied with everything, but I was concerned by the tremors. After we went back to his office he examined me, with Kamal in the room, and told me that the baby was fine and that I would need to come back every week.

When we got into the car, the first thing Kamal asked was if I noticed that his hands were shaking.

"Yes, I did..." I replied with a slight hesitation.

"You sure you don't want to go to the military hospital?"

"Since we're going to do a natural birth like we did with Layla, he won't be operating. I think it'll be okay. Just make sure you're in the room with me."

"This is not the States, *Habibti.* I don't think they even allow men in the delivery room here."

"It's an American hospital. Please insist!" Just knowing he was there would bring me great comfort.

He eventually gave in, joking that he would be the laughing stock of Tripoli.

There were many times in Libya when I saw the conflict my husband felt between doing what he believed was right and what he felt had to be done in order to conform to custom. Even though at times I felt his battle was hypocritical, particularly in minor inconsequential situations, I chose to trust his judgment.

I remember one time when we were going to pay respects to a family member who had passed away. Kamal insisted that I wear the Libyan *Urrday* and wrap myself with the *Farashiya*, the traditional white covering, cloaking over everything, including my head. His father disagreed, and said I did not need to. I wondered why it was that my husband, educated in the United States and desperate for change, could be more conservative than his father. Kamal finally gave in to his father's objections. Even though he was not happy about it, I ended up going as myself and loved my father-in-law more for standing up for me!

I started going once a week for checkups, always accompanied by Kamal, unless he was out of the country. I was due mid-June, but by the end of that month I was only getting bigger and hotter, and there was still no sign of the baby coming. Dr Watson said that even though I might be overdue he was not going to induce labor for another couple of weeks.

Mary accompanied me on one of my last visits to the doctor when Kamal was in Morocco. On our way back to the city, I noticed that the car behind was tailgating me. The road was very narrow, and there was hardly any room for me to move over for it to pass without stopping. It was so close that I was afraid he was going to crash into my little Fiat, which was so small that my huge stomach was actually touching the steering wheel.

Mary and I started cursing the driver of the big black shiny car behind us, who we were sure was just showing off and trying to intimidate us. When I did not move over to the side of the road to let him pass, he slammed on the horn impatiently and continuously.

"What should I do?" I asked Mary, afraid that he would purposely ram into my car and hurt my baby.

"Just stop on the side and let the idiot pass!"

I did that, but not without shouting insults at the driver as he passed us. I remember calling him *kalbe ya hud* or dog of the Jew, the worst curse I knew in Arabic, even though Kamal had told me never to use it.

The driver knew we were cursing him, but he just looked at us and laughed as he slowed down to wave his thanks. I thought he looked familiar. His car was followed by a black Peugeot with four men in it who were waving and laughing at us, pointing to the car that had just passed us.

"Oh shit, Esther, is that who I think it is?" Mary asked with her hand over her mouth.

It immediately registered with me who he was. I can't believe that he had almost run us off the road and that I had so loudly shouted that awful curse. He was the prime minister of Libya, Abdel Salam Jalloud, the second most powerful man in the country. The men in the car following him were obviously secret service.

"Oh, my God!" Mary and I kept saying, realizing the trouble we could have gotten into. Thank goodness he and his goons had some sense of humor – or we very well might have ended up in prison.

I was uncomfortably large and overdue by July, and expected every day to be "the" day. It was stifling hot and dry, and it was becoming too difficult for me to be outside the house. Not sure if it was going to be a boy or a girl, we had a difficult time deciding on names, even though I favored Alia and Adam. I was hoping for a son, so that I would not feel obligated to keep trying until I produced one. The Libyan ladies – especially those who had sons! -- kept telling me that I had to give Kamal a son. The ones who only had daughters insisted that it did not matter anymore.

Mary and Ahmed came almost every evening after work to keep us company, as it was too difficult for me towards the end to continue entertaining a house full of guests every night. Kamaria cooked all my favorite Singaporean foods that I was craving, which luckily everyone, including Kamal, loved as much as I did. We spent our evenings playing cards or watching American movies Mary borrowed from Occidental Oil Company, where she worked. Mostly though, Mary and I would just sit and talk. We would sometimes laugh so uncontrollably over the silliest thing that our husbands would look at us and shake their heads in bafflement.

It was, by all accounts, an exceptionally hot summer. I would fan with my hand and not feel any breeze. I was

153

getting so big that it was difficult to walk, sit or sleep. Kamal kept teasing me that I looked like I was carrying twins, which would have delighted him to no end. My legs started cramping every night, and Kamal would wake up at my slightest movement to massage them. One night, I had apparently groaned in my sleep and he shot out of bed thinking it was time to leave for the hospital, scaring me in the process.

In the early hours one Friday morning, I told Kamal that I felt the baby was coming, and that he needed to stay home. The phone services were not always reliable, and I was afraid I would be unable to reach him.

"Okay, *Habibti*," he said, "but you know you have been saying that every day for one month?"

"I know, but I didn't tell you to stay home before."

I was sure this was the day. I felt as if I were carrying a ton of bricks in my stomach, which had suddenly dropped.

Around eight that morning, my water broke. I got ready to leave for the hospital, while Kamal called his family in Khums and Mary and Ahmed, who managed to arrive just before we left. They were going to take care of Layla for the day and keep her entertained. When Layla got a little upset that she was not going with us to the hospital, Mary bribed her by promising to take her to the beach and out for gelato later.

By the time we got to the hospital, my contractions were getting closer and closer, but after almost ten hours the baby still hadn't arrived. I could feel my strength giving out, and I was told later that in my delirium I created quite a ruckus. Kamal tried to make jokes and tell me stories to distract me, but I had lost my sense of humor. He told me later that I had ordered him out of the room, and when he got up to go, I ordered him to stay. Then towards the end, I was calling for anyone and everyone to come and put me out of my misery.

Finally, at 11p.m., I gave birth to a beautiful, healthy boy weighing a whopping ten pounds. He had so much hair that when his head first emerged, one of the nurses in the delivery ward thought it was a girl. When I regained my senses I was very embarrassed and ashamed of my behavior, but only briefly. He was, after all, a big baby, and I had done it all naturally. Holding my beautiful newborn in my arms, everything was forgotten.

Kamal cried when he first held his son in his arms, and after they took the baby to be washed, Kamal came and sat on the bed with me, and kissed me.

He held my hand to his lips and whispered his first love name for me, "My Stora, you have given me the two most precious gifts in the world, and I want you to know that I have never been happier in my life as I am today. Don't worry, *Rohay*, I promise you that everything will be okay."

My first visitor early the next morning was my darling daughter, from whom I had never spent a night apart since her birth. She was brought to the hospital by Mary and Kamaria. They had dressed her up in a pretty new sundress, and I'll never forget how wonderful it felt to have both my children in the same room for the first time. After examining her baby brother, Layla was more concerned with when I was going home. Kamal and I later decided that we had to make sure she did not feel the new baby was going to get all the attention.

My mother- and father-in-law came later that afternoon, and told me that every Ben Ramadan household was slaughtering a lamb that day in honor of the baby's birth. We still had not decided on a name, so the four of us spent a long time going over names. I suggested Adam, but Kamal nixed it. Kamal wanted Hisham, but I nixed that.

It went on and on between the four of us all afternoon, and after dozens of names, we all agreed on Tarek. It was actually Ibrahim who suggested it, but he wanted to be sure I agreed and gave the final okay. I loved the name, which made my father-in-law very proud that he had chosen it.

I was put in a lovely, spacious private suite with my baby in a small crib right next to me. There was twenty-four hour service, and I could order from any restaurant in Tripoli if I wanted. After the birth, the hospital stay was almost like a holiday. When my husband and guests were gone, the British and American nurses would come by to chat, and one of the Egyptian nurse's aide would come every morning and night to massage my legs and arms. She even washed and styled my hair for me before I left. I made sure to try every restaurant I could, given my short stay, and Mary and my sisters-in-law all came every day to visit.

I could have stayed longer if I wanted, but I missed my daughter too much, so I went home on the fourth day. Kamal came that morning to take Tarek and me home. On the way, he told me rather casually that we had to have an *Esbua* in three days, as was customary. I had no idea what he was talking about, but after he explained, I wanted to go back to the hospital.

"I have to give a party in three days?" I exclaimed, "You're kidding?!"

In accordance with Libyan custom, a celebration of the baby's arrival is expected on the seventh day of birth. This entailed inviting friends and family to the house. It also meant preparation of meals for a lot of people. Not only was the Ben Ramadan family quite large, but many of the extended family as well as friends would feel obligated to come out of respect. I was still so tired from the birth I didn't know if I could pull off an all-day party for over a hundred people involving lunch, tea and dinner. Also, I knew we did not have enough utensils, glasses and china to accommodate a hundred or more guests.

The next day, Kamal and I went to a small department store to get everything we needed. He told me that his father and brothers would be bringing several lambs to be slaughtered, and the women from the family would take charge of making the couscous as well as other dishes. The day before the celebration Mary drove me to our favorite pastry store, where I bought about two hundred pieces of assorted pastries, including *baklava, kanafe* and *paspusa.*

On the day of the *Esbua,* my whole family converged early at our house and everyone sprang into action. I was ordered by the women to stay in bed and to just get myself ready for the party. They took care of everything under Rogaya and Lamia's directions. The only thing I had to do was serve one cup of tea to each newly arrived guest. My mother-in-law was in charge of making the tea, the maids were instructed to keep washing and tidying up, Kamal would welcome the men while Lamia welcomed the women.

Serving the tea meant collecting a small silver tray filled with shot glasses of hot tea from Rogaya, and handing each individual female guest the first round of tea. Because I had such a difficult labor, I knew it was going to be a little painful for me to stoop and serve so many people, but it had to be done. The one thing I have always respected in traditional cultures are customs such as these. With all the help I had from all the family, Tarek's *Esbua* turned out to be an enjoyable, festive celebration.

My newborn son was sleeping peacefully in our air-conditioned bedroom, but when his grandfather arrived that morning and saw him, he was appalled. Even though it was the middle of summer, Ibrahim did not trust air conditioning, to the misery of his daughters in Khums.

"No, Hiba, not good for Tarek to sleep in air condition-room," he gently admonished me.

He proceeded to turn off the air-conditioner and kiss his grandson on the head, taking in a deep breath.

"He smells like a Ben Ramadan," Ibrahim pronounced, beaming, as if he had just made a brilliant discovery. He was so very proud and happy to have another grandchild.

Starting from about eleven in the morning until nine that night, a steady stream of people arrived. Everyone wanted to see the baby, all of them tucking money into his clothing. His grandfather watched over him like a hawk, quickly moving the money away from the crib as soon as the person left, complaining that it was dirty. By the time the last guest left, over three-thousand dinar had been put into the crib, which amounted to almost ten thousand dollars.

I realized what an important day it was for Kamal, as a means of assessing who came to show their respects. There were obviously no formal invitations issued, but solely by word of mouth almost two hundred people had attended. Their presence was considered an honor and a sign of respect for Kamal and Ibrahim.

Following tradition, many of the guests addressed me as "Um Tarek", mother of Tarek. It was that day when I felt officially accepted as a Ben Ramadan.

CHAPTER 10

KHUMS

Khums, located on the shores of the Mediterranean coast, about sixty-five miles east of Tripoli, was founded by the Phoenicians around 1100 BC. In 146 BC the city became part of the Roman Republic. The Roman Emperor, Septimius Severus, was born in Leptis Magna, about one and a half miles east of Khums. He turned his hometown of Leptis Magna into one of the most beautiful cities in his empire. Today, the ruins at Leptis Magna are considered to be finest example of preserved Roman architecture outside of Italy.

The Ben Ramadan family compound borders the land where the ruins stand, atop remnants of a civilization built before the time of Jesus Christ and Mohammed.

The family home was built by Ibrahim the year before his marriage to Rogaya. It was originally a small, three-room stone house, situated on about a hundred hectares of land overlooking the Mediterranean. As the years passed, Ibrahim added rooms to the house to accommodate his growing family. Though the house became larger, it remained simple and unpretentious, sitting amidst lush groves of olives, dates and orange trees. Sheep, goats, chickens, and the occasional cow roamed fenced-in sections of the land, providing the family with meat, fresh milk, cheese and butter. The forgotten ruins nearby became the personal playground for my children whenever they went to visit their grandparents.

Fridays were always spent at Khums. We all looked forward to our visit to the coast and to seeing everyone. We would leave Tripoli after an early breakfast for the hour and a half drive, with the children and Kamaria in tow. For the other servants, it was a day of rest, as we would not be returning to the city until after the late evening meal.

The narrow highway to Khums was usually desolate on Fridays, as everyone else would also be home with their families. A few trees here and there would color the bleak landscape, and a few old stone buildings would be visible from the road. We would inevitably see abandoned cars on the empty stretch of road, sitting there week after week.

We knew we would be seeing Amir and Ali there, as well as their wives and children. Unless someone was sick or out of the country it was taken for granted that the children and grandchildren would all be there. Rogaya and Ibrahim in particular lived for Fridays. For them it was a day of celebration, and their excitement was shared by their daughters, who looked forward to news and gifts from the city, as well as seeing the children. They were loving aunts who doted upon the children. Sometimes one of them would return to spend the week with us in Tripoli, a special treat for all of us, especially the children.

When Kamal had first told his parents that he was marrying a foreigner, an American, he said that his mother had locked herself in her room and cried for three days. However, now that we were married and had children, Rogaya made a point of treating me like her daughter, maybe even better! She was the definitive matriarch. I never saw or heard anyone show her disrespect—not out of fear, but out of love. She was a gentle, soft-spoken woman whose life centered around her husband and her family, and she was in her element on these Fridays. Yet she was never shy to voice her opinions, which always proved to be fair and accurate.

I loved my mother-in-law's cooking and enjoyed teasing the girls, who were just as inquisitive and opinionated as me. Being able to relax and enjoy food from her kitchen was also a very nice break from my routine of entertaining guests almost every day.

Every Friday, as soon as Ibrahim finished his favorite breakfast of *assida* (boiled dough made with flour and served with date honey and clarified butter), he set out for the local market to buy the finest food and delicacies, and whatever else Rogaya and the girls wanted. Ibrahim would have already slaughtered a lamb in the morning, so he purchased the nicest looking fruits and vegetables he could find. Every shopkeeper he approached offered him their best. He was, after all, the patriarch of one of the largest and most respected tribes in the area.

He would also sometimes buy dresses and shoes for the women, and presents for his grandchildren, which delighted them and him alike. Even when the girls criticized his choices, he would laugh and brush them off. His daughters were not always as appreciative, as they would rather go to a nice dress shop in Tripoli to pick their own clothes.

Whenever he bought me gifts I made a point of showing him my gratitude. He didn't have the best taste in women's clothing, but I truly loved the man and the thought behind his efforts. It reminded me of how Kamal once used to take such pleasure in buying me presents.

Ibrahim finished his shopping by eleven so as to be home when his sons arrived. The men would then go together to the mosque for *Jumaa* (Friday prayers). His only regret was that his youngest son was still in Italy. *Malesh*, he consoled himself, in a few years he would come home for good, and he would be the first lawyer in the Ben Ramadan clan.

Ibrahim knew everyone in Khums, and everyone he saw greeted him with respect and reverence. He always responded with a smile, followed with the placing of his right hand over his heart. In spite of his age, Ibrahim was still strikingly handsome and had a commanding presence. He was tall and robust, but moved with the upright, confident gait of one with authority. The twinkle in his extraordinary light-gray eyes offset the thinning of his once luxuriant gray hair.

Except for his trips abroad, Ibrahim always wore the traditional white Libyan *Holi*, an outer garment reminiscent of the Roman toga, atop impeccably clean white trousers and shirts, matched by a white *tagiyah*, cloth cap. He held himself with splendid dignity.

The overall unassuming simplicity of the man belied the stubbornness of his strong convictions. He was an attentive listener, respectful of the other person's ideology but unassailable in his own. He reminded me of the character Zorba the Greek, played by Anthony Quinn. Physically, they looked remarkably similar, but Ibrahim's demeanor was gentler and more polished. He had charisma, which Amir inherited, while Ali inherited his father's smile and gentle disposition.

Kamal, I realized, was the favored son who inherited his father's intellect and his love of politics.

As he made his way home on the dusty and bumpy road back to the farm, Ibrahim would thank Allah for all the blessings He had bestowed on him, even for his foreign daughter-in-law. He told me many times that he loved me like one of his own daughters—maybe more he insisted, because I was so far from home. Though he wanted me to learn Arabic, he enjoyed practicing his English with me and discussing politics and culture in the U.S. He was ecstatic when I produced a son, for Kamal's sake as well as for the family. He loved smelling Tarek's head when he was a baby, telling everyone again and again that he smelled like a Ben Ramadan. He adored all his grandchildren, declaring that they were the future of Libya, and that they would be the ones to change the country.

He always honked as he drove through the gates into the compound, knowing that the grandchildren would come rushing out to see what he had bought them. Yet for all his wealth, Ibrahim was a frugal man who lived simply. Like his wife, his joy was his family. Once a year he would go for a visit to Italy to see his son who was studying law in Modena. He enjoyed the pleasures of the Italian culture, of which he was very fond, and the opportunity to practice his Italian, which he spoke fluently.

One summer, Ibrahim invited Kamal and me to join him on one of these trips, and he was the perfect host and guide. We stayed at his favorite hotel in Rome, the same one he had stayed at for years, where he was well known and liked by the staff. He took us to his favorite restaurant close to the Spanish Steps, and told us this was also the Shah of Iran's favorite restaurant. My fondest memory of that trip was at a lunch we all had there together. A violinist was playing, and my little Layla got up and danced. She twirled and danced all over the restaurant, oblivious to anyone, amid encouraging shouts of "*Bravo*" and "*Bellisima*" from the other patrons. My father-in-law was at first surprised, maybe even somewhat embarrassed, but soon beamed with pride and happiness.

He often told the story of that lovely day and laughed every time he recounted it, especially recalling Layla's uninhibited dancing, something that would be unheard of for a little girl to do in public in Libya.

After the men returned from the mosque, the women would start preparing three large trays of food for us all. A large silver pot and bowl would usually be passed around by one of the sisters for the men to rinse their hands before eating. It was perceived more as a ritual of respect and tradition than one of functionality, as everyone had already washed their hands. Unless they were babies, the young boys would usually sit with the men. After the men were given their tray of food, the other trays would be brought into another room for the women and children.

The food was always delicious and plentiful. We usually had couscous, and I would spice mine with Rogaya's homemade *harissa,* and chives when they were in season. My favorite dish was *bazeen,* boiled dough made with barley flour, and eaten with an aromatic lamb sauce. Sometimes Rogaya would prepare my favorite salad, *Korbsa Mafusa,* made with pieces of homemade bread, sun-dried tomatoes, onions and lots of pounded fiery hot chilies.

After we finished, the children would run outside to play, while the men got ready to go to their friends' houses to have tea, play *Scuppah,* and discuss politics. It was a weekly ritual. To my disappointment, the ladies did not play cards

The brothers would go to visit their friends together or separately, depending on the agenda. When they returned in the evening after supper, we would sit around and listen to them recount the stories they had heard. Since Ibrahim never played cards, and did not go out visiting with his sons, the weekly ritual provided him with the opportunity to hear the political talk from them. He was not interested in hearing idle gossip. He would tease us by saying that was reserved for women.

Actually, unlike many of the other women, Rogaya did not like to take part in any gossip either.

Kamal once told me a story about Ibrahim and an Italian girl who lived in the village many years ago. Ibrahim wanted to ask for her hand in marriage but knew he had to first get his blessings from Rogaya.

The Italian girl was willing to convert to Islam and become Ibrahim's 'second' wife but Rogaya refused, and threatened to leave with her three sons. Kamal told me the story of how he ran away from home because he did not want to leave Khums. Apparently out of love and respect for his wife and children, the matter was abruptly dropped and never again mentioned by Ibrahim.

After hearing that story and the story of Kamal's birth, I understood the strong bond between Rogaya and her son. I was somewhat ashamed at my insistence to have special care for my delivery, nonetheless glad that I had. Over the four years I was there, Rogaya retold the story of Kamal's birth to me many times, until I knew it well enough without translation. She was resilient but never expected much from anyone else. She worked from dawn to bedtime, only stopping to sit down to make tea for her family. She chose to do everything herself, if not with the help of her daughters, rather than pay for strangers to work in her house. At the same time, she was never envious of her sons' wives for having servants and some of the finer things in life. In fact, it gave her pride. There was never any hint of female competition. To this day, I think of her with respect and love. She was so sensitive and thoughtful, always gently reminding Kamal to be more considerate of me because I was a foreigner.

Though arranged marriages were still occurring in Libya and accepted by many, it was not the case in the Ben Ramadan family, where the girls were determined they would have the last word. Their mother not only agreed but was adamant that her daughters be allowed to choose their own husbands.

When we went to Khums after a visit to the States, one of the sisters excitedly told me that a prospective groom of Yasmine had asked their father for permission to marry her. I was so excited I ran to ask Yasmine if it were true. Sometimes the sisters would tell me stories, and have a good laugh after I fell for them.

"Is it really true, Yasmine? Are you getting married?"

She smiled shyly, but from the glow on her face I knew it was true. I was thrilled for her because it was obviously what she wanted. I couldn't wait to hear all about it.

The women all sat on *flokati* rugs on the terrace while Rogaya started to brew a pot of tea and Rania went to fetch pastries. I was surprised to hear that Yasmine's fiancé was the boy next door, and teased her about sneaking out to meet him. We all laughed, but Rogaya somewhat nervously.

When I finished interrogating Yasmine, my mother-in-law turned to me with twinkling eyes and a cheeky smile, and asked me, point blankly,

"How did you meet Kamal?"

I was surprised, because no one from the family had ever asked me. I think it was out of bashfulness or respect. I later told Mary jokingly that maybe they were afraid I had met him in a bar! Many Libyans perceived American women as loose, which was one reason they didn't want their sons bringing home American wives.

I told the tale as best I could. Even in my halting Arabic, and with some necessary translation, Rogaya hung on to every word I told her (though of course I omitted a few details). She found the story delightful, smiling the whole time and nodding her head in approval. At the end of the story, she told me that she was grateful and happy Kamal had found me.

Yasmine's wedding was planned for the following year. The women in the family were predictably more excited than the men, who were more cautious and reserved. Whenever I tried to talk to Kamal about it, he acted as if it was his own daughter getting married, obviously disconcerted whenever the topic was mentioned. When I told the sisters about his reaction, they laughed. They said he just didn't want to think of his sister with a man. During the next year, we happily and busily prepared for a wedding despite a growingly tense political environment.

One day in April 1977 Layla and her little cousins were watching *The Three Stooges* while the women lazed around after lunch on *mindars*, idly chatting. It was the only show on television, and only on for an hour once a week on Fridays. Layla especially loved it because it was in English. Otherwise, television was dominated by Gaddafi, and no one watched except to mock his nonsensical propaganda. Nevertheless, it was usually turned on for background noise just to remind people that there was such a thing as TV, and that maybe one day there might actually be more entertaining programs.

Layla, who was only three at that time, came running into the room, excitedly calling for me to go look at the television.

"Mummy, Mummy, come look! They hanging!" she cried, emulating a person hanging, with her hand around her neck.

She was our little story-teller, always coming up with preposterous stories, our Radio Layla, as we called her, so at first I did not take her seriously. However, the gesture of hanging bothered me. How would she even know such a thing existed?

"Quick, Mummy, quick!" she insisted, pulling my hand.

I let her lead me into the main salon, where the other children were sitting, their eyes glued to the screen. I looked at the TV and was momentarily confused. It did not look like *The Three Stooges*, or any other show for that matter. With disbelief, it dawned on me that it was real life. Two men were hanging, obviously dead, in what looked like a public place.

My first instinct was to run to the room where the men were having tea, talking quietly, and urge them to see what was happening on the television. My face must have reflected my horror because they all immediately rushed back out with me.

Only then did I think to order the children—still watching intently—to go back to the room where the other women were. I could not understand what was being said by the commentator, but from the looks on the men's faces, I knew what was happening was monumental. Soon the rest of the household joined us and we – with some difficultly – tried to convince and eventually ordered the children to play outside.

Ibrahim and Kamal later somberly explained to me that Gaddafi was not going to tolerate any criticism or opposition to him or his regime. Anyone who opposed him would be eliminated. Reluctantly Kamal admitted to me that it was not the first public hanging.

We later learned that the two men who were executed were teachers at the University of Benghazi. Gaddafi had personally ordered their executions as a reprisal for their participation in student demonstrations. Their names were Kamal Dabboub and Mohammed bin Saud.

We were all in shock, sickened by the boldness and brutality of his actions, and understanding with unwanted clarity that we were in the midst of a violent chapter of history. As many feared, blood began flowing freely in Libya after that day, at the hands of the man who had been entrusted to be the leader and the savior of the nation.

In order to protect me, Kamal had not elaborated on how grim the political situation in Libya had become. I knew he was frustrated with the slowness of the bureaucracy, but I had no idea that we were on such a bloody path. For the first time since arriving, I felt real political terror, something I had never experienced in any of the places I had lived. My mind was reeling: *How could those men be hanged without benefit of trial?*

After we returned to Tripoli that night, and after the children were put to bed, I insisted that Kamal tell me what was going on.

"Hiba, it is better that you don't know too much."

"Kamal, Layla just saw two men hanging!" My voice rose in frustration. "You have to tell me what's happening here!"

CHAPTER 11

GADDAFI

I sat in stunned silence that night as Kamal told me in detail about the reality of Gaddafi's abuse of power. There were already indications he had become a tyrant to be feared even before we left the United States. In 1973, only four years after the revolution, or *Fatah*, as he liked to call it, Gaddafi decreed in Zuwara that anyone opposing him was a deviant, and any talk or even rumor of dissent by "deviants and perverts" would result in imprisonment or execution. In the same speech, he announced the creation of the *lijan thawriya*, revolutionary committees all over the country, to be his eyes, ears and judges of the revolution, answerable only to him. In this way, he gave these committees extraordinary powers, including the right to seize land and property. In return, of course, they owed him their absolute loyalty and were placed under his complete control, ready to do his bidding.

I realized then that all those nights in Tallahassee, when the Libyan students gathered together to talk, drinking cup after cup of tea, they were in fact trading stories and talking through their disbelief about what was happening at home. *No wonder Kamal had not told me anything.* He obviously did not want me to know that the honeymoon period with Gaddafi had ended before ours began. Listening to him tell me everything now was a shock. I don't know what I would have done if I had known, but I wished that I had at least been prepared, or given the opportunity to decide.

"Why didn't you tell me this before?" I asked with sadness, feeling that he had lied to me by omission.

"I'm sorry, *Habibti*," he shook his head, looking contrite, "I did not want to scare you, and I swear, I was so sure the situation would get better."

When I arrived in Libya in early 1976 I didn't know that Gaddafi was already hated and feared by many Libyans, even though most were resigned to having him around. As early as January 1976, days before we landed in Tripoli, he had executed several students from the University of Benghazi for protesting against government control. Like so much I would learn in the days to come, no one had wanted me to know how bad the situation was.

Muammar Gaddafi was born in a tent in the desert outside of Sirte in June 1942. His father was a Bedouin farmer who barely supported his family by growing barley and raising goats and sheep. Despite his humble beginnings, Gaddafi was considered very smart, so the village elders arranged for him to attend school in Sebha and Misrata. He went on to graduate from the University of Libya in 1963 and subsequently joined the Libyan military. After receiving his commission from the army, Gaddafi was sent to the Royal Academy at Sandhurst in England for advanced military training. Upon his return home, he started to rise within the ranks, and was appointed captain in August 1969. One month later, on the first of September 1969, supported by almost the entire Libyan army, twenty-seven-year-old Gaddafi led a group of officers to successfully overthrow the government of King Idris in a bloodless revolution. He replaced it with a Revolutionary Council of twelve officers and conspirators, and in the process promoted himself to colonel. His newly formed council included Abdel Salam Jalloud and Khweldi Hamedi, two of the original members of the Gaddafi-led coup. Jalloud went on to become Prime Minister, and Hamedi, a distant relative of Kamal's, was appointed Minister of Interior.

The Libyan love affair with Gaddafi's revolution ended as soon as it became evident that the love he had for himself was more than his love for Libya. Discontent was voiced only in whispers and among family and close, trusted friends. Just as his pictures were posted on every street and in every building, so too were spies and secret police. The early enthusiasm for the so-called liberator started to turn bitter within a few years.

I had never been in a country where people lived in abject fear, at the mercy of one man, so it was difficult for me to understand the gravity of the situation, and why it was tolerated. Kamal, as well as my limited Arabic, insulated me from what was happening on a daily basis. Every time I asked, I would get the same casual answer, "He's *majnoon*, crazy!"

When Gaddafi's *Green Book* was published in 1975, there was no more doubt that the country was controlled by an irrational man. I did not realize the extent of its foolishness until I tried to read the book after it was translated into English. It was too excruciating.

In 1976 Gaddafi replaced the Libyan Constitution with *The Green Book*, the manifesto of his political, economic and social philosophy. He envisioned it as being the Third Universal Theory, comparing it to Mao's *Red Book*. In actuality, *The Green Book* was a series of simplistic, nonsensical ramblings and inane tirades based on his own warped philosophy.

In his section on women, the "philosopher" muses: "It is an undisputed fact that both man and woman are human beings...But there is no absolute equality between them as regards their duties."

Sadly, these declarations were required reading for two hours a week for all school children in Libya from the ages of eight up. In fact, it was mandatory for every Libyan to read *The Green Book* and for every household to own one. It was distributed for free.

When I talked to Kamal about it, he would shake his head despondently, and shrug off my concerns. "The less you know, the better. Don't say anything outside of the family."

For him to feel the way he did about the man whose picture he had carried in his wallet only a few years ago was disconcerting. I am a realist, and I have never heard of an insane dictator becoming sane. If anything, they got worse.

I became frightened to raise my children in a country that was ruled by a mad man, but knew there was nothing I could do except pray for change. My husband was reluctant for me to know too much; perhaps in a way I did not want to know too much either. I didn't want our lives infected by fear. For my children's sake, I wanted to at least be able to pretend that we were living within a certain amount of normalcy.

When fear turned to terror in 1977, it was difficult to have much hope left. After the televised hangings, Gaddafi no longer bothered to hide his true agenda: the elimination of all political opposition. The mere hint of discontent or criticism was grounds for arrest, torture or execution. There was no such thing as the benefit of a trial. Conversations revolved around who was missing, or who had been arrested, tortured, or executed. Everyone began living in a state of paranoia.

There were more public hangings, and often people were seen being taken off the streets or from their homes, sometimes never to be heard from again. On many occasions, traffic downtown would be diverted so motorists would be forced to drive by public hangings. On those days, Kamal would insist that I stay home, without telling me why. Bodies were put in wooden boxes and deposited on the doorsteps of their families. For the grieving and distraught, there was no authority to report to— even if anyone dared. The more fortunate were released after intense interrogation and torture, with dire threats of deaths to them or their families if they dared speak against Gaddafi. Army officers were periodically condemned to death for allegedly plotting coups, and any acts of resistance, whether real or fabricated, were quickly suppressed by still more executions.

His "cultural revolution", reminiscent of Mao's, included raiding bookstores and burning subversive or "perverse" texts. In 1977 he deviously arranged for a "literary festival", inviting prominent and promising Libyan artists and writers to attend. After all the participants showed up, he had them arrested and jailed, where they were interrogated and tortured; many for almost ten years.

For the few hours each day that the TV worked, it was completely devoted to Gaddafi's repetitive speeches, punctuated by shots of Libyans cheering him and his revolution, shouting "*Fatah*" over and over, on cue. Even at the time, it seemed surreal that he was able to have any type of following.

Most of those cheering him in the squares and places where he appeared had been bussed in from schools and work. There were probably just as many secret police and Gaddafi thugs in the crowd, so it was crucial that everyone appeared enthralled and enthusiastic.

His favorite venue was atop of the Red Castle Fort, where he'd orchestrate a dramatic scene: adorned in outlandish and colorful costumes of his own design, accented by designer sunglasses, and habitually shaking a threatening finger in the air.

Tripoli's Red Castle Fort Museum, overlooking the harbor on one side and facing Green Square on the other, was rebuilt by the Italians in 1919 to house a spectacular collection of Libyan and Roman antiquities. After Gaddafi came to power in 1969, he wasted no time in adding a wing to commemorate himself and his revolution.

Gaddafi's dream of power went beyond Libya. Early on, he envisioned himself as the leader and savior of the Arab world and Africa. The only person Gaddafi idolized as much as himself was Egypt's President Nasser, who was the only Arab leader in modern times able to unify the Arabs emotionally and ideologically.

After Nasser's unexpected death, Gaddafi had aspirations of taking over Nasser's role, but he failed miserably. In the process he alienated himself from Egypt, Tunisia, Sudan and other Arab countries, where he attempted to orchestrate plots to overthrow their leaders. The Arabs had no intention of accepting him, and laughed at his efforts.

Undaunted, Gaddafi turned his attention and his money to Africa and terrorist organizations all over the world, pouring out billions of dollars to gain not just their loyalty and support, but also to seduce them. Some African leaders went so far as to bestow on him the title of "King of Kings".

Unaccounted billions of dollars were given to African nations and terrorist groups, while Libya and Libyans remained in a miserably stagnant economic state. Gaddafi's reach extended as far as America: on one of his business trips to the United States, Kamal was instructed to deliver a large amount of cash to Louis Farrakhan for the Nation of Islam. The same generous gesture from Gaddafi was repeated for several other Muslim organizations in the United States. Like other Libyans in sensitive positions in the government, Kamal had no choice but to do as he was told. The option of refusing such an order would mean certain arrest or the necessity of leaving the country, as many intellectuals, professionals and businessmen were doing.

Through it all, Gaddafi stood arrogant and defiant, ruling by fear and with full control of Libya's oil money. While he was robbing the country and filling his personal bank accounts abroad, he was depriving his own people. Foreign nurses and secretaries were making more money in Libya than Libyan doctors and university professors. Unless they had support from their families, like Kamal did, many professionals had to leave the country in order to provide their families with a better life.

Yet, unbelievable as it may seem, throughout it all, the thinnest thread of hope still existed. There were rumors that Gaddafi was going to change the Libyan currency for new currency. I heard from an American friend of new Libyan currency being printed in England, and that plane-loads of the new money were going to be flown in to replace the old one.

I tried to convince my father-in-law to convert the cash he had into foreign currency, but he refused to believe that would ever happen. The older generation found it difficult to admit to the severity of what was going on in the country, in part because they were trying to restrain their children from rebelling or leaving. Out of fear, most of them were resigned to accepting the situation.

"That is communist!" Ibrahim exclaimed, "He cannot do that!"

But he did. Within a month after hearing the rumor, three Boeing 747s flew into Libya, packed with the new currency. Only 1,000 dinar of the old currency could legally be redeemed at the bank, rendering the old currency worthless.

In addition, it was decreed that no one was allowed to own more than one home. This gave permission for squatters to take over empty houses and tenants to co-opt the places they had been renting. My father-in-law, who had spent his lifetime working and investing in real estate, lost almost everything overnight to squatters and members of Gaddafi's revolutionary committees. It amazed me how philosophically and stoically Ibrahim accepted his loss. It also made me admire him even more.

In 1977, Gaddafi instigated marches towards the Egyptian border to protest against the peace accord Anwar Sadat had signed with the Israelis, and threatened war by sending Libyan tanks to the border with Egypt.

I was frightened. We all were. Luckily this lasted only three days before the Libyan army retreated, following a successful Egyptian retaliation. However, Gaddafi's mindless foray spurred a lot of anti-Egyptian sentiment in Libya, which I was occasionally subjected to because I was often mistaken for an Egyptian.

Many of our friends started talking about leaving Libya—Libyans as well as foreigners. Kamal, however, refused to consider that as an option. He strongly believed that the only way of bringing the regime down was by working from within. He also felt confident that the military would eventually execute a successful coup.

But Gaddafi had been clever enough to deflate the power of the army by minimizing it and by keeping a vigilant eye on its officers. He surrounded himself carefully with his inner circle, consisting mainly of members from his own tribe and foreign mercenaries. Despite these precautions, he too began living in a state of paranoia. It became common knowledge that he slept in a different place every night to avoid assassination.

I became increasingly fearful for Kamal, and begged him to at least prepare for the likelihood that we might have to escape, and to consider the job offers he sometimes received from the United States.

"If every educated Libyan left, what would happen to the country?" That was his answer every time. And: "Don't worry," he would tell me while trying to allay my fears, "the military or someone close to him will get him soon."

Day by day people we knew started leaving, out of fear or disgust. And day by day I saw Kamal becoming more disillusioned and angry. I feared that his animosity toward Gaddafi would start to show through.

Around this time, Kamal took me to a function where Gaddafi had invited senior employees of various ministries and organizations to attend. Of course these "invitations" were considered orders. After waiting almost two hours for his arrival, everyone was instructed to form a receiving line, where we would greet him individually.

I couldn't help but notice how much charisma the man still exuded, despite the evil he embodied. He was tall and striking and, like all dictators possessed that certain intangible quality that charms people into wanting to believe in them. People were taking turns to kowtow, kiss and praise him and, in turn, he acted the role of the benevolent leader.

It was bizarre, since I am sure at least half of the people in that room would have killed him if they could. I told Kamal that I could not bear touching the hand of a man who had killed so many innocent people. We both felt so repulsed by the whole scene that as soon as we had the opportunity we discretely slipped.

Every day, all over Libya, the public – children as well – were ordered to main squares and different venues to join in the chanting and singing of praises and support for this megalomaniac. Those staged events would be filmed and run over and over all day long on the single TV station to demonstrate his "popularity". I couldn't understand why no one had been able to kill him, despite several botched attempts.

We soon started hearing of threats against the dissidents who left Libya. Gaddafi reviled them as "stray dogs", and promised to hunt them down. Their families in Libya were questioned and threatened, sometimes thrown in jail.

One day, Kamal came home from work and told me that Hadi, a friend of ours, had disappeared. Hadi's family had looked all over for him for three days, and knew something was very wrong. Two days later, we learned that his mutilated body had been left by the gate outside his house that morning. He had been badly tortured before dying, and stuffed in the pocket of his bloodied shirt was a note saying this was what happened to traitors.

CHAPTER 12

MOSCOW

In 1979 Kamal was asked to represent Libya at the International Political Science Association (IPSA) World Congress, scheduled to be held in Moscow that August. I never traveled without my children, but by now they were older, so I convinced myself that they would be well looked after by Kamaria and our family in Khums. Since arriving in Libya and realizing how brutal the political situation was, I had become fearful of letting the children out of my sight. However, Kamal insisted that I accompany him, and I knew we needed time to ourselves. I had forgotten what it was like when it was just him and me, free from children and family.

I was surprised at how excited he was when I told him I would go. He playfully picked me up off the floor in a hug and danced around kissing me, promising that it was going to be like a second honeymoon.

"I love you so much, *Rohay*," he whispered in my ear. "I'm so sorry I haven't been a better husband, but I'm trying everything I can to make you and the children proud of me one day."

"I am proud of you, Kamal," I assured him—and I was.

"All I really want is for you to just spend a little more time with me and the kids. We hardly see you anymore, even when you're in the same house."

I hated to complain, but I sometimes felt I had to remind him he also had a family who needed him. We had begun to see less and less of each other, as he was spending a lot of time with Gaddafi and at the Foreign Ministry. Sometime I saw so little of him I wondered if it would have made any difference to him whether the children and I were there or not.

"Hiba, I owe it to Libya and to you and the children to change this rotten government. We're living in very dangerous times, but the only way I can make any change is by working in the system."

I believed he was right, but I still didn't want it to be him doing it. I wanted to scream, and tell him, like I had many times before, that I was terrified for him. I was terrified that he would disappear one day, or that his lifeless body would be thrown on our doorstep. It was happening all over the country to men who disagreed or even whispered their discontent of Gaddafi into the wrong ears. I loved Libya, and I loved my Libyan family, but I despised the man suppressing what could have been a great country.

"I'll buy you a coat in Moscow—the most beautiful fur we can find," he said. "It'll be my second honeymoon present to you!"

He was trying to change the subject, and I let him. Seeing him acting frivolously for a change reminded me of our early days together, when we would find fun in everything we did. For the past four years Kamal had become so serious and distracted that he hardly joked or smiled anymore. I missed my husband very much, and so decided to look forward to Moscow, thinking we would have time to be ourselves again.

Within days of our conversation, even before we applied for our visas, I had my first encounter with the KGB.

I had just returned from my daily shopping excursion, and was honking from the driveway for Abdo to open the garage door, when a car drove up next to mine. A nice-looking, well-dressed, European man emerged. I was puzzled, but also instinctively fearful. He tried to reassure me with his smile and gestured that he was not a threat to me. I slowly rolled down my window.

"Good morning, Madame Ben Ramadan!" He spoke in English, and I was startled he knew my name. I was certain I'd never seen him before.

"My name is Boris... I work with the Russian Embassy here in Tripoli. I'm here to help you with your visa to Russia."

I did not get his last name, but it didn't really matter. I also didn't know how to reply; Kamal would not have wanted me to talk with him. At the same time, I was curious about how he even knew I was going to Moscow with my husband so soon after I had agreed to go.

Then, of course, it dawned on me: KGB. I was becoming more savvy, but I still felt a shiver run up my spine.

Since my first encounter with the CIA at the American Embassy I had become more cautious about how to deal with these types of situations. It was obvious that Kamal, with his PhD, and his close involvement with the Libyan government, would be observed and even courted by both agencies. There was a fine line between what the Americans could do to help Libya and how much information they needed to get the job done. The Russians, as far as most Libyans were concerned, did not enter into the equation of a future democratic Libya.

"Oh! Thank you, but I'm sure my husband will make the application for me." I was nervous, but managed to answer graciously and calmly.

"I'll take care of it then, Madame." He ignored me gently. "We'll make sure to give you a detachable visa. If there's anything else we can do for you, please let us know."

It was awkward, because I knew what he was doing but I wanted to pretend I didn't.

I quickly thanked him again, by which time Abdo was standing next to my car glaring at him, looking at me for instructions. He was fiercely protective and, for a small man, rather fearless. If he had known it was a stranger, I am sure he would have chased him away.

As Boris cheerily drove off, waving to me as though we were old friends, the significance of the encounter dawned on me: the Russians were making a concerted effort to track our every move. We had already been warned by the Foreign Ministry that we might be spied on during our stay in Moscow. *It's going to be an interesting trip*, I thought, not least because I had never been to a communist country.

When I told Kamal what had happened, he just nodded and told me not to talk to strange men again. I reminded him that it was I who was being approached, outside of my own house.

A few nights later we heard the main doorbell ring, and after a few minutes Abdo came in with a package, which he said was left by the same man I had spoken to the other day. Kamal opened the box, and nestled inside the wrapping was a bottle of very expensive Cognac. The card with it read:

To Doctor & Madame Ben Ramadan,
Best wishes for a good visit to Moscow, Boris.

Kamal and I looked at each other. He was furious.

"How dare he come to my house again?" he cried out at Adbo in Arabic, ordering the nervous-looking man never to accept anything from the Russian again.

It was inappropriate in those days for someone from a foreign Embassy, or even a foreigner for that matter, to simply drop by a Libyan home. If someone from the secret police had seen him and wanted to make an issue of it, Kamal would have had a difficult time explaining.

We ended up giving away the cognac to Christian friends, who were very appreciative.

Before leaving for Moscow, James Moore contacted me, asking me to please go to the embassy. He said he needed to talk to me about our pending trip. When I told Kamal, he shrugged and said it might be because I was an American, and mentioned something about the Cold War. I took that as permission to go, and also thought it would be a good idea to let the Americans know where my children were in case something happened to me. When we were in the Bubble Room, he briefed me on my visit to Moscow, which he already knew about.

"You will be contacted by the KGB," he warned me. "They will try to compromise you."

How ironic, I thought, and told Mr Moore about Boris, hoping it would let him know that I was not so completely naïve about him either. I told him also about Boris's third and last visit to us.

To his aggravation, Abdo was no match for the Russian when he returned the next time, when he insisted that it was imperative Abdo give Kamal an "important" package. After the second bottle of Cognac, Kamal had ordered Abdo to let him know the next time he came by.

Kamal invited Boris into the house on his third visit.

Boris seemed taken aback, mumbling a few awkward compliments on our home as he walked into the large foyer. But only a few steps inside, Kamal made his real purpose for the invitation clear: "We thank you for the gifts, but you should know we do not drink alcohol."

Boris grinned sheepishly, and shrugged.

"And," continued Kamal, sternly, "if you come to my house again, I will be forced to report you to the Minister."

Kamal gestured toward the door and a chastened Boris left without a word. That was the last time we saw him.

Moore listened to my version of the encounter, but made no comments, as though he already knew what I was telling him. Before I left, he gave me a few more warnings of what to watch out for in Moscow, and by the time I left the Embassy I felt I was going to be embarking on quite an exciting journey.

We left Tripoli on the tenth of August. I was exceedingly anxious about leaving the children; my prevailing fear was the plane crashing and my children left orphans. On the other hand, I was intrigued by Russia, and looking forward to going on a trip with Kamal.

Adding to my excitement was Kamal's unmistakable joy that we were going on a "honeymoon", as he kept referring to the trip. Moscow was going to be a desperately needed opportunity for us to spend time alone. In the four years since we had moved to Libya we had not shared more than a dozen evenings together. However, I also felt guilty about complaining when so many people around were in worse situations.

We checked into the palatial Hotel Rossiya on a beautifully clear day. It was located only a few blocks from the Kremlin, and the young man at the registration desk informed us in perfect English and with much pride that it was the largest hotel in the world.

As we were shown into our room, I noticed that an attendant was sitting at a table that had been set up on our floor across from the elevator. Seeing my surprise, Kamal turned to me and said discreetly, "We delegates are assigned 'attendants'."

"Is that really necessary?" I asked, not yet grasping his meaning.

"The Russian government believes so. They're here to monitor our comings and goings..."

On our first night we decided to eat at the hotel since we were both tired and really didn't know where else to go. The huge dining room on the top floor was almost empty, as the conference was not scheduled to open for another two days. I had been anticipating my first Russian meal, remembering a popular Russian restaurant in Singapore I'd frequented called the "Troika Room", which served dishes I particularly loved. My appetite had been whetted to experience the real thing.

The menu was substantial, bound in leather. However, we found that nothing we had chosen was available. I looked over to another table in a corner, and saw to my delight that the couple had in front of them a large silver tray piled with lobsters and other shellfish.

The occupants were a heavy, garrulous older man who appeared to be very drunk, talking to a beautiful young girl, blond and scantily dressed, and effusively nodding to everything he was saying.

"May we please have what they're having?" I asked our waiter, pointing to the scrumptious seafood tower. This was exactly what I had in mind.

"I'm sorry, Madame, but that was specially ordered for the gentleman." He looked genuinely apologetic and insisted there was nothing left in the kitchen.

Kamal and I understood the situation immediately. The "gentleman" was a high-ranking bureaucrat accompanied by an expensive call girl. I felt like going over and asking if we could share his lobsters, since his platter was piled so high that there was no way they could have finished it all. Kamal nixed my suggestion, and we eventually ended up ordering Chicken *Tabaca*, which we found for the next week to be the only thing available on the menu, besides sturgeon and tomato and cucumber salad.

After dinner, we walked through the quiet, empty streets around the hotel, holding hands, finally venturing down to the Red Square where the Basilica was. It was a magnificent sight, despite its peeling paint. It was difficult not to feel overwhelmed by the size and historical significance of the city, and I was anxious to start exploring it.

There in the shadows of the Basilica, my husband held me tightly to his chest and kissed me with a passion that assured me, for the moment at least, that I was his world once again.

"You are, and always will be my Hiba, my desire and my gift from God," he whispered, stroking and breathing me

192

in with his old passion. "Please forgive me for acting like a *hamar* sometimes, but I love you with all my heart and soul."

He knew it made me smile when he called himself a donkey. We walked until we got too tired, reliving some of our funny moments together, letting everything except ourselves fade away.

When we finally returned to the hotel we encountered the same attendant, who avoided looking at us and simply gave a slight nod when we wished her a good night. In the days to come, we learned that these attendants were on twenty-four hour shifts.

The next morning, the Libyan Embassy sent a car after breakfast to take us to the embassy for our meeting with the ambassador, who had invited us for dinner that evening. After pleasantries and a brief tour, the ambassador offered us the use of his chauffeur so that we could sightsee and visit the University of Moscow, where the conference would be held.

The wide boulevards and grand old buildings of Moscow were awe-inspiring. It was when we visited the museum, however, that it struck me how badly most of the buildings were in need of repair. Some of the magnificent and priceless treasures were exhibited in cases with cracked glass, and there were no English translations for the exhibits, which I found frustrating. It reminded me of Libya, where Gaddafi had banned all signs in English. I had no doubt the idea came from his Russian friends.

After stopping at a charming dacha outside of Moscow for lunch, Kamal asked the driver to take us to a store where I could look at fur coats.

When we arrived at what was supposed to be the best store in all of Moscow, I was stunned. The small selection was so old-fashioned that, much as I searched, I could not find one I would ever wear. There were, however, larger selections of fur hats, some of them attractive, but unless they matched a coat, it would have looked ridiculous. I left there utterly disappointed.

Kamal tried to cheer me up: "Just look around, *Habibti*, and see what else you would like." But I knew he was as disappointed as I was.

After a scrumptious dinner at the embassy with several other diplomatic couples, the driver returned us to the hotel, assuring Kamal that he would be there in the morning to take him to the conference.

There was a different person at the table on our floor this time, a grim and stern-looking older woman, so forbidding that we didn't even bother to wish her goodnight.

As we were lying in bed talking, Kamal turned his head toward me. "What will you do while I'm at the conference?"

"I'd like to look around, maybe see if I can find some galleries." I loved visiting art galleries whenever we traveled. "I'd really like to find some contemporary Russian art. Maybe if I see a piece I like I'll buy it, since we couldn't find a coat."

"That sounds good, *Habibti*. But be careful, okay?"

I knew what he was referring to, but our first two days had been uneventful, and I had almost forgotten about being paranoid.

Kamal left early the next morning and I lounged in bed for a while before getting dressed to go downstairs to one of the less formal dining rooms for breakfast.

Since it was past 10 a.m., I wasn't surprised to find the place almost empty. I picked a table by a large window so I could look out onto the street, and ordered a simple European-style breakfast.

While waiting for my food to come, I saw a very handsome, well-dressed man enter the dining room. He looked like an American, and dressed like one, I idly thought. He saw me looking at him and to my surprise sauntered straight to my table.

"Good Morning, Madame," he said cheerfully in an American accent, but I could tell that he was not an American by his mannerisms. "Do you mind if I join you?"

Had he been older and unattractive, I would have been less hesitant, but he was tall, blond, blue-eyed and extremely suave. I knew if my husband walked in and saw us together he would have been upset. The place was empty, and it was obvious that he didn't need to share a table with me. However, I did not want to be rude, and since we were in a public place I felt safe enough. Besides, I was curious.

He sat down and introduced himself as Michael something or other, not a Russian-sounding name. He asked for the same breakfast I was having, and we had a casually banal conversation. He could not have been more charming.

Just as I was nearly finished he told me that he was going to visit a very good friend of his, who was regarded as one of the foremost contemporary artists in the USSR.

Seeing my eyes light up, he asked, "You have some interest in art?"

"Very much so," I replied. "I majored in art at college."

"Well then, why don't you come with me? My friend has a lovely studio not far from here."

Already on guard, I politely thanked him but declined his offer. If he had offered me the Hope Diamond along with the visit, I would not have gone anywhere with a strange man. "If you don't want to ride with me in my car, we could take the subway."

My suspicions were confirmed. He was definitely a KGB operative. I reckoned he'd known about my background in art all along.

I was anxious to end the conversation, so I told him that I had plans to meet my husband for lunch, thanking him again for the offer as left the table.

That night at dinner I told Kamal what happened. He listened intently, and when I finished he shook his head and told me he had a similar experience that day.

"After I presented one of my papers I had lunch with some people I knew, and after lunch decided to take a walk around the grounds to have a cigarette. A very attractive young woman came up to me and asked me for a light. After lighting her cigarette, I was about to walk off when she put her hand on my arm. She said she thought I was very kind and handsome, and wanted to show me her city!"

"What did you say?" I asked, incredulous.

"I told her that I was married and not interested in prostitutes."

He said he told her in a very matter of fact way, and that she did not seem surprised or offended.

He then took my hand and kissed my palm, looking unwaveringly at me.

"I also told her that I have a very beautiful wife who melts me every time I look at her." Though he was teasing, I saw a hint of the old Kamal I knew, the one who charmed me with his adoration.

"You should have told her that your wife is a crazy *majnoona* who would tear her eyes out!"

"Well, it was obvious she was trying to compromise me."

When we got back to the hotel, Kamal made a thorough sweep of our room before finding a bug in the radio speaker. We had actually tried turning on the radio the first day, but found that it didn't work. Sure now that we were bugged, we decided to play along and give them something to listen to that night and every night for the rest of our stay.

I spent a lot of time alone wandering around the city, doing the tourist routine of visiting museums, Lenin's Tomb in Red Square, and going into various cafes and shops. Except for the usual souvenirs, there was nothing I really wanted to buy. Half the shelves in the grocery stores were empty, and the available selection was limited.

Even when there were a lot of people on the streets, it was eerily quiet except for the occasional sound of traffic. In some of the stand-up cafes scattered all over town where I stopped for tea and a snack, there was rarely any laughter or loud chat. Sometimes it was so quiet I thought I could hear a pin drop.

The only time it was different was at night. The Russians drank a lot of vodka, and when they drank too much they became loud and boisterous. I only saw Kamal in the evenings, and though we went to several recommended restaurants, the only thing available on the menus everywhere was the same: Chicken *Tabaca* and tomato-and-cucumber salad.

I got so fed up that one night I decided to order the sturgeon Kamal had warned me against. He was right: it was too strong and oily for my taste.

All the delegates and their wives were invited to a special performance of the Bolshoi Ballet one night, and the Moscow Circus on another. Both were thrilling; experiences of a lifetime. Kamal and I commented afterwards how difficult it was going to be to watch a ballet or the circus again without comparing them.

An odd thing that happened often in Moscow was people offering to buy things from us, sometimes literally off us. Every taxi driver would ask what perfume I used and if he could buy it from me. I had people stopping me in the streets offering to buy my handbag, my watch—whatever I had on. Kamal was asked the same, especially his Kent cigarettes, which he often gave away. One time a woman actually came up to me on the streets and asked how much I would sell my Levis for—the ones I was wearing!

We enjoyed ourselves greatly during that seven-day hiatus. Kamal was in his element on that trip, among other academics and intellectuals. He was more relaxed than I had seen him in a long time, constantly teasing me and making me laugh, agreeing to do anything I wanted. It felt like our early courting days in Washington all over again, and there were times I even forgot we were married and had kids. We talked a lot about our life in Libya and what he hoped to accomplish. For the first time, he confided to me that he felt his hands were tied and that he had not been able to do many of the things he had hoped to do.

"Gaddafi has surrounded himself with Libyans he has paid to be afraid of him, and foreigners who're paid to tell him anything he wants to hear."

I could see the frustration and disgust on his face for the man who was once his hero.

"He's destroying Libya, Hiba, and we don't know how to stop him."

For the past two years, every time I heard of murders and tortures performed by Gaddafi's secret police, I couldn't stop myself from imagining it was happening to Kamal. I was terrified that they would know of his hatred for their lunatic leader, and that he would one day simply disappear like so many others.

"Will you consider working abroad," I asked. "At least until the political climate improves —"

"No!" he interjected, unwilling to hear any more of it. "The only way Libya is going to change is from within. I have to be here when that happens."

Though we had a wonderful vacation and spent more time alone together that week in August than we ever had since moving to Libya, I missed my children very much and was ready to go home. Except for a few obligatory wooden painted souvenirs, we left Moscow empty-handed but happy and relaxed. We were both looking forward to seeing the children, and Kamal promised that he would take us all for a nice vacation in Florida at Christmas time.

When we changed flights at Kloten Airport in Zurich, I headed directly for the duty-free shop. I wanted to stock up on chocolates for the bleak months ahead of us in Libya, and take them as gifts for the family. Kamal laughed when he saw the pile of chocolate boxes in my cart.

"Are you planning to feed chocolates to everyone in Libya?" I told him what I was doing, wondering if I had bought enough.

"Don't worry, *Habibti.* Things will get better."

I wanted to believe him, but suddenly I realized I had no more faith in those words. And when I searched Kamal's eyes, I saw he didn't either.

CHAPTER 13

KAMAL

When we moved to Libya, Kamal was immediately appointed Director of the Strategic Studies Center and Chairman of the Arab Development Institute in Tripoli. He immersed himself in his new position, eager to be a part of the development of his beloved Libya. Finally, he felt he could serve his country in a capacity that might produce substantive change.

Considering the scope of his duties, as well as his educational background—which included two master's degrees—he was shocked at how modest his salary was. He was earning only slightly more than what the janitor in his department was making. In time, we learned that almost all professionals working for the government were deliberately underpaid, a psychological ploy by Gaddafi to devalue their worth.

Kamal often worked twelve-hour days, but I understood he was doing what he wanted to do, and felt he had to. He was seldom home, and when he was it was usually in the company of friends, either personal or professional. As the weeks and months went by, I saw less and less of him. After a simple breakfast with the children, he would leave the house by 8 a.m. and return at 2 p.m. for the main meal, with a male guest or two in tow. On the few evenings when he was not working, he would usually play cards with his friends either at our house or theirs. On special occasions we would take the kids for a drive after supper and then go pick up gelato or *sphinx*, a fried pastry we all loved.

Kamal often tried to take a short nap in the afternoons, knowing that he still had a long day ahead of him. It was usually then, before dozing off, that he would tell me a little about his day. In the beginning, he was optimistic about the changes he thought would come about; he hoped that with the immense infusion of oil money Libya would prosper and become a model Arab country. However, as time passed, he became more disillusioned and bewildered by the stupidity of the people he had to work with. It was difficult for him to understand how some of them were not as angry as he was with Gaddafi's policies.

When Kamal was not at the Institute or travelling, he would usually be working with Ahmed Shahati at the Foreign Ministry. After Shahati introduced Kamal to Gaddafi, Kamal would be personally summoned by him at all hours of the day or night. These conferences became routine, with Gaddafi querying Kamal a flood of questions on foreign affairs, but inevitably cutting him off in mid-sentence to claim his own points. Gaddafi disliked anyone thinking they knew more than him, even if he was the one asking the questions. He had a habit of contradicting every-one, even when he was clearly not listening.

Within months of arriving in Libya, Kamal was appointed one of Gaddafi's foreign advisors. The position sounded prestigious, but the reality was far from it. Kamal found himself growing increasingly frustrated because no matter how much work he did on any subject, or whatever prudent advice he gave, Gaddafi's mind seemed locked into doing exactly what he wanted to do from the beginning. As an added insult, he gave more credence to some of the Eastern European advisors hovering around than his own people, many of whom were well-educated like Kamal— and obviously more in tune to Libyan political and cultural interests.

Gaddafi managed to alienate many of his neighbors. He also unnecessarily interfered in far-flung rebel movements throughout the world. He supported the IRA in Ireland, the Muslim rebels in the Philippines, Idi Amin in Uganda, and was particularly interested in the growing Muslim movement among the blacks in the United States. He wanted to support his "brothers," as he called them, and helped finance several groups, including the Nation of Islam.

While throwing away billions of dollars into support for dubious movements around the world, and essentially exposing himself as irrational, Gaddafi was at the same time keen to gain recognition by the West, in particular the United States. He sought for the exchange of ambassadors between the two countries, and recruited Kamal to take part in the negotiations, promising to appoint him as Libyan Ambassador to the United States if he succeeded. As a result, Kamal flew back and forth between Tripoli and D.C. at least ten times over the course of a six-month period, often flying on the Concorde between London's Heathrow and Washington's Dulles Airport.

Though the U.S. State Department was willing to accept Kamal's credentials as ambassador, they presented the Libyan government with a set of conditions in order for a formal diplomatic exchange to occur. One was that Gaddafi ceased supporting terrorism. Gaddafi balked at being told what he could or could not do, and was unwilling to concede to any of the conditions. In the end, negotiations fizzled out, and he became more brazen with his support of terrorism abroad and more brutal treatment of political prisoners at home.

Failing to make headway on his terms with the United States, Gaddafi turned his attention to Europe. He decided to support Francois Mitterand, leader of the French Socialist Party, in his bid for the French Presidency. Kamal met with Mitterand on Gaddafi's behalf several times, contributing to his political campaign and reporting back to Gaddafi his assessment of the man and his political viability as president, which Kamal found inevitable given the political mood in France at the time.

Kamal liked Mitterand, and apparently the feeling was mutual. On one of his trips to Paris, Mitterand invited Kamal for dinner at Le Fouquet, after which he insisted on taking him to the Crazy Horse, in Pigalle.

In September 1978, Billy Carter, the brother of President Jimmy Carter, was invited to Libya at his own instigation. In reciprocity, the American Embassy invited Ali Treki, the Foreign Minister, Ahmed Shahati and Kamal to a reception for the president's brother. I was also included in the invitation, but it turned out that I was the only woman from the Libyan delegation who attended.

It was rather disorienting for me to be in Libya and see alcohol being served so openly, and even more surreal to see Billy Carter walking around with a can of his signature Billy beer in hand. When we were introduced, Billy genially conversed with me for a few minutes, graciously inviting Kamal and me to visit him in Plains, Georgia.

"It's only a few miles up the road from the Florida border...." he said with a quizzical grin.

Kamal and I offered a perfunctory laugh.

As I was still trying to wrap my mind around the bizarre encounter, Billy turned and asked me with a wink, "You sure you don't want a Billy beer?"

I was sure.

Kamal felt discomforted by Billy's presence in Libya, since he knew that he was being used, and that Billy had just accepted $200,000 as a gift for his visit. Kamal knew there was no way the president would give in to dealing with Gaddafi's people through his brother, and was sure that in the end Billy was going to be the one humiliated. He saw it as clumsy and undiplomatic, and was thoroughly embarrassed by the whole episode.

During the time I spent in Libya, I met many interesting and brilliant men, both Libyan and foreign, but one of the most charming was the former U.S. Vice-President, Spiro Agnew.

Kamal's brother, Amir, acted as a liaison between the government and foreign companies, and was instrumental in buying military equipment, uniforms, and telecommunication supplies for the army. Businessmen from the United States would often visit him in Libya, and he would sometimes include Kamal and me in his social interactions, which was always a treat for me. On one of his business ventures, he invited Spiro Agnew to Tripoli to present his proposal for a sale of helicopters to Libya.

I ended up being seated next to the former vice-president at a small, but very elegant dinner that Amir hosted. Agnew was sharply dressed, attractive and charming. He teased me about going to Hood, the girl's college I had attended in Maryland. Of course he knew all about it since he was from Maryland, and mentioned some Hood girls he knew. I found him fascinating, and we talked freely about a range of subjects. I thoroughly enjoyed our conversation, but I had to control myself from monopolizing him after seeing disapproving looks from the other male guests at the table.

Ever since I had known Kamal he had told me that one of his goals was to create a political model for Libya based on a blend of democracy and Islam. He said it would be different from any other model used in the Middle East, and that it would be successful because it would be tailored to fit the Libyan cultural, religious and socio-economic makeup. It was only shortly after arriving in Libya that Kamal realized he and his peers would never be given the opportunity to present their vision for a free and democratic Libya under Gaddafi.

As we sat on our verandah one night after dinner, on one of the rare occasions that we had to ourselves, Kamal looked at me, his face drawn with sadness.

"This man is destroying Libya, Hiba, and I don't know what to do."

I had never seen him this low.

"I'm so sorry for bringing you into this mess," he continued, "But I can't just walk out. This is my country."

I understood, and held his hand in mine. We talked for a long while, and for the first time I saw true hatred on his face and heard defeat in his voice. He could no longer pretend to believe in the man he once idolized.

"He is so well protected that the only way to get rid of him is by a coup."

The weight of this declaration hit me full force. My mind reeled with questions. What events lay before us, and what role would Kamal play in them?

He continued pensively, "The risk of someone close to him trying to kill him is too high, especially if they fail, and that's why it hasn't been done. He would punish not just the family, but the entire tribe."

Around 1977 Gaddafi decided that he wanted to subsidize Middle East Study Centers at major universities in Europe and the United States, and sent Kamal to make the necessary preliminary arrangements. As a result, Kamal was gone even more than before, and when he was home the children hardly saw him. I teased him that his children hardly recognized him in person as they saw him more on the television. Of course the only programs on TV were political propaganda, and often Gaddafi would order that Kamal be present, much to his chagrin.

I accepted my husband's absences as necessary, and coped by keeping myself occupied with the children and our own social activities when he was gone. My friends Mary and her husband, Ahmed, who had no children, showed my children and me a side of Libya I would otherwise not have been exposed to.

Mary was my closest and only American friend in Libya, the only woman I knew there who understood my past and how it related to my present, as all good friends do. Unlike Kamal, Ahmed was more liberal, and took Mary to restaurants and the beach. Only once during our four years in Libya did Kamal agree to go with the children and me to the beach, and that was only after a lot of cajoling from Mary and Ahmed. They practically had to shame him into going, for his children's sake.

The beaches Ahmed took us to were spectacularly beautiful and almost always deserted. There was a lovely beach in Khums, where the glistening, desolate sand seemed to stretch for miles, but I was forbidden by Kamal to go there with the children in case anyone from the town recognized us. Luckily there were many other beautiful beaches around Tripoli, like in Zanzour, and only occasionally would there be anyone around. I knew Kamal did not approve of me going to the beach, and he continued to express his disapproval of me using a swimsuit in public, even though I always wore a shirt over it.

"It's different in America, where men are used to seeing women half naked," he would say.

Since he was not offering an alternative for the kids and was too busy to spend time with them, I did not feel too guilty defying his wishes for our children's chance to frolic in the Mediterranean Sea. I was very grateful to Mary and Ahmed for including us on their excursions, and I promised Kamal that I would put on my robe if there were any strange men within a mile!

One of my favorite places in Tripoli was the Shati Hotel. I loved sitting on their long terrace, gazing out at the Mediterranean in the late afternoon, and if we were lucky, there would be a breeze blowing. Mary and Ahmed often invited us to join them, but I think Kamal only went with us a couple of times to placate me. While the adults sipped espresso or drank Italian sodas, the children would happily slurp their gelatos as we all watched the sunset.

Kamal did not like going with me to public places because he was not comfortable with strange men looking at me, at least not in Libya. He told me it was a sign of disrespect for men to look at a woman in the eyes unless they were family. And while Kamal was liberal when we lived in the United States, he seemed to change the moment he stepped back on Libyan soil. He repeatedly insisted that he was simply trying to protect me—responding to external pressures—but sometimes I wondered if the changes were not internal as well.

After our return from Moscow, Kamal told me on several occasions that he was being followed. He was also being closely questioned by some people about his American connections. When I inquired further, he indicated only that they were Gaddafi's people. He suspected that he was being implicated as pro-American and a CIA agent at the instigation of certain Eastern European elements surrounding Gaddafi. He was furious, as the accusations were completely false but difficult to disprove. I knew that professionally he had been under a lot of strain over the past two years, but despite many warnings he refused to give up and leave.

"That is exactly what they would like me to do," he said bitterly, "but I refuse. I have no choice except to try and work within their damn system."

He said that millions of dollars were spent educating Libyans, yet when they came home they were not allowed to put their education into practice. Unless they were kowtowing to Gaddafi, the intellectuals and progressives who wanted democracy were deliberately suppressed.

"Maybe we should go while we can," I continued to suggest on several occasions. My priority was simple: the safety of my husband and children. My other fear was that if Kamal were arrested, I could be asked to leave the country without my children.

"I'm not running away!" he would insist.

I was scared for him, afraid that he might suddenly disappear and never be heard from again, relieved each night he came home, terrified every morning he left.

By this time Amir and his family had already left, and so had my friends Mary and Ahmed. I didn't want to leave my Libyan family, but I also didn't want to see Kamal in prison or killed.

I knew from my conversations with his mother that she too was feeling very conflicted. She was hoping that perhaps Kamal's friend in the cabinet would be able to protect her son from harm. She kept telling me about her premonition that one of her sons would die in a foreign land. I knew she meant Kamal.

Spies and secret police were everywhere, and fear and suspicion permeated every household.

"Don't ever mention Gaddafi's name or talk politics to anyone outside the family" was the catchphrase *du jour*. Many families were leaving, especially the ones who had been educated abroad, and those who had the means. Men were disappearing daily: professionals, students, teachers, and military officers, anyone who opposed the man who was the self-appointed tormentor of Libyans. Dinner conversations and social interactions revolved around who was killed, imprisoned, or simply vanished.

Kamal was in a vulnerable position. False charges were becoming the norm and he had no way to defend himself. I too could conceivably come under suspicion of being an

American spy. It was all unthinkable, farcical, and ludicrous. Yet it was our reality.

Kamal walked in one October morning, as I was preparing to go out to the S*ouk al-Hout* to shop for dinner. He'd never come home so early, and seeing the expression on his face, I knew immediately something was wrong. He held out his arm, and gestured.

"Come to the bedroom, Hiba, I've got to speak with you."

From the tone of his voice, I knew it was something serious. I was scared, thinking for sure that someone we knew had died or had gone missing.

I followed him. He closed the door quietly after me, and sat down with me on the bed, taking both my hands in his, squeezing them hard and bringing them up to his lips. He kissed them, in the way he always had. "I have to leave the country immediately," he said, in a steady, low voice.

"What? Why? What's happened?"

"You remember what happened to my cousin?" he prompted.

Of course I did, but I nodded hesitantly, afraid of what he was going to say next.

About a year ago, Mustafa had left home at the usual time to go to work but never returned. He vanished without a trace. Efforts by the family to find him were met with warnings from the authorities to stop, or else every male in the family would also "disappear."

Kamal continued, "Mustafa's wife found his body this morning outside their house. He'd been tortured, probably beaten to death just before they dumped his body."

I knew of many similar stories, but this was different because it involved Kamal's cousin. As I sat there trembling

211

with shock, Kamal told me exactly what happened that morning.

Shortly after his friend, who had brought him the news of Mustafa, left his office, Kamal was summoned to Central Intelligence. As he was preparing to leave, knowing he could not disregard the order, he received another call, this one from Khweldi, then Minister of Interior, insisting that Kamal come to his office immediately. Kamal's instinct was to trust Khweldi, so he went to see him first.

Khweldi and he spoke for a few moments of pleasantries, and then Khweldi passed him a note, placing his index finger on his lip to remind Kamal about the recording devices in the room. What was written would change our lives forever:

Gaddafi has given orders for your immediate arrest. I cannot help you. You must leave the country at once!

As casually as he could, Kamal left Khweldi's office, went out to his car, and drove straight home. He knew his old friend would never have warned him to leave unless the situation was life-threatening.

Kamal explained to me that he was going straight to the airport, and hopefully with the help of the airport chief, Mohammed, he would be able to take the first flight out, to wherever it was going. Arrangements would be made for the children and me to leave Libya, and he would be waiting for us eventually in America.

"Don't worry, *Habibti,* Ali will take care of everything. He'll find some way for you and the children to get out as soon as possible. You have to be brave for them, and for me.

And whatever happens, don't leave the house under any circumstances unless Ali is with you."

In that instant I was coming face to face with what I had feared for the last four years: if Kamal were caught I'd never see him again, or if I did, it might only be when he was dead, like Mustafa, discarded on our doorstep. What I feared also was being arrested or deported myself, my children taken from me.

Everything began to happen so fast, and I was in such a state of shock that I don't remember anything I said except asking if I should pack a bag for him. He said there was no time. All he was taking was his briefcase.

I had long considered the possibility we might eventually have to leave, but I hadn't imagined it would be like this. I had a million questions, yet all I could think of was him going without having packed a change of clothes.

"Don't be afraid, Hiba. They won't do anything to hurt you or the children."

I called the children into our bedroom, and told my four-year-old son and six-year-old daughter to kiss their father goodbye. Naturally they had no idea of the magnitude of the situation, assuming their daddy was simply going on another one of his frequent trips abroad.

"Will you bring me back a present, Daddy?" Layla asked playfully. He'd never failed to bring the children something back from his trips.

"Of course I will, *Habibti*!" he said. Then he turned to Tarek: "You're the man of the house now. Take care of your mummy and sister, okay?"

"Yes, Daddy, I will!"

My heart nearly wrenched apart, seeing my little boy's face, determined to be a little man.

Kamal held me tightly for a long time, and told me that no matter what happened, to always remember that he loved me and the children more than life. He kissed the children goodbye, and gave them all kinds of instructions to be good.

Then we heard the doorbell ring.

I jumped, thinking the secret police were at our door.

"No, no, it's okay, *Habibti*," he reassured me, "It's only Ali."

We followed Kamal downstairs and were greeted by a somber-looking Ali, who took the time to kiss the children as they rushed into his arms. By that point I felt I was in an out-of-body experience in slow motion. Before I knew it my husband was gone, and my children had gone back to playing as if nothing had happened.

I felt hopeless and terrified, and had no one to talk to. Mary had left, and I knew my phone was tapped, so I couldn't even call my family in Khums. I had not smoked in years, but I wanted a cigarette so badly that I searched all over the house for one. When I finally found one of Kamal's packages of Kent in the parlor, I broke down and cried. I quickly went to the bedroom and shut the door, trusting that Kamaria would take care of the children. So many things went through my mind that I could not concentrate on a single one. I just prayed that Kamal would be able to get out of the country safely without being detained at the airport.

That afternoon Ali and my father-in-law came to discuss the situation. I could see that Ibrahim was crushed; he knew he was about to be indefinitely separated from his grandchildren as well as his son. Plans had to be made to get us out of the country, as we were legally unable to leave without Kamal's written permission. He had left in such a hurry this had not been done, but under the circumstances it would not have been approved, since there was already a warrant out for his arrest. That would have been a reason enough to hold me hostage.

There was no question, at least within the family, that the children and I had to leave. Ali said he would make all the arrangements, and Ibrahim said he would get hold of as much American money as he could for me. Since we did not have a US bank account, we would literally be going back to Tallahassee without a dime. Under the new law, Libyans were only allowed to take 1,000 dinars out of the country each year, which was hardly enough to start a new life anywhere. I knew the money Kamal and I had in our bank account in Tripoli would now be confiscated, and it would not be safe for me to withdraw anything, much less close out the account.

Later that evening Rogaya and two of my sisters-in-law, Yasmine and Maia, came to stay with us for a few days. With their help and Lamia, Ali's wife, we determined what to do about the house, and divided up all the personal effects that had to be left behind.

It was a depressing time for all of us; we knew the family was about to be broken up yet again. Amir and his family were already gone, now Kamal, and soon the children and me. It was certain that we wouldn't even be able to come back to visit as long as Gaddafi was in power.

Rogaya hugged me that night, crying for her son and for the grandchildren who would soon be gone. Once again, she mentioned her fear of her son dying away from home, in a foreign land. She hugged me and told me how much she loved me, and that I was like her fifth daughter. I felt so sad for her, thinking of her pain at losing a part of her life.

"I am not only losing my son and grandchildren," she wept, wiping her eyes with a handkerchief soaked in tears, "I am also losing a daughter."

CHAPTER 14

LAST DAY IN LIBYA

I had never even heard of Libya before I met Kamal. Because of my love for him I had changed my name, left my country, and given up everything I had known in another life to make a new one with him there. Now, alone in an increasingly hostile country, I didn't care what happened to me—but I was terrified for my two small children.

If for some reason I was arrested, I could be deported without my children or thrown in jail. I didn't want them to grow up without a mother, in a country embroiled in political turmoil and terror. I had absolutely no knowledge of where we were going, or even how. All I knew was that I was ready to do whatever necessary to get them out. The day Kamal left our home, secreted away by Ali, I packed a suitcase for each of us, but I was desperately waiting to hear that he had got out safely.

Ever since that terrible day we were on constant alert, ready to escape at a moment's notice. Ali warned me not to leave the house in case I got picked up by the secret police. I crammed my one suitcase with only a few changes of clothing, leaving room for my children's photographs and irreplaceable personal items. I had been instructed by Ali to pack light, as though we were going on vacation, so as not to raise any suspicion of a defection. I hoped to be able to explain the photographs and personal items as gifts for friends and family back in the States.

Inside my black Dior handbag were our most precious lifelines to freedom: Layla's and my American passports and about 100,000 US dollars, which my father-in-law had somehow very quickly been able to put together, at a very high price. I knew the risk I was taking was enormous and that at some point I might be forced to get rid of my daughter's passport as well as the money. It could be used to buy our freedom, but to be caught with it could also result in instant arrest, not that they even needed an excuse. Besides, it was all the money we had to start a new life wherever we went.

There were three plainclothes secret police who took shifts daily in the empty lot across the street. They sat around, lounging in their cars all day and night, making no attempt to hide their presence. Since the phones were tapped, I had no way of calling my parents and telling them what was happening, but I hoped Kamal had already called to explain in a way that would not alarm them unduly. I was also unable to use the phone to alert the U.S. Embassy of our predicament and impending departure; however, I knew what I had to do from previous conversations I had with Moore.

In order to protect Kamal and me, the embassy had not issued a passport for Tarek, and had strongly advised me to get rid of Layla's American passport in case of a search. Since Layla had been born in the United States, it would have been easier to argue the reason for her possessing one; still, if I were to be detained, I could be charged with trying to smuggle my own children out of the country. Then I could be deported without my children or imprisoned, as the children would be considered Libyan citizens by virtue of their father being Libyan. By law, the children would then be put into the custody of their Libyan grandparents.

The American consul at the embassy explained that under the circumstances, and even without passports, the children could be easily paroled into the United States. I was instructed that if I had to leave Libya under dire circumstances I was to go to the US Embassy of whatever country we entered, and arrangements would be made for our return to American soil, with or without papers.

"We have all your information at the State Department, and at most you would only have to wait a week for all the paperwork to be ready."

Moore's reassurance kept ringing in my ears whenever the flood of panic would wash over me. The thought of being stranded and stateless was overwhelming.

I packed as much of the children's clothing as possible into two suitcases. They also each had a little knapsack filled with a few of their favorite toys and snacks. Kamaria crammed two suitcases with clothes and souvenirs I had bought her during her years with us. She was the only one who could legally leave, and had more than fulfilled her four-year contract, but she insisted on accompanying us. I was grateful, and relieved to have her with me.

Like every morning for the past two weeks, the whole household awakened before dawn to a substantial breakfast prepared by Nabila, who wanted to be sure that when we left it would at least be on a full stomach. I was going to miss the delicious Tunisian dishes she prepared, especially the breakfasts and late-night suppers.

219

If it had not been for the children, who filled the house with their laughter and play, the tension would have been unbearable. For their sakes, the adults had no choice but to maintain some sense of normalcy. Yet, no matter how hard we tried to hide our anxiety I am sure the children still managed to sense it—especially Layla, who continuously watched and questioned every move I made. Tarek was the only one who seemed oblivious, reacting only to me. Whenever I seemed upset or looked worried, he would say, "You okay, Mummy?" Coming from a four-year-old, those words gave me the determination to make it okay for them.

One day, with nothing to do except wait, I walked slowly through the house we had called home for the past four years, taking stock of our life there. Before long, I knew that strangers would move in and claim everything we left behind, courtesy of Gaddafi and his thugs.

The servants would also be leaving soon, returning to their homes in Egypt and Tunisia. My father-in-law had promised to give them each the equivalent of three months' salary, and I told them to take whatever they wanted from the house. However, since their mode of transportation was by overland taxi or bus, space was limited.

I sadly looked at the things I had selected on our many trips abroad, bringing back memories of happier times filled with hope: Chinese antiques from Singapore, china and crystal from Europe, and paintings I had collected from various artists everywhere we went. It was all meaningless now.

What I regretted leaving most were the children's belongings such as the bassinet and crib they had both used as infants, shipped over from Florida, and various knick-knacks I had used to decorate their rooms.

Every other room in the house was furnished with exquisite gold-gilded Italian and French pieces, none of which I had chosen. Heavy velvet curtains draped every window which, when drawn at night, would blanket the entire house in darkness to the city outside, cloaking us inside with a false sense of protection. Enormous gold-plated chandeliers (when they worked) dappled uneven, flickering light throughout the house. Because the furniture was so expensive and had been a gift, I could not get rid of it. Instead, I had learned to live with it, just as I had learned to accept living in Libya, with all the good and the bad.

About a week after Kamal left, Ali told me that time was running out. He said that if he could not get us on a flight soon we would have to drive across the border from Libya into Tunisia, by hopefully avoiding or bribing the Libyan border patrols.

The Tunisian border was almost ninety miles west of Tripoli, but there were several checkpoints before then. How I was treated would be up to whomever was there. I dreaded that, for the children's sakes as well as mine. Also, since Ali couldn't go with us, our fates would depend on the reliability of our driver, and I was scared to trust anyone outside of the family. Libya had taught me to be paranoid.

It was November, and even though the days were cool and pleasant, the nights in the desert could be very cold. A flight out of Tripoli was our best hope, though they were usually booked up for weeks or even months in advance, and everyone leaving the country needed an "exit visa". A married woman had to have her Libyan husband's permission to leave the country, and children their father's.

With Kamal gone, the proper legal documents were impossible to obtain, and to be caught with forged documents would seal our fates. Yet despite these risks, forged papers were obtained and signed by Ali and given for me to present in case we were stopped at the airport or the border.

Ali explained to me that our best hope was to depend on a friend of the family, Mohammed, who had helped smuggle Kamal out of the country by simply taking him straight to the plane after bumping off another passenger. Each time the family had left or entered Libya, Mohammed had been there to escort us, ushering us straight from the plane to the terminal to avoid the long lines at immigration and customs. He was always friendly and polite. I sensed that he was a very decent man with a difficult job. Like all Libyans, he had no choice but to do what he had to do to survive.

Based on past experiences, Ali and Kamal also trusted him. The previous year, when Kamal was getting ready to return to Tripoli from an international conference in New Delhi, Ali had called to alert his brother that a warrant had been issued for his arrest. Apparently, Kamal had been too vocal at the conference, on issues relating to political maneuverings and manipulating by the Russians and Eastern Europeans in Libya. He had presented a paper on Arabs, and more specifically Libyans, needing to find their own political model. He went on to elaborate that neither the Western nor the Communist model would be a good fit for the Libyan culture, and particularly not the communist model. As a result, the Soviet delegates reported back to the Libyan Foreign Ministry that Kama was sympathetic to the Americans, insinuating that he was working for the CIA.

With Mohammed's help, Kamal was able to slip into Libya without being detected at the airport. Ali had arranged for a meeting with Prime Minister Jalloud, to whom Kamal explained what happened, thus bypassing the notorious secret police. That time, with Jalloud's consensus, the situation was diffused.

I prayed that Ali was right about Mohammed, as the children's lives and mine depended on it. All Mohammed had to do was alert the secret police and I would be arrested. He could potentially be very well rewarded for reporting us.

Ali's plan was simple, but fraught with uncertainty. Seats would be made available by Mohammed bumping off four passengers on a booked flight at the last minute. Precision and timing had to be perfect. A contact in immigration would pass us through, and Ali and Mohammed would stay with us until boarding. Unfortunately, the secret police were always on the lookout for dissidents trying to flee. They swarmed the airport, targeting anyone with or without reason.

Still, I preferred this option over an escape through the desert. If things went wrong at the airport, I could make a scene, and hope that maybe someone would alert the U.S. Embassy. My biggest fear was no one knowing where we were or what might happen to us in the desert.

Every morning, after the children had finished their breakfast and been dressed by Kamaria, our routine was to sit in the spacious main hall and watch them play while we waited for Ali to come. I could not even let them play in the garden. And every morning Ali came, and every morning he would say that today was not the day. Still, we had to be prepared and ready to leave at a moment's notice.

At 8 a.m. one morning, I jumped at the shrill sound of the doorbell echoing from the servants' quarters. It was earlier than Ali usually came, but I prayed it was him. My heart lurched every time the doorbell rang, each time fearing it might be the secret police.

I motioned to Kamaria to take the children and leave the room.

"Hush!" I told her. "Try not to make any noise." I needed to make sure it was Ali.

As she had been instructed to do many times before, Kamaria grabbed the children and hurried to hide in the secret room until I told her it was safe to come out. The children thought they were playing hide and seek, and the servants had been given instructions to always tell strangers that we were not home. Only the family and trusted servants like Kamaria knew about the room. Luckily, Amir had had the foresight to have this room constructed when he had the house built. Its original purpose was to be a safe room for housing jewelry, money and precious items, and was therefore highly secured. It was just large enough to squeeze in about four people.

I joined them as soon as Nabila's husband went to answer the door. The children, Kamaria, and I all huddled on the floor in the small, darkened space. It was behind the mahogany bookshelves that lined one wall of the large hallway between the enormous main dining room and another smaller formal dining room used by women on special occasions. The entry could be secured from the inside, so that, short of breaking through the bookcase and the wall, access from the outside was well concealed.

We waited silently, except for some soft giggling from the children.

After what seemed like an eternity, especially with the children fidgeting and waiting to be "found", we heard three soft knocks followed by another two, then one. It was our predetermined signal.

I opened the door slowly, and with great relief saw my dear brother-in-law—dressed in full military uniform—looking tired and worried, but smiling as always. The children adored him. They jumped into his arms shrieking with delight while he covered them with kisses.

As he carried them out, he turned to me and said quietly, "Hiba, we have to leave immediately. A warrant has been issued for your arrest, and they will be here soon. My car is in the garage."

"Why?" A stupid question, but I was terrified, now that the time had come.

"They don't need a reason," he stated matter-of-factly. "They know Kamal's left the country, so they'll hold you until he comes back."

My heart pounded so hard I could feel it in my throat. I felt like I was going to choke to death on it.

"Don't worry, Hiba," Ali said. "Once we get to the airport, Mohammed will put you on the flight to London without any problems."

He went over the plans with me, saying that my Lebanese friend, Mohammed Ajami, would be informed of my arrival time and be at Heathrow Airport to meet us. He also told me that Kamal had been in contact with Mohammed.

I was flooded with relief. Until then, I had not known for certain if Kamal had got out of Libya safely.

"There's a Libyan Airline flight leaving for London at noon. You must get on that, but we must hurry!"

I quickly finished preparing the children and myself, while Ali and Kamaria collected the bags.

Sensing that the time had come, the servants gathered together, waiting for us downstairs as we rushed to the garage. They were all quietly crying, including Abdo, hugging and kissing the children, knowing it was likely they'd never see us again. Ali told them to say their goodbyes quickly. Everyone understood the urgency.

I thought my heart would burst out of my chest as it pounded even more when I saw the soldier standing next to Ali's car. He was carrying a machine gun.

"It is okay, Hiba," Ali assured me. "He answers only to me, and I trust him completely. We might need him."

Ali is a man of few words, so whatever he says is noteworthy.

The last phrase echoed in my head: *"We might need him..."*

I looked at Ali, and my heart filled with respect and gratitude for this gentle, strong man, who was risking his own life to help us. He was one of the highest-ranking generals in Libya, and what he was doing could cost him his life.

CHAPTER 15

JAMAHIRIYA AIRPORT

Driving away from the house that morning, I was over-whelmed with sadness at the thought of leaving behind my life in Libya, and not knowing when the children and I would see our family there again. All the memories we had shared over the last four years rushed through me from every direction.

I tried to get hold of myself and listen to Ali, who was giving me last-minute instructions: "Don't say anything. I will speak for you and stay with you until you board the plane. If I can…"

I had complete faith in Ali and was prepared to let him take care of everything. I knew he loved the children, and would not allow any harm to come to them.

I instructed Kamaria that in case I was detained she was to immediately tell the Ajamis everything as soon as she got to London, and call my father in Singapore, as I didn't know if Kamal was going to be in London.

As we got closer to the airport, the magnitude of my situation hit me anew—as well as the danger it posed for Ali. I prayed that God would guide us through the next few hours.

I looked outside the window at the road that had once led to the promise of a new life. Though the sun was shining and the November air outside was fresh and crisp, my heart cried for what could have been, and for all that was lost.

Mohammed Ajami, who was to meet us in London, was married to a friend of mine, Daisy. We had spent a lot of time together in Tripoli prior to their departure. She often visited me at my house, and we were invited several times to theirs. Mohammed was granted permission from his company to be transferred to England a few months prior, as they were getting exasperated with the living conditions in Libya.

After we arrived, and while we waited for Tarek's passport to be processed, the children and I were to stay with the Ajamis in Richmond, a lovely town on the Thames and only a short drive outside London. The prospect of being in a free country again was almost too good to be true. First, however, I had a potentially dangerous hurdle to overcome at Tripoli Airport, which Gaddafi had renamed Jamahariya Airport. Ali kept reassuring me that everything was going to be alright.

I thanked God the children were oblivious to what was going on and were just looking forward to getting on the plane. They each had a small knapsack, and the only hand luggage I carried was my handbag and an antique Chinese gold panel carving my mother had given us as a wedding gift. I was afraid not to take it because I knew she would be furious if I left it behind. It was irreplaceable as it was almost three-hundred-years old. I had carefully wrapped the carving in many layers of paper days ago.

My handbag contained Layla's passport, as well as my own, and the cash my father-in-law had given me. It was all the money Kamal and I would have to start a new life in the United States, or wherever he decided to go.

When we arrived at the airport, I was surprised to see that it was packed with people leaving. Super-sized suitcases, unopened electronics, cardboard boxes, and every imaginable container conveyance was shoved around among the swarming crowd.

I was really scared by then, and hoped that perhaps no one would notice me and the children sneaking onto the plane. I didn't know from this point on what to expect. Ali was busy giving instructions for our suitcases to be unloaded and beckoning us to follow him into the terminal. Trying as much as I could to be inconspicuous, I followed with my children and Kamaria in tow.

As we made our way toward the terminal, I kept thinking of an American lady I had met, whose Libyan husband, Yusef al-Azmarly, had been shot and killed at the OPEC conference in Austria in 1975. It took her two years of appealing to Gaddafi to grant her permission to be able to take her children out of the country. I remembered her telling me she used to sit outside his office for hours every day, until she was asked to leave. Fortunately, her persistence paid off. The irony was that upon her husband's death, her aged in-laws were granted custody of the children, and not her.

Amazingly, even in the midst of the melee, the children and I were quickly separated from the rush of bodies and high volumes of arguing, pleading and indignation. We were thankfully whisked past long lines of people waiting to have their bags opened and their contents publicly inspected. The chaos was startling; utter confusion reigned.

By now I was starting to feel more confident that every-thing was going to be okay and go according to plan. Ali's soldier was carrying his gun, as well as the Chinese carving I had so carefully wrapped. Kamaria was carrying Tarek, while I was holding Layla's hand as she walked beside me. Ali led the way, following a very official-looking man in a dark suit and tie. I wondered if he worked for the airport or the secret police.

The man led us to an empty table at one corner of the terminal, indicating to the porter pushing our luggage to put it all on the table. He spoke with Ali, and from his expression I could see that it was with reassurance and respect. I understood that he was telling Ali not to worry, that he would take care of everything.

"Hiba," Ali turned in my direction with what I detected was a faint look of relief, "this man said he will take care of you. He said they don't need to examine your luggage. You just go inside, and wait for your plane to London. Mohammed will be there, and my soldier will help you. Everything is okay. Don't worry."

He said all this slowly, with a brave but sad smile. I know he was sorry to see us leave, yet relieved that the children and I were going to make it out safely. Putting his arm around me, Ali led me a few steps away and lowered his voice so only I could hear.

"He says I don't need to go inside, but he said my soldier can go in and help you until your plane leaves."

I understood from the way he told me that he did not want to argue with the man, or it would seem as though he didn't believe him—and if he didn't, then maybe there was something to hide.

Ali took Tarek from Kamaria, tenderly kissing his little nephew and sweetly instructing him to take care of his mother and his sister. He then squatted down and took Layla in his arms, holding her tightly. After saying goodbye to the children and Kamaria, Ali hugged me and whispered to me once again that everything would be all right.

"Mohammed will be waiting for you inside. He will stay with you until he takes you all on the plane."

I was frightened but knew I had to wait without displaying any hint of fear or guilt. I had seen Ali presenting the phony "Exit Visa" to the man in the suit, who brushed it off with "*Malesh.*" It's okay!

I followed the soldier, still carrying his gun and my antique package, through the gate. I turned to look one last time at my dear brother-in-law. His face was drawn and his body looked tense. If only all armies had generals like him, and if only more men were like him, I thought, this would be a better world. I waved goodbye one last time, and I think at that moment we both wondered if our paths would ever cross again.

After walking past the gate, we approached the escalator, with Ali's soldier leading the way. By then Ali was out of sight. Having the soldier with his gun escorting us gave me a false sense of security.

Out of nowhere, two men dressed in black suits came up to our soldier and barked orders in Arabic for him to leave. He was confused, answering that he had been given instructions by General Ramadan to help me, whereupon one of the secret police pointed a gun at him and told him to hand over the package and go away.

"*Imshi! Imshi!*"

The poor man handed over the package and walked away in shame, his eyes to the floor to avoid looking at me.

At that point, everything started to happen so fast that I was thrown into a complete state of bewilderment. It was as though another person came into my body and took over, because I was in total shock.

The four of us were ordered to an area where there was a long table with our suitcases already opened and their contents strewn all over. We watched as the two men examined every item, including the hems of dresses and pants. It was humiliating. I could see other passengers walking on the other side of the hall furtively glancing at us with sympathy.

After every single item from the bags was examined, the men carelessly threw them back into the suitcases and asked to see the children's knapsacks. They took everything out of the children's bags, once again examining every item meticulously. One of them took out a penknife, slitting holes in the back of my daughter's doll and my son's teddy bear to make sure there was nothing stuffed inside.

To my surprise, the children took it all in their stride. Perhaps they sensed they were supposed to so that Mummy wouldn't get into trouble. Kamaria kept stroking them, quietly reassuring them that she would sew the toys back together as soon as we got to London. It took every drop of self-control in my body not to scream at the men.

Then one of them, who I assumed was the person in charge, looked at me and pointed to my carry-on package.

"What is that?" he asked suspiciously.

He was a very tall skinny man, dark, and his face looked badly scarred, as if it had been burnt. His expression was dour and accusatory.

"It's a present for my mother." I answered, as civilly as I could under the surreal circumstances.

He proceeded to put it on the table in front of me, and without a word, used the penknife again to cut the strings and tear apart the wrapping. All the care I had taken to wrap it for nothing...I forgot where I was, and got very annoyed with the nonchalance of the man ripping apart my handiwork.

"You'd better wrap that back up!" I snapped in English, unable to control myself.

He completely ignored me.

Of course there was nothing to find, but at least he did clumsily attempt to rewrap the carving, tying a loose piece of string to secure it.

I was starting to get more upset than scared by this time, but thought that maybe now they would leave us alone and let us go. He rudely gestured for us to move on down the corridor towards the plane.

I could feel everyone around with their eyes on us, probably thanking God it was not them. I walked down the corridor, holding my son's hand tightly in mine while Kamaria stuck close to me with Layla in tow. Surprisingly, the children were extraordinarily quiet, no doubt sensing something was wrong as children often do.

Halfway down the corridor, I saw two women in uniforms watching us coming, and as we got closer, one of them waved me towards her. As I got there, I was wondering what she wanted, because she kept using a word I did not recognize. When I shook my head, she finally said, "Search body!"

I had traveled all my life, over four continents, to many countries. Never once had I ever been strip-searched. I was appalled at the thought. When they pointed to the children and signaled for them to go into a small room, I thought I was going to lose it and started arguing with them. One of the women yelled at me,

"*Ascoti!*" Shut up!

At that moment something clicked in my head, and I knew that I had no choice but to play by their rules. I asked the woman to let me talk to my children first, so they wouldn't get scared. She shrugged, which I took as consent.

"Listen darlings, these ladies want to play a little game with you, okay? They think that you are hiding a little kitty, so they are going to see if they can find it."

It was a weak explanation, but the only thing I could think of so quickly.

Tarek was okay, but Layla thought it was silly. She nonetheless agreed to go along after a little bit of persuasion. Thankfully, they allowed me to go into the room with my children when they examined them.

When they were done, I took them outside while Kamaria went in next behind the closed door. I had a few minutes then to decide what to do with my handbag. If they searched it, it would all be over. As Kamaria was coming out of the room, I went up to her and surreptitiously shoved it against her body. She very quickly slipped it out of sight under her coat.

When I went inside, one of the women closed the door while the other asked me to undress. After a humiliating and infuriating search of my body and my clothes, I was told to get dressed and get out. More than anything I wished for Ali to come and get us, to take us away from these people. I knew he would if he could. I wanted desperately to be with my family in Khums, where the children and I would be safe.

I thought of the time when I went for a walk by myself at the farm, and suddenly two wild dogs starting chasing me. I screamed at the top of my voice and ran like the wind, but of course no one heard me, as the wind was blowing towards the sea and not the house. I got backed up to the wall surrounding the house, and managed to fend the dogs off with garden hoses and a big empty tin can and lid I used to hit them with. Their mouths looked enormous, foaming with saliva, barking at me with deafening sounds. I kept thinking that perhaps the only way I could save myself was to rip their mouths open. I was not ready to leave my children without a mother. I was sure I was going to die, and it crossed my mind what a freakish death this was going to be. Just then I saw Ibrahim come running, ordering the dogs away. He gathered me into his arms and helped me back to the house, where Rogaya and the sisters fussed over me. A little later I heard two shots, and Ibrahim came into the house carrying a gun. All he said was, "Never again!" He never wanted me to be scared of going to visit his house. It was that simple.

As Kamaria and I were gathering the children and our carry-on bags, the same man who had ripped apart my carving came up and told us brusquely that we could board the plane. I could see that the corridor to our flight was empty now, and as the four of us walked I could hear my heart beating so loudly that I was afraid someone else would also hear it and not let us leave.

After what seemed like an eternity we finally got into the cabin. I could see the look of pity on everyone's faces. The stewardess showed us to our seats in first class, and Kamaria and I prepared the children for takeoff. *Please God,* I prayed, *help us get to London safely. Please God, let my heart stop pounding so loud and so hard.* I kept on praying while the plane started moving to taxi down the runway. Thank God for Kamaria, who kept talking non-stop to the children, to distract them, because I was incapable of words or movement.

As soon as the plane taxied down the runway, all the passengers started clapping and cheering. I looked around the cabin, confused. Slowly I realized that it was for us. They were cheering our escape from the goons at the airport. They had seen what we had gone through and knew our desperation...but they had celebrated too soon.

When I had gone to Libya almost five years ago, my future had been fraught with uncertainty. Now, again, I felt as if my life were on a precipice. I had not been able to talk with Kamal since he left, so I had no idea what we were going to do. All I knew was that once I got to London I would be able to talk to him, and he would reassure me that everything was going to be all right again.

I looked out the window as I felt the plane slowing down, and realized with horror that we were turning to taxi back to the terminal. I had no doubt then that they were coming to get me.

"Kamaria," I leaned across the aisle, hurriedly giving her instructions. I figured that they would have no reason to detain her, so even if the children or I were to be held, she would be able to tell the Ajamis everything and contact my parents. I held my daughter tightly, trying to reassure her. "Everything is okay, my love. We'll be seeing Daddy soon."

I prayed that I was not lying to her.

My son was thankfully already starting to nod off, exhausted by the long day. Our flight had already been delayed for three hours as a result of the search, and it was definitely now going to be even longer.

As the plane came to a stop, a dreadful silence permeated the cabins, and I could feel all eyes on me.

I gave Kamaria my handbag, and waited for the thug in the black suit. I couldn't believe they were doing all this for an American passport. They didn't even know how much money I was taking out of the country. By now my savvy nanny had my bag tucked out of sight, wedged behind her back.

I held my daughter's hand as the plane door opened and, just as I had expected, it was the same man. He rushed onto the plane with such an air of importance and urgency, coming straight for me. Pointing towards the door, he yelled at me, very loudly

"*Imshi!*" Go!

I stood up, trying to muster as much dignity as I could with my heart practically hanging out of my mouth.

"Where you bag?!" he shouted in broken English.

It took me only a second to fathom his meaning. This was why they'd called the plane back. They realized that no one had examined my handbag!

There was nothing I could do now, so I reached for it behind Kamaria. It was the first time the poor lady exhibited panic, looking at me with wide questioning eyes. I told her in Malay that it was okay and to take care of my children.

"If I miss the flight," I reminded her quietly in Malay, "you call my father the moment you land in London, okay? He will take care of everything."

At that time, I didn't even know how to contact Kamal. I think the poor woman was more afraid for me than herself.

"Mummy, Mummy, where are you going?" Layla sensed something was not right, and I was afraid she was going to start crying.

"It's okay, darling. Mummy will be back. I love you infinity. Listen to Kamaria okay, baby?"

I walked towards the door, with the strap of the bag burning into my shoulder and my captor behind me. Once we were out of the plane, he unceremoniously pushed me into the terminal.

"*Imshi! Imshi!*" He was shouting now, but I didn't care, knowing the children couldn't hear. Suddenly, we were joined out of nowhere by another black-suited thug I recognized from earlier. One on each side of me, they steered me towards an inconspicuous-looking door somewhere inside the terminal. I was aware of many eyes on me, but it didn't matter anymore. I knew I was in serious trouble. I automatically adopted a feeling of resignation, and in doing so I was suddenly able to calm myself.

One of the men lightly knocked three times on the door before opening it and ordered me to go into the room. Inside, an older, somewhat stocky man was sitting behind a large desk talking on the telephone. As soon as I walked in, he told the person on the other end in Arabic that "she is here," before abruptly hanging up.

He looked at me as though he was studying a map, very seriously and slowly.

"Sit down!" He ordered, pointing at the chair across the desk. He then signaled the two men to leave. After they hesitantly left the room—probably wishing they could stay to see me humiliated—the older man turned to me.

238

"Give me your bag, Madame Ben Ramadan."

I handed it over to him as calmly as my nerves would allow and sat back, hoping that I did not look as terrified and guilty as I felt. Lying has never been one of my strong points, a result of getting caned often by my mother for the most insignificant transgression. I decided that I would be as truthful as I could without hurting Kamal or his family.

As he unclasped my bag, he poured out the entire contents onto the desk and picked out the passports and the cash, which I had secured in an envelope. Slowly, he went through each of the passports and counted the cash.

"Why does your daughter have an American passport?" His English was excellent. I felt somewhat relieved that at least I would be able to communicate and explain myself better.

"She was born in America, and since we go often to Singapore, it is easier to go with an American passport because she doesn't need a visa." I was answering carefully, but I could hear my own voice cracking.

"This is a lot of money, Madame. Do you know it is illegal to take so much money out of the country?"

I did not answer him, hoping he would surmise that maybe I was not smart enough to know Libyan laws. Mercifully, he let it go.

"Where is your husband, Madame?" His delivery was slow and calculating.

I looked him straight in the eye and answered truthfully. "I swear I don't know."

He looked at me for what seemed like a long time.

"So, what other illegal items are you taking out of Libya?" The sarcasm was blatant.

"Nothing...." I managed to choke out softly, my resolve starting to crumble.

He studied my face without saying a word. After what felt like an eternity, he grimly said, "You know I can arrest you, right? You know, there are some people who want to put you in jail until your husband comes back to get you?"

I numbly nodded, and noticed that he was looking me straight in the eye. I knew that the rest of my life depended on my answer: whether I go on the plane, or was sent to a Libyan prison indefinitely.

A calmness swept over me as I searched his face for an inkling of sympathy. Never in my life have I begged with my eyes like I did those few moments.

And then I saw it, a glint of kindness. Emboldened, I took a chance and appealed to his humanity.

"*Sidi*," I said, using the Arabic word for master, a term of reverence and respect—a term I have only used for my father-in-law, Ibrahim. "I have two small children who need me, and they are my life. I would die without them. All I care about is them. I love my family here, and I love Libya, but I need to leave for a while. I cannot stay by myself without my husband."

I knew I was begging, but I didn't care. He was my only hope left. I tried to cry, but crying does not come to me easily.

The pause was excruciating. Finally, he began to slowly put all the contents back in my handbag. He gave me a long hard look, stood up and said very gently, "Bon voyage, Madame."

I couldn't believe what I heard. I wanted to hug him and thank him over and over again, but all I could do was barely whisper, "*Sukran, thank you.*"

Even now, I thank you, from my heart to yours. You are a good man, and I shall never forget you or your face.

He walked me to the door and opened it for me. I looked at him one last time and gingerly smiled at him with gratitude. Without a word, I walked past the two thugs who were standing outside with smirks on their faces.

I was shaking so much inside that walking back to the plane was more difficult than it was coming out. I wanted to run, but my knees felt as if they would buckle under from the shaking.

Somehow, I managed to find my way back, and as I went into the safety of the plane, I crumbled into my seat. Sensing I needed no words, Kamaria kept Layla quiet, but I could see the look of relief on both their faces. My little boy, bless his heart, was fast asleep by now.

The whole plane was silent.

This time, the plane finally took off into the sky after taxiing down the runway, but there was no clapping. Instead, it was quietly somber, as though everyone was sharing in my relief, too powerful to warrant any words, and afraid perhaps that any noise would break the spell.

I looked down at the city that had been my home for four years, thinking of all the people I loved whom I was leaving behind. My first day in Tripoli almost five years ago replayed into my mind. I had been awakened early that morning by the sound of the *Azan*, the Islamic call to prayer from a nearby mosque. The voice of the *muezzin* in the moments before sunrise was hauntingly beautiful and moving. I wondered if I would ever wake up to that sound again.

Suddenly, the tears I had buried in my heart now flowed as sadness overcame me—not just for my own circumstances, but for the tragedy of an entire nation.

CHAPTER 16

TALLAHASSEE

After we arrived at Heathrow, many of the Libyans from my flight came up to me at the baggage area to ask if I was okay. Several even apologized for the treatment I had received. It was this kindness and sincerity that restored some of my hope. One day, perhaps this vast majority of decent Libyans would rule the country, rather than the hired thugs of a maniacal tyrant.

As we left the gate, I caught sight of Daisy and Mohammed. Suddenly what had transpired earlier that day seemed more like a nightmare. I tried to remind myself that I was now where law and order prevailed, where it was illegal to be seized from your home or off the streets, and never be heard of again. I should have felt liberated, but I had lived with fear for so long that it had become a part of me. When Daisy hugged me, I became so overwhelmed that I started crying again, falling into her arms with relief.

On the drive from Heathrow to Richmond, I briefly filled them in on the details of the day, hardly believing it myself. Sensing that I needed time to recollect myself, the Ajamis stopped asking me questions. I looked out at the cold night, lit up by the lights of a favorite city, and remembered a happier time not so long ago when Kamal had waited on the steps of my flat, and our lives had become one.

Now I looked at the dampness outside in the passing English countryside and felt such sadness for Kamal, for losing everything he had worked towards and dreamt of. Gaddafi was a cruel, but for now, invincible opponent, banked by monies from one of the largest oil-producing countries in the world. I could not wait to hear my husband's voice again, to reassure him that somehow we would find a way to go on.

I called my parents and Kamal as soon as we arrived at the Ajami's. He had been checking in daily with Mohammed, and though he knew I was due to leave Libya that morning, he was worried when he heard the flight had been delayed. When he heard my voice, I could hear in his that he was fighting hard not to break down.

"Hiba! *Habibti*! I have been dying from worrying! Are you alright? How are the children?"

After hearing everything, he was relieved and ecstatic that we managed to get out, and told me that he had already rented an apartment for us in Tallahassee, where he now was.

The Ajamis were very hospitable, and the break in England was a good transition for all of us. I took the children into central London a few times, but it was already cold and became dark early, so we would go back to Richmond in time for tea, one of my favorite English traditions, inherited from growing up in colonial Singapore.

I talked to Kamal every day, and he told me that though he was unable to speak directly with his family without compromising them, Ali was able to send messages through other sources. He also found out that the reason I was repeatedly searched was because they were looking for secret documents, which they suspected I was trying to smuggle out for Kamal. Ali's main fear was that the children and I might have been held as pawns.

Tarek's passport was ready within a week, and I quickly made arrangements for our return to Florida. Kamal was anxiously awaiting our arrival, and I was impatient for us to be together again. It had been almost a month since Kamal had left Tripoli, and I could hear in his voice that he was desperately missing us.

Once again I had to say goodbye, this time to friends who had given us shelter. I had grown close to Daisy in Libya, but we became even closer after almost two weeks in England. We didn't know when we would meet again, but at least we now had the freedom to be in touch whenever we wanted.

When the children, Kamaria and I arrived at the airport in Tallahassee, we were met by Kamal and our dear friend, Ismail. They were cheering and clapping as we came out.

Kamal rushed up and took me in his arms. The weight of the last few terrible weeks melted away. I was back in America and safely home with my husband.

Kamal had secured a teaching position at Florida State University, which was a relief since we no longer had the security of his job and family in Libya. We could no longer expect his family to help us financially, and there was no possibility of recovering any of the money from our bank account in Tripoli. What I wanted now was a house, and after looking for a few weeks I found a small two-story place for us in a quiet residential neighborhood. It was modest in comparison to what we had in Libya, but it was as much as we could afford with the money from Ibrahim. To me it was perfect. Never again would we have to live in the shadow of tyranny.

I had been raised a Catholic, and attended a convent school in Singapore, and I wanted my children to have a similar education. To my surprise, Kamal agreed to let me enroll them at a Catholic school close to our home. Mercifully they were happy, effortlessly adjusting, and soon thriving. They easily made new friends, and I did everything I could to shield them from what was happening in our lives financially and politically.

Though I no longer had all the material luxuries I had in Libya, and though I missed the love and warmth of our extended family, I also did not have to worry every day that Kamal would be arrested or murdered. To me, such freedom was worth everything.

Within two weeks of returning to Tallahassee, we were warned by people we trusted from Libya that we were on Gaddafi's hit list, including the children. The threat seemed surreal while living in a quiet southern town and Kamal and I chose to not let it interfere with our lives by telling ourselves that Gaddafi would not dare do anything to us on American soil.

Once we were settled, Kamaria felt the need to return to her family in Singapore. Though I was sad to see her go, I knew she was feeling homesick. Surprisingly, she had been content in Libya, making friends with the other maids in the family, and learning to speak Arabic as well as how to cook Libyan food. Unfortunately, it was more difficult for her to adjust in Tallahassee. She was sad to leave the children after having cared for them for four years, but I knew it was in her best interest to go home. When we took her to the airport we all cried, promising to see her in Singapore one day. Our paths never crossed again, but I shall always remember our gentle and loving Malay nanny, and be grateful for the nurturing role she played in our lives.

For the first time in years I was without help, but eagerly looking forward to being a regular housewife again and taking care of my family by myself. Compared to Libya, everything in American was easier and quicker to accomplish, especially grocery shopping and navigating around town. The Libyan students we had become close to before we left for Libya had all returned home except for Ismail, who had married an American and decided to make his home in Tallahassee until the political situation in Libya changed.

There were only a few other Libyans in town, but except for Hisham, an older graduate student, Kamal decided it would be prudent to keep a low profile. It was not unrealistic to expect that one of the Libyan students might be spying for the regime. However, we often had Libyan friends from out of town who would come and stay for a few days. Inevitably after dinner, the men would stay up all night talking politics and drinking glass after glass of Libyan tea, which Kamal was getting good at making himself.

Sometimes he would go and visit Libyans in other parts of the country. He remained secretive about these trips, explaining only that he was meeting with dissidents, and trying to talk to them about getting organized. I didn't question him much because he would always tell me that for my own sake, the less I knew the better. I just hoped that whatever he was doing would help ease his frustration and anger at being forced out of his own country, and make him feel he was doing something constructive towards achieving his wish for an end to Gaddafi's rule in Libya.

"*Habibti*," he once told me, "if sitting in jail or being killed would get rid of that monster, I'd do it. I'd do anything to destroy him, the way he has destroyed thousands of Libyans!"

I understood what he meant, and even though I was not prepared to accept it, I knew that if the time came I would probably have no choice in the matter...

Kamal's brother Amir and his family had settled into their new life at Violetta Farm outside of Tallahassee even before we arrived. I had helped renovate and decorate the old house on the property the previous year when we spent our Christmas vacation in Florida. It was humble in comparison to the mansion they had in Libya, yet it sat on a 1,600-acre plot. In addition to eleven huge tobacco barns, which Amir had told me to give away (neither of us realizing their value), there was a large pond for fishing and an abundance of deer, which they sometimes hunted.

Unlike Kamal, Amir made sure early on to transfer money out of Libya. He was astute, and had done very well for himself financially, but he too had been forced to flee. I was happy that Kamal at least had his brother close by, even though for some reason I never got to see Noor as much as I would have liked. There was such a stark difference in her lifestyle, and even though her husband tried to make her life in Tallahassee as comfortable as he could, I am sure she was feeling the loneliness of being away from her family and her country, and not adjusting as easily to life in America as Amir was. I felt sorry for her, and wished we could have been closer, but for some reason I did not understand until later, Amir did not encourage our relationship.

We often took the kids out to the farm to play with the horses or fish with George, the caretaker, who watched them like a hawk. He was a good, gentle, black man who took care of the family, as well as the farm, with great pride. Amir appreciated George so much that he built a small new house for him and his wife on the property, equipped with all the latest modern conveniences. Till this day I remember how the dear man would always have a basket of blackberries, or whatever fruit or vegetable was in season, ready for me to take home whenever he knew I was coming.

Our children continued to thrive, and despite all the upheaval Kamal and I were starting to settle down again. I was so busy building a new life for us all that I didn't notice when the change in Kamal began. I do know, however, the moment our lives took a turn from almost normal back to fear once again. It was in February 1980, only three months after we had left Libya.

Late one night, the phone rang, waking us both up from a deep sleep. We had been entertaining some friends and their children that evening, and I was exhausted. Half asleep, I switched on the lamp next to my side of the bed, thinking it was perhaps an overseas call. Kamal answered, and by the time I turned to look at him, his face was tight with rage. I knew something was terribly wrong.

He slammed down the phone and could not speak for anger, so I waited for him to be ready to tell me what happened.

"That son of a bitch said that all of us will be going back to Libya in wooden boxes if we don't return by June!" He was so furious he could hardly spit out the words.

My immediate instinct was to run to my children, hold them in my arms very tight and hide them somewhere safe. I was terrified that we had been given an ultimatum, but I was also furious. Surely, the arm of the Libyan secret police could not reach a small American town so far from Tripoli. Kamal had said we would be safe because Gaddafi would not dare harm American citizens, especially in America...

I wondered how they had found us so quickly, as we had tried to be careful who we associated with. Only our families and closest friends knew where we were. Obviously someone had betrayed us.

"Hiba," Kamal looked at me, emphasizing as clearly as he could, "it was an American."

I was incredulous, as it was something I had never considered. *Oh, my God*, I thought, *now we have to worry about paid American assassins!*

"I'll report it tomorrow. Please don't be afraid. They're just trying to scare us."

Neither one of us slept. I brought both the children to our bed while Kamal went downstairs to the living room, where he sat on the couch keeping watch all night, drinking coffee and smoking cigarettes until dawn.

The calls kept coming, usually late at night, from different people, most of them with Libyan accents. Kamal would curse at them and tell them they should be ashamed of themselves, but the threats became uglier. There were nights when I would sit on the floor in our living room peeking out between the slats of the wooden blinds, watching and waiting, in case someone came to kill us.

Kamal tried to assure me that they would not dare do anything, but I did not believe him. Gaddafi had actually formally decreed that all Libyan dissidents had to return to Libya by June or be "liquidated like stray dogs."

1980 was the year of terror for Libyan dissidents. A Libyan journalist, working for the BBC in London, was shot to death outside a mosque in April, and one month later a Libyan lawyer was shot outside his office in Kensington. There were many other incidents of Libyans targeted and murdered abroad, especially in Europe and England, but the most horrific was the attempted murder of two Libyan children in London. They were given poisoned peanuts and sweets by a family friend after he was unable to persuade their father to return to Libya.

When I heard this, I immediately took precautions, such as alerting the children's schools and teachers, and keeping a constant and vigilant eye on them myself, never letting them out of my sight. Only a few of my closest friends in Tallahassee knew about the ominous situation we were in. It was impossible for most people – few of whom had ever lived outside of the US and unversed in the ways of brutal dictatorships – to understand what was happening.

I spent my nights going from room to room, peering carefully between the slats of blinds from all the windows of my house. I never got used to the phone ringing late at night; every time my heart would pound so loudly it seemed to deaden all my other senses. I begged and pleaded with my children daily to not talk with strangers and not go with anyone, not even family acquaintances, anywhere, no matter what they were told.

Our fears heightened in October. Faisal Zagallai, a relative of Kamal's who was attending graduate school in

Colorado, was shot twice in the head when he opened his door to someone posing as a salesman. Miraculously he survived but was blinded in one eye. His perpetrator was arrested four months later, but was incredibly only charged with two misdemeanors for assault. The assassin, Eugene Tafoya, turned out to be a decorated green beret who claimed he was hired by the CIA. In fact, he had been hired by an ex-CIA agent who'd gone rogue to work for Gaddafi.

About two weeks following the Colorado episode, Kamal and I experienced a terrible scare at our house. One night after the kids had gone to bed, we were sitting in the den downstairs watching TV when I thought I heard a noise in the garage. I was sure I had closed the garage door, but I got up to check in case I had forgotten, thinking that maybe a bird or a small animal had been trapped inside.

Peeking through the blinds, which covered the top half glass of the door, I saw a man coming towards me.

I screamed, but by the time Kamal rushed to open the door the man had disappeared. In his pajamas, Kamal ran down the driveway to the street, and dashed all over our surrounding neighbors' yards looking, but could not find him.

After calming me down and making sure the house was secured, we debated whether to call the police. I wanted him to, but in the end he convinced me that there was nothing they could have done, and there was no point scaring the children. From the very brief look I got, I was almost sure the man looked like a Libyan. The next day, Kamal told me that he had reported the incident to the CIA.

"The police here can't do anything," he explained to me, "because it involves a foreign government."

252

As I became more worried about the precarious situation we were in, Kamal adopted an attitude of resignation. Everything was *Inshallah,* left to the will of God. To make matters worse, he was gone more, even though I didn't know how he managed to maintain his job while travelling as much as he did. I understood, however, that he needed to do something to feel that he was contributing towards the cause, and to find platforms to publicize the horrendous situation in Libya under Gaddafi.

His efforts soon started paying off. He began being interviewed by major media, and he was invited to give lectures and seminars around the United States, and sometimes Europe. He and Dr David Ward, Chairman of the Political Science Department at Florida State University, published several books and articles together, which became invaluable resources for scholars on Libya.

It was around this time that Kamal told me he was already actively involved in an opposition party, and said that he was trying to recruit others to join him. He had committed himself to a group of his peers of elite Libyan dissidents, which included intellectuals, businessmen and professionals. They were getting organized, and Kamal told me they had already successfully solicited contributions from wealthy dissidents as well as from other Arab sympathizers. He mentioned having to go to Sudan to attend a meeting, and said that he needed to find another source of income as he would be traveling a lot. I was worried, because I did not know how he was going to find the time or the money, or how much his involvement would affect us.

Needless to say, I was frightened to be left alone with the children on even more of his trips away from home. I tried to discuss with him the possibility of not traveling as much, to perhaps find a way of teaching at the university even while working for the opposition. The children were too young to be without a father around, and I didn't know what I would do if anything happened to him. He brushed off my entreaties as insignificant, trying to emphasize to me that there was something more important than all of us at stake, and that he could not be active unless he was able to be more flexible.

"Can you imagine me, Kamal Ben Ramadan, being happy teaching college in a small town?" His eyes flashed disbelief at my absurd proposition. "This is not what I have worked my whole life for!"

He raised his voice so dramatically that it surprised me.

"I promise you one thing," he continued, "I'll do whatever I have to do to get rid of that *shaytan*, that devil!"

It was a watershed moment in our relationship. I realized at that moment how far apart we had become, because I was not willing to sacrifice my children's present to gamble on Gaddafi's future. For Kamal, the Libya of his dream was in shambles, and I could see that our life in Tallahassee was never going to be enough for him. He was looking for a solution somewhere else to restore his dream, but for me, my children overshadowed every other concern. They were my dream for the future.

Amir was also receiving threats on a regular basis, and we got word one day that Ali had been arrested. No one was able to get any information about what happened to him except that he was taken to the Abu Salim Prison in Tripoli, which was already overflowing with political prisoners. We were devastated. For weeks, Kamal and Amir sat by the phone in abject despair, waiting for news. They never heard anything more about Ali, and it was not until many years later that his fate was revealed.

Amir and Kamal were both put on notice by calls from Libya, presumably the secret police, that unless they returned by a certain date, their father and all the male members in his family would be arrested and charged with plotting to overthrow the government. It was a difficult decision, because there was a strong chance that he would be killed, but inevitably, Amir knew he had no choice but to go. It was decided that Kamal would stay to continue his work with the opposition party.

Amir left the farm and everything he owned in Quincy to be sold by auction. Every single item in the house, as well as the property and everything on it was under the hammer: Christofle silverware, Limoges china, Persian carpets, a Napoleon chess set, everything, down to his Bruno Magli shoes. There was no money left from the sale after all his creditors were paid off.

Amir's homecoming was as bad as we feared it would be. He was arrested upon his arrival and transported to Abu Salim Prison, where he was tortured and placed in solitary confinement for a year. When he was finally released, he was wearing the same clothes he had worn on the day of his arrival, unwashed and almost totally torn apart. He had been tortured and nearly beaten to death. Since the only people he had been in contact with were his interrogators and torturers, he never saw nor heard anything about Ali when he was there.

The departure and imprisonment of Amir affected Kamal profoundly, and drove him even more desperately to search for ways to combat a regime that was becoming more brutal and seemingly invincible.

One day, Kamal told me that if everything worked out, he might have found a solution to our financial problems that would also give him the freedom to travel and maintain contact with the opposition abroad. He had met a woman from Qatar when he had given a presentation at Columbia University in New York. Her name was Wafa. She was apparently so impressed by his work that she arranged for Kamal to be invited as guest lecturer at the University of Qatar.

Within two weeks, Kamal received a first-class round-trip ticket to Doha as well as a paid contract for the three-day lecture equivalent to his one month's salary at Florida State. He also saw it as the perfect opportunity to meet with opposition members in the Middle East and Europe while he was in the region.

Kamal's first lecture was so well received that he was offered a permanent guest lecturing position at the university, where he was very handsomely compensated. Under the contract, he would lecture six days a month. Since he was paid so well in Qatar, he was able to restructure his position at Florida State and spend more time traveling.

Kamal started going often to London and Qatar, and would usually be gone for about ten days at a time, once a month. I was beginning to see that my husband could never accept being a small fish in a big bowl, and I had no doubt he felt more important there than he did at home or at the university. Apparently, Wafa was from one of the wealthiest families in Qatar. He told me that whenever he went to London she would send a chauffeur-driven Rolls-Royce to pick him up at the airport. He also had a standing invitation to stay at her family's house in Belgravia, which was staffed by a full-time maid and a cook.

Regardless of the justifications he had for accepting her hospitality, it made me very uncomfortable to know that my husband was spending so much time with a woman I had never met. I asked Kamal on several occasions to invite her to Tallahassee so I could meet her, but somehow the timing was never right for her. I found it disconcerting that a single woman, especially an Arab and a Muslim, felt so free to take the liberty of accommodating a married man without being related to him or even knowing his family. However, whenever I tried voicing my misgivings to Kamal he would get indignant that I should question his integrity and her intentions.

"The only type of relationship we have is professional," he protested. "She's a good Muslim who prays five times a day and carries her Koran everywhere."

Seeing that I was not satisfied with that answer, he continued: "Hiba, she's extremely dedicated to her work, and she's been very supportive of the opposition party. Don't be silly. I love you, and I've more important things to worry about. Besides, she's much older than me."

He kept giving me so many reasons and excuses why there was and could never be anything between them that I started to feel ashamed for doubting him.

Throughout that period, though, I was seeing a change in Kamal that worried me. He was growing increasingly arrogant and self-absorbed, and behaved as if the children and I were no longer of any importance to him. I knew his heart was in Libya, but I wanted some of it for us, too. He seldom laughed or even smiled anymore, and even the kids were learning to accommodate his mood swings as I did. I kept telling myself that I had to forgive him because of the excruciating pain and sense of guilt I knew he was feeling due in part to the imprisonments of Ali and Amir because of him. I felt it, too, but I was trying very hard not to allow myself and the children to be more victimized than we already were.

Apart from this, with two small children to care for, I did not have the time to sit around bemoaning the fate of Gaddafi and Libya. I empathized with Kamal, but there were times when I was also frustrated that he was distancing himself. I wanted to ask him how he could manage to take on a revolution if he was unable to take care of his own family, but I did not dare. He was like a time bomb waiting to explode.

Kamal held no illusions that the Americans would get rid of Gaddafi any time soon. While doing research for his dissertation he had surmised, in his interview with the former United States Ambassador to Libya, that the CIA had been instrumental in helping put Gaddafi in power. It was obvious then that the United States was not as anxious as the Libyans were to get rid of Gaddafi.

One day Kamal told me that we were going to have a visitor from the State Department by the name of Paul. When he arrived the next afternoon, it did not take me long to guess his real position. Later, Kamal informed me that he was indeed the head of the CIA Libyan Affairs Division.

Throughout his visit, I had to suppress a smile, because he was the quintessential picture of the CIA's answer to James Bond. The man was perfectly stereotypical: not only was he tall, well-built and movie-star handsome, but he was also well-spoken, charming, impeccably dressed and well-mannered. He even wore a khaki military-style trench coat and dark glasses. It would have been funny if the context hadn't been so serious.

Paul told us that a Libyan man had been arrested at a motel in Panama City, two hours away from Tallahassee. From phone records they were able to ascertain that the phone number at the hotel was the same one that had called our house several times with death threats. My heart dropped. The man they arrested had a lot of cash in his possession, two guns, and a list of Libyan dissidents. Kamal's name was on the list, as well as mine. He insisted that he was working for the CIA, which of course turned out to be a lie. Paul said he didn't know if there were more paid assassins out there, but he suspected there probably were, and warned us to take necessary precautions. I wondered if the man arrested in Panama City was the same one who had been in our garage. Before leaving, Paul also told us that there was a student at the university who was spying for the Libyan Embassy.

"Who?" Kamal asked, not surprised,

"Hisham…" Before he could even finish his sentence, Kamal started cursing. Besides Ismail, Hisham was the only other Libyan we trusted in town. We had shared many meals at our house with him and his wife, and we had all been very open about our feelings for Gaddafi's regime. It made sense now how the Libyan secret police had so much information about us even though we had been so careful.

After Paul left, Kamal told me that the State Department had produced a psychological report on Gaddafi, deeming him mentally ill. He also said that they had offered to pay him $10,000 to write a report on

Gaddafi, which he instantly turned down. He was adamant that he would never put himself in a position to be accused of working for them or the CIA. He insisted that he had to maintain contact with them to gain information and maybe support for the benefit of the opposition party. Likewise, he realized they kept tabs on him and other Libyans to gauge the mood of Libyan dissidents in the United States. He was cautious of his interactions with them, selectively telling them only what he thought they needed to know. In fact, Kamal wondered sometimes whether the CIA was on the side of Gaddafi or the dissidents. Perhaps, he said, they just wanted be to on the winning side. We had no doubt that our phone was tapped by the CIA, just as it had been in Libya by Gaddafi's people. However, in order to succeed, the dissidents needed more than a dream. They also needed the support of America and the Western governments.

A few days later, while I was having morning coffee with two friends in my kitchen, chatting about schools and our children, my doorbell rang. I got up to see who it was, and when I opened the door I saw a tall, lanky middle-aged, clean-cut man in a dark suit. I made a mental note not to open my door to strangers again, even Americans.

"Mrs Ben Ramadan?" asked the stranger, who may or may not have been harmless.

I numbly nodded, thankful for my friends in the kitchen.

"I'm Agent Romano from the FBI, ma'am, and I wonder if I may speak with you for a few minutes."

I was stunned, but managed to say something in my state of confusion at the unexpected and unwelcome intrusion.

260

"Mr Romano, I'm sorry, but I can't talk to you now. I have some friends here... A call would be more appropriate. I'm sorry, but I don't want to scare my friends."

"Mrs Ben Ramadan, let me give you my card, and you feel free to call me any time. We just want you and your husband to know that we are willing to offer your family protection."

"Thank you." I managed to say, feeling somewhat guilty at having been so ungracious. I wondered if something else had happened.

That afternoon, Kamal called to tell Paul what happened. Apparently the CIA must have told the FBI not to get involved because we never heard from Agent Romano again.

Shortly after, we had another surprise visitor; this one a welcome guest, someone we both highly respected and admired. Mansur Kikhia, an old friend of Kamal's. He was a human rights activist, a former foreign minister, and a diplomat. He was Libya's Ambassador to the United Nations, a position from which he had just recently resigned. I had met Mansur when he visited us at our home in Tripoli, and I was happy to see him again. He was gentle, well-spoken and unassuming; it was *haram*, a sin, that Gaddafi was driving away men of his caliber from Libya.

Mansur had obviously flown to Tallahassee to discuss some serious and private issues with Kamal so after dinner I took the children upstairs so the men could talk privately. He only spent that one night with us, but he and Kamal used every second they had together, staying up almost all night.

After lunch the next day, I kissed Mansur goodbye, and invited him to come back anytime. I never saw him again. Years later, in December 1993, while attending a civil rights conference in Cairo, Mansur was kidnapped, apparently by Egyptian agents, and handed over to the Libyan regime. He was later murdered on orders from Gaddafi.

That evening, after the kids were in bed, Kamal told me that Mansur had requested and received political asylum from the United States after his defection. Mansur had come to Tallahassee to discuss the different political opposition parties that were forming against Gaddafi, and to reach out to Kamal to join the one he was involved in. Kamal told him that he was already committed to the National Front for the Salvation of Libya, which was headed by another friend, Mohammed Magariaf, who had been the Libyan Ambassador to India until his recent defection.

Interestingly, shortly after Mansur's defection, Kamal was asked by the Libyan Foreign Ministry to replace Mansur as the Libyan Ambassador to the United Nations. The only condition was that Kamal return immediately to Tripoli to be briefed. I asked Kamal what he told them.

"I told them to go to hell."

In no way would he ever be associated with Gaddafi again; besides, he was sure that the offer was nothing more than a ploy.

In October 1981 Kamal left for what he described as a secret trip to Sudan. He assured me he would tell me all about it upon his return. When he got home, he confided to me that he had been in Khartoum for a press conference to officially announce the formal establishment of the National Front for the Salvation of Libya. It was founded and led by Magariaf, with the support of Libyan dissidents like Kamal and his peers. They had strong financial backing, as well as the support of several governments, including the United States. The Sudanese government, headed by Numieri, had offered to issue them Sudanese passports so that they could use them for surreptitious trips into Libya.

Kamal was excited and optimistic, and made it clear to me that he intended to be heavily involved with the NFSL, and that I should be prepared for him to be away a lot more. He told me they would be working closely with Libyans inside the country and that they would be training fighters outside, probably in Sudan and Chad. To accomplish their ambitious goals, they were going to need a great deal of money and some powerful backing.

I had long accepted the fact that Kamal could never be satisfied being a university professor patiently biding his time, but I also didn't know how he could possibly be so heavily involved in such an operation so far away. Our resources were simply too limited. Every Libyan dissident wanted to go home; they all hated the lunatic dictator who ran the country with fear, but Kamal became a man obsessed, no longer the man I married. He was becoming someone I sometimes didn't recognize. He was becoming more secretive and less communicative, and I was finding it harder and harder to reach him.

In December 1981 we all drove to Iowa to spend Christmas with my best friends Mary and Ahmed. We had been together almost every day when we were in Libya, and I'd truly missed Mary, especially with what I had been going through. It had become difficult to talk to Kamal, and I had no one else to confide in.

I was rather surprised but so delighted when Kamal accepted Ahmed's invitation to visit. I knew it would be exciting for the kids to play in snow for the first time in their lives, and I hoped the trip would alleviate some of Kamal's tension. Mary and I had laughed our way through a lot of our difficult times in Libya and I hoped she could help me understand what was happening with Kamal.

The children had a wonderful time in Iowa with Mary and Ahmed, who played with them in the snow and taught them how to make snow angels. We went on day trips to little towns around Cedar Rapids, and drove around different neighborhoods at night to see Christmas lights. It was our first vacation as a family since we had left Libya.

It would have been more fun if Kamal had not acted as if he were above all our frivolity. His silence and misery were embarrassing, but the rest of us were determined not to spoil the children's holiday. Finally, when we had a little time alone, Mary asked me what was wrong. I told her Kamal was perpetually agonizing over the political situation, unable and unwilling to adjust to life in a small university town, and seemed to be haunted by a hundred different reasons not to want to be where we are.

"So what?" answered my pragmatic friend, "We all feel that way. It doesn't mean that we stop living."

Like so many times before, she had been able to express what I could not.

I told Mary that I had tried everything to make him happy, but the harder I tried the worse he reacted. Sometimes I even wondered if he had gone crazy, lost some of his sanity from all the paranoia and despair Gaddafi had created for him and his family. Mary tried to comfort me by saying it was only temporary and that he would eventually accept the fact that he needed to go on and appreciate what he did have, namely me and the children. After all, a lot of people were in his position. We all had to be patient and make the best of a very difficult situation.

I later found out that Ahmed had tried talking to Kamal, but did not get anywhere. Kamal was too caught up in his own world, refusing to budge in changing his attitude, even for that short visit. It was as though he felt guilty for having a good time, and resented that we did. I am sure he was also feeling guilty for being free while two of his brothers were imprisoned.

From Iowa we drove south to North Carolina, to visit Kamal's sister Yasmine and her husband Jamal. It was good to see them and I tried to be happy, but it was forced and painful, especially since Kamal did not even bother to mask his gloom. I didn't know if Yasmine realized that something was very wrong with her brother, but I didn't want to burden her with our problems as she was pregnant with her first child.

When we got home after the trip, I told Kamal he had ruined what could have been a really pleasant and much-needed vacation for all of us.

"If you're so miserable here, where do you want to go?" I asked, prepared to go anywhere to get him out of his wretched misery. It felt as if I were married to a zombie.

The answer, however, was always Libya.

One day, he raised the possibility of returning to Libya. He knew he would be imprisoned, but didn't care. His concern was who would support the children and me.

I grew irate. I had accepted, a few years before, that his love for his country surpassed his love for his family. But the reality of living with a man whose wife and children were no longer a priority for him was unbearable. I looked at him, and no longer saw the man I knew.

I felt so hopeless that I wished he would just go back to Libya and leave his fate, as well as ours, in the hands of God. For the sake of the children, I tried to forge ahead as if nothing was wrong, but inside I was desperately unhappy. I could not tell anyone, not even Mary, because sometimes misery cannot be adequately expressed without giving the impression of self-pity.

I was profoundly hurt by my husband's neglect of our family, and deplored the defeatism that exuded from every pore of his being, every day and night. At the same time, I also felt deeply sorry for him and tried to do everything I could to lift his spirits, but nothing I did pleased him. I was living with an angry stranger, a man who hated himself so much that he was completely unable and unwilling to appreciate anything or anyone around him.

Divorce was never an option for me, so I was resigned to letting him do what he wanted, waiting for something to change. It took almost a year to happen but when it did, I was completely unprepared.

CHAPTER 17

THE BETRAYAL

After one of Kamal's trips to London I unpacked his suit-case as I usually did, and found a Danielle Steel novel, *The Promise*, tucked away in the bottom of the bag. I had never once seen him read a novel like that. Instinctively, I knew something was wrong.

I approached him calmly, with the book in my hand. "Where did you get this?"

"What?" he said distractedly, or perhaps just feigning distraction.

I held it up, "This book...this romance novel!"

"I've never seen it before."

"I found it in your suitcase, Kamal."

"Hiba, I've no idea how it got there!" He answered too fast and dismissively.

Kamal had just returned from attending a conference in London, so I immediately suspected who must have given it to him, or had perhaps planted it there to be found by me.

"Did Wafa give you this?" I asked him directly, and as I said the words, it felt right. I felt sick to my stomach.

"Please tell me the truth." I pleaded with him, not want-ing to sound like a paranoid woman for nothing. "Is some-thing going on between you and that woman?"

"Of course not!" he snapped at me. "I've told you before. You need to see a psychiatrist if you think there's anything!"

He walked out of the bedroom, slamming the door behind him.

As I lay in bed that night pretending to be asleep, I silently cried for what was and what could have been. I knew my husband was lying to me. He had been painting a picture for me of a relationship with Wafa that was purely professional and political, based on a common cause, but I had been doubtful. Now, a lot of things that had not made sense suddenly became painfully clear. I could not sleep that night, the pain stabbing at my heart, my mind seeing and remembering, trying to analyze, but my heart still wanting to excuse.

I started to look at Kamal differently. Until that evening I had been sure he loved me too much to ever cheat on me, and that his sense of family loyalty extended to me, his wife. Trust and fidelity was something that had never been an issue in our marriage before. When I had recently mentioned to him that one of my friends had found out her husband was having an affair with someone in their church choir, he had commented without hesitation: "She should kick the bastard out."

I tried to convince myself that a man who'd react that strongly could not himself be involved in an affair.

I had been excusing Kamal's mood swings and sense of defeat for the past two years as stemming from being cut off from his family and the country he loved, but now I questioned myself. I thought of Ibrahim, who I missed desperately. I wished I could talk to him, knowing that somehow he would make everything right again. My father-in-law was such a strong and down-to-earth man; he would never have allowed Kamal to behave like a victim. But of course I could not call Libya. It was almost impossible to get through, and the phones were tapped.

The next day, I dropped by the university to see our friend David whom I trusted. He and Anne had married the previous year, much to my and Kamal's delight. I knew he would tell me the truth if I asked him. He had visited us in Libya, and I remembered that he had also met Wafa once in Qatar, when he had attended a conference with Kamal. When I told David what I suspected, he thought I was crazy.

"No way, absolutely no way!" he said, throwing his head back and laughing at me.

He went on to explain what he knew about Wafa, and he was sure that their relationship was strictly professional.

"Believe me, you have nothing to worry about. She's controlling and abrasive, which bothers Kamal. He told me that himself!"

"Maybe he's encouraging her?"

I realized I could not help if women were attracted to Kamal, but I had to be sure that he reacted with integrity.

"Well," David answered in his analytical fashion, "she can do what she wants, but Kamal's no fool, he's not going to jeopardize losing what he has with you and those beautiful children."

It turned out that I was, in fact, married to a fool.

In the summer of 1982 the children and I went to visit my parents in Singapore for two weeks. I wanted Kamal to come, thinking the change of scene would be good for him; however, he insisted he had an article to finish writing and that it would be a good time to do it while we were away. I didn't put up much of a resistance, as I was so emotionally and mentally exhausted from his behavior that I almost welcomed the separation. Besides, I thought, he might miss us and appreciate us more after we returned. The visit in Singapore went by quickly, but all the while I was anxious about returning to Florida. He called us a few times while we were in Singapore, and told me how much he missed us.

Kamal seemed very happy to see us back, and for a while we became a regular family again, doing things together and even having fun. I was hoping that maybe he was finally making an effort to adjust and trying to make the best of his situation. There was no more mention of Wafa, and he avoided any conversation regarding London or Qatar. But around the beginning of fall, my life changed forever.

I called Kamal at work one afternoon. Frances, the department secretary, answered. I had known Frances since Kamal had been a student working on his PhD in the same department. I admired her candor and outspokenness, usually uncommon with Americans, who generally try to avoid "stepping on toes". Kamal and David had both told me that she was not shy to dish it out to the staff, including the professors. Frances and I had always been on good terms, and always chatted about the children, or what I was doing, but mostly about Kamal. She was very fond of him.

"He's been on the phone for a while now, honey," she drawled in her southern, matter-of-fact voice. "That woman from Qatar calls him every day."

Though my heart was in my throat, I pretended like it was natural for the woman from Qatar to be calling my husband daily.

"Thanks, Frances. I'll just call him back later. Thank you…" I murmured, hardly able to get the words out as my heart was palpitating so hard, and my mind was screaming. I had no doubt now what was going on.

I knew Frances was giving me a hint, but what she didn't know was that she had just dropped a bombshell on me. In a way, I was grateful to her for putting an end to the deceit. There is no emotion in the world to me worse than the feeling of betrayal. I could not forgive this, because it reveals a person's true feelings, but most of all, his character. It took my breath away to know that my husband, the man I had loved so deeply and for so long, could have betrayed me.

From that moment I have abhorred anyone who uses religion, any religion, to characterize the virtues of themselves or another. I couldn't help thinking how stupid I had been, to believe that someone I didn't know might be virtuous simply because they carried around a Koran and a prayer rug. I hardly ever saw my family in Libya praying or reading the Koran. I know they did, regularly and religiously, but it was all done discreetly, just between them and their God. Their faith was not a show conducted for the eyes of those around them, and they never once preached to me about Islam.

According to Kamal, I was the crazy one for even thinking he would be interested in another woman at such a chaotic time of our lives. Sometimes I even wondered if he was right, that maybe there was something wrong with me for not trusting him. But at this point, I didn't care what he thought. My whole world had been put into a blender that would not turn off. I only knew that finding the off switch was going to take time, but that eventually it would have to be done. However, I still needed definite proof before making any decision. If this game between them had been going on for the past two years while I was living in fear for our lives, it would redouble my pain and anger.

That night, I could hardly stand to look at him, and it took every ounce of control for me to even talk to him with civility. Somehow I managed, but only for the sake of my children.

The next day was a Saturday. Kamal was playing with the kids in the backyard but glancing inside once in a while to see what I was doing. When I saw him becoming more distracted by the children, I took his briefcase upstairs to our bedroom and locked the door.

Frantically rifling through some papers and other knick knacks, I found two bundles of letters held together by a rubber band, a few with their envelopes mostly postmarked Qatar. There were about fifty letters, all in Arabic. It crossed my mind what a prolific letter writer she was.

I opened several of them, looking for some hint of their contents, still desperately holding out faint hope that these were business-related, but at the end of some of them were one sentence in English, as if the writer wanted me to know they were love letters. One read: "I want the whole package", another: "I will wait forever." Some were smudged with teardrops at the end. The boldness and obviousness of the deception stunned me.

In a state of shock, I took the letters and left the house without saying anything to Kamal. I got into my car and drove to the house of Ismail, whom I thought would help me sort it all out. Maybe there was still a chance to salvage the situation. When I got to his house, I gave him a few of the letters I had taken with me and handed them to him.

"Ismail, please tell me what is going on."

He had hardly glanced at the first letter before shaking his head.

"These are stupid letters," he said, handing them back to me.

"They mean nothing, Hiba. Please, just forget about them!"

Much as I pleaded with him, he refused to translate them for me. On looking back to that day, I don't think the letters were a surprise to Ismail.

I got into my car and thought furiously how I could get them translated. I had many Arab friends in D.C. whom I knew would do it for me, but I couldn't wait so long. Then I remembered Nina, a Lebanese lady I knew who lived in Tallahassee. I was sure she would help me.

I stopped at a phone booth outside a convenience store and called her. I asked if she could please meet me, telling her only that it was extremely important. We arranged to meet at a pizzeria close to my house.

After ordering our Cokes in the dark empty restaurant, I filled her in on the sequence of events leading to my call. I asked if she would translate the letters for me. When she agreed, I asked that she not try to spare my feelings, but to give me a verbatim translation. She promised she would.

As she sat there and read the first letter, I could tell from her facial expression that what I was about to hear was not going to be good. It wasn't. After translating only ten letters for me word for word, I had heard everything that I needed to know.

The letters had begun two years previously, in 1980. They were beautifully written, and reminded me of the love letters Kamal used to write me when I was in Singapore. He used to tell me how rich the Arabic language was and, as I now saw, how powerful and seductive. At times, the brazenness of this woman's declaration of love for my husband made me feel that perhaps I had been remiss in not talking to him like that more. She promised him everything, more than I ever could. She was going to help him liberate Libya, change the Arab world, take care of him, and raise my children in Qatar as Muslims and Arabs.

The letters went from declarations of love, to frustration, to pleas of allowing her to take care of him and his health, and providing him with a better life. The words were so powerful they almost evoked sympathy from me! The fact that there were so many over such a long period of time proved that he had not discouraged her enough, and had valued them enough to save them. Nina tried to console me, saying that Kamal was acting like a drowning man, reaching out for any promise of help.

I knew I had to be sure of everything in order to make my decision, but at that moment I wished my whole being would suddenly cease to exist, to relieve a pain so searingly deep and hurtful, and all the more intense because it had been caused by someone I loved, and trusted, and to whom I had chosen to give myself and the most precious of gifts: our children.

I had a difficult time convincing Nina that I was okay enough to drive home. She let me go when I told her I really needed to be alone to think. I sat in my car in the parking lot for a very long time, slowly going over the events of the past two years.

As I drove home I thought how easy it would be to end the agony that I was sure would never leave my heart. I kept hearing her words, suffocating me every time I tried to breathe, shattering everything I believed in.

I looked at every tree along the roadside, wondering which one was big enough to cause instant death if I ploughed into it fast enough. I luxuriated in this feeling, though only briefly, until I remembered my children. No woman in this world could ever love or care for my children as I would.

I suddenly became livid, and decided that my children were the only thing that mattered to me in my life. She could have Kamal, but over my dead body would either one of them have my children.

When I walked into our house, Kamal was in the kitchen with the children. As calmly as possible, I asked them to go play upstairs in their rooms. After I was sure they were out of earshot, I looked at my husband, who I desperately wanted out of my sight.

"I am going to give you one last chance," I said, throwing the miserable bundle of letters on the kitchen counter. I managed to articulate my choice of words while shaking with anger and fear of what I knew I might have to do. "Tell me the whole truth and I'll see if I can work this out with you, but if you lie to me anymore it will be over."

I could see his eyes darkening, and for the first time in two years I could feel my strength returning. I was determined to take charge of my own life again.

"There's nothing going on, I swear on my children," he mumbled.

He went on protesting and trying to explain – perhaps Ismail had already called to warn him – but I knew he was lying. He was like a helpless child caught doing something naughty. He was clutching at straws to convince me, but it was too late. The bond that had been holding us together through many difficult times had been severed by his deceit. While I had been living in fear for our lives, my husband was exchanging love letters.

"I understand," I whispered, slowly nodding my head. "You sold us out..."

I did not say a word to Kamal the next day. I knew he was hoping the whole subject would simply go away, but I also knew I could never pretend that nothing had happened. On Monday, after taking the kids to school, and after Kamal left for the university, I went upstairs and packed up everything belonging to him into several suitcases and put them in the garage. I called a friend who was a divorce attorney and asked if I could make an appointment for that afternoon. When I got there, I told him what happened, and asked him to file for divorce immediately.

Divorce had never been an option for me until I read those letters. It then became the only option. I knew in my heart that the thread of trust and respect could never be rewoven. I had lived in absolute terror for almost three years, sometimes not sleeping in case someone came to hurt my children. I spent many nights alone in fear, while my husband was travelling all over the world having his ego stroked by someone who promised him a more comfortable future than what he had with us. I was indignant, partly because he had something here to build on. He had become a sought-after spokesman on Libyan politics, and

276

was well respected in his profession. He had forgotten that he was a Ben Ramadan, and that it was he alone who held the key to his future.

During the next few months before the divorce was final Kamal and I made a few attempts to talk, but our discussions were hopeless because he was unable to be completely honest. I knew he was miserable but by that point I had no strength left to care about anyone except my children. They were my only priority, and I had to preserve some semblance of sanity and self-respect in order to protect them.

Layla begged her father to come home but he always said, with tears, that he couldn't. Whatever was holding him back must have been very strong because he could not even explain to his closest friends what happened, except to say that he wished it hadn't. Many innocent people were affected, but at least one person had her wish come true. What she did not realize was that the man she took from me and my children had died the day he left Libya. The man I married would never have done what he did. He would have had the pride, integrity and strength of a Ben Ramadan to know that the solution was within him.

Since we had been married by Islamic law as well as in the American civil court, Kamal also had to divorce me the Islamic way. In Islam, all a man has to do to divorce his wife is say "I divorce you" three times. This was done shortly after Kamal moved out.

He came over one night to help me get the children ready for bed. After the children slept, we went downstairs together. He asked me to sit down at the dining table with him, and for the first time since I found the letters, he told me he needed to talk to me.

"I have never loved a woman the way I love you, and I never will again. Please, I beg you, never forget that." He looked at me the way he did that night years ago, as we sat at another dining table, in the International Student House in Washington, D.C., where it all began.

In a steady but choked-up voice he started talking, pouring out the love he had for me and the children, saying it was the only thing of beauty that was left in his soul. Words of torment and pain flew from his mouth like the *ghibli* sandstorm. I remained speechless, each word flying at me like sharp particles of sand. He spoke of the agony of losing everything he had ever dreamt of, his obsessive hatred for the man who caused it, and his vow to dedicate his life to destroying him at any cost. His only regret, he said, was the pain he had caused me and the children, and the shame he felt for not being the man and husband I deserved. He revealed a lost and tortured soul, wanting something I knew I could never give him.

"One day, I swear I'll tell you everything, and I'll make it all up to you and the children." His face was shattered with sadness.

At the end, he put his face in his hands and with his head bowed towards me begged my forgiveness, never explaining why, but in my heart, I already knew.

In an almost inaudible voice, he explained that he was only going to divorce me verbally once, so that he could remarry me again one day if I would have him back. I was not aware, until then, that in Islam, if a husband divorced his wife three times verbally, she would have to marry someone else before he could remarry her.

Then he said it, in Arabic, one time, "I divorce you."

"I will always love you, my Stora," he whispered, holding me tightly in his arms for the last time.

"Even if God forgives me, even if you forgive me, I will never forgive myself for what I have done, as long as I live."

When he let go of me, his eyes were red and his face wet with tears. He took my hand, and for the last time brought it up to his lips.

"Hiba, my love, I want you to know that when I die, all I will ask from God is to have you by my side again in heaven."

He looked into my eyes with such pain, still holding my hand to his face. He then held me tightly to his chest and kissed me softly on my head before quickly turning to leave.

I had not said one word the entire time.

I turned off all the lights, and went upstairs. I carried both my sleeping children to my bed and held them in my arms all night. I finally feel asleep as the sun was starting to rise. In the morning I found my pillow had soaked up the tears of the night.

CHAPTER 18

THE JOURNEY ENDS

"Mummy, Mummy!" My daughter's soft crying would always turn to screams soon after putting her to bed. "Mummy, my heart is crying!"

Layla cried herself to sleep for six months after her father left. It was excruciating for me to hear her, night after night. I would have done anything to stop her sadness, but all I could do was hold her in my arms and reassure her that both her father and I loved her. She kept asking why he had to go, asking if it were her fault. My little boy, on the other hand, kept everything inside him, and tried to act very strong and brave for my sake, even though I knew he was hurting. He was only six years old, filling in for his father the best he could. At those moments, knowing the pain he had caused his children, I truly despised Kamal and what he did.

Our American divorce was final four months after I had found the letters. Kamal's first words to me after the brief and cold proceeding would haunt me for years to come. Going down the courthouse steps, the very same steps from which we had once descended in happier times as newly-weds, he stopped me, saying he had to tell me something.

"I cannot tell you why, Hiba, but I have to leave. I swear to you, I have no choice…" He told me this standing in the lightly drizzling winter rain, his head bowed and his shoulders slumped with the weight of the past and the future.

"One day you will know the truth and understand, and I hope you will forgive me…"

I knew Kamal was hiding something, because a lot of things he had told me did not make sense. It would have been better for both of us if he could have just been honest and told me the truth—no matter what it was—but he was either too ashamed or too afraid, or perhaps he was protecting Wafa. At times I felt so sorry for him that I was glad he had someone ready to console him. Kamal moved to Qatar the next day, and married Wafa shortly afterwards. In the years to come, I forgave Kamal for everything he did to me, but I never forgave him for the pain he caused our children.

Under the terms of our divorce Kamal had to pay child support until the children finished their college education and alimony until I remarried. He assured me that I would never have to worry about having to work, as he wanted me to stay home and take care of the children. I considered moving back to D.C., but finally decided that living in Tallahassee would give them the roots and stability they needed.

I thanked God for my children. Without them I don't know how I could have found the strength to carry on. Overnight, I had to assume the role of both a mother as well as a father. I was afraid, but I told myself that no matter what happened my love for my children would somehow carry us through. Being alone and totally responsible for two small children was perhaps the most challenging time of my life. With no family around, however, the most difficult everyday role as a single mother was not having anyone to share my children's problems and triumphs with. I swore to myself that I would always be there for them until my last breath.

And I was lonely. I missed not having a husband to talk to, to share my children's stories, laughter, and growth with, and I missed not having a big family around. Now, it was just the three of us, and for the first time in my life, I was truly on my own. I was always afraid I would not be able to give my children everything they needed. At the same time, I knew how lucky I was to have them, and I was determined to make things work out for us.

I quickly learnt that divorce was like a contagious disease. Except for Anne, many of my married friends suddenly disappeared, probably afraid that they would be infected by it. Also, apart from Mary and Ahmed, who kept in constant touch, not many of our Libyan friends contacted us to see how we were doing. Including Ismail, whose wife told me that she would prefer that I not be part of their lives since Kamal was gone.

"I just don't want my husband getting too involved with you and your problems," she told me quite blatantly.

Her unkindness left me mortified, but I never heard from Ismail again. I could not help but feel that somehow he had let us down.

However, the most painful and difficult part to understand was the silence from Kamal's family. My children often asked for their grandparents and their aunts and uncles in Libya, but I didn't really have an answer for them. I did not understand it myself. No one from Kamal's family contacted me after the divorce. It was as though we had never existed. I could not call them because Kamal warned me not to, as it would put them in jeopardy. However, I did send short notes and photos of the children. I kept waiting, thinking it would only be a matter of time before I heard back from them, but not a word. Over the years we learnt to live with the silence. If only they realized how much it would have helped us to not have also been divorced from the family we loved, and whom we thought loved us. It was only because of Mary that I was able to preserve the link to Libya for my children.

For a long time after Kamal left I felt I lost my identity as a woman. I had been with him for almost fourteen years, had adapted myself to life as a Libyan wife and mother, and had even changed my name. Besides being a mother, I didn't know who I was anymore. After finding the letters, "Hiba" ceased to exist, but it would take a few years before I became Esther again. I never stopped yearning for the love and warmth of the Libyan family I had left behind that fateful day.

Having been with only one man for so long, I felt hesitant and shy about dating again. When I finally did, my relationship with Kamal took a turn for which I was totally unprepared. When he found out I was dating, he got very angry with me. He forbade me from going out with any man. In fact, he said, I was not even allowed to have any man in the house. I was shocked by his reaction and tried to remind him that we were divorced.

"I don't care!" he screamed at me all the way from Doha. It was the first time he had ever done that. Never, in all our years together, had he cursed or yelled at me.

"You're still the mother of my children, and you will do what I tell you!" I told him that under the circumstances he was being a hypocrite.

When he found out later that I was still dating, he immediately cut off child support and alimony. He called one day to tell me that if I did not stop dating completely, he would cease sending money permanently.

Finally, on the advice of a friend, I talked to an attorney by the name of Joe Stevens. He helped me understand my legal rights, which made me feel less intimidated by Kamal and his threats. Over the next few years, Joe helped me survive one legal and financial blow after another, and guided me through many issues I was completely unprepared to face alone. There were times when he knew I did not have any money, and during those times, he never sent me a bill. I tried looking for work, but it was difficult after having been out of the job market for more than ten years. It seemed I was always either over or under-qualified. Even though my parents were aware of my situation, my mother refused to allow my father to help unless I agreed to return to live in Singapore.

Meanwhile, the little money I had started to quickly dwindle away. I lived from month to month, not knowing if or when Kamal would be sending us money, but no one knew how desperate I was. Months would go by sometimes when he would not send me anything, and rather than tell anyone, I resorted to selling my jewelry, including the exquisite emerald and diamond set Amir had given me, and the beautiful diamond pendant from Ibrahim and Rogaya. I remembered then what Amir's wife, Noor, had told me about jewelry being a woman's dowry. I wished I had listened.

One day, I had a surprise visit from friends of mine from Benghazi. They had heard about the divorce, and had flown to Tallahassee to spend a few days with us. When the children went outside to play, Hassan said that he had something to tell me. He looked uncomfortable, so I geared myself up for bad news.

"Hiba, I am so sorry to tell you this, and I debated about doing it, but I think you should know." He avoided my eyes as he talked, nervously smoking, his thick glasses shielding his embarrassment

I couldn't imagine what he had to say.

"I have a very good friend, Nasser, from Qatar, who told me that the rumor there is that the reason Kamal divorced you was because you were having an affair."

I was shocked, and repulsed when I realized the implication. Regardless of what happened, I couldn't imagine that Kamal would generate such a lie about me, the mother of his children.

"Don't worry, Hiba. Anyone who knows you will not believe that. I swear to you it will never be repeated in my presence again without a severe scolding from me."

I knew how much Hassan cared for me and the children, so I had no doubt he would not have told me this unless he was absolutely sure of the source. I wondered if that was the reason why I never heard from Kamal's friends or his family in Libya.

"There's more," he continued, painfully.

"Nasser also told me that his wife heard from one of Wafa's cousins that she and Kamal were married by Islamic marriage contract, *"Katb el-Kitab"* before your divorce..."

Hassan's revelation was the final twist of the knife, but it was also what freed me from Kamal.

CHAPTER 19

DEATH IN A FOREIGN LAND

In 2008, after fifteen years of not hearing a single word from her father, Layla received a call from Kamal. Though she was happy to hear from him, she was also guarded.

Understandably, it was difficult after years of unkindness followed by over a decade of silence, to allow him back into her life without reservations. The calls from him started to come regularly, and though they meant a lot to my daughter, there were still tears that had not dried, and many missing years to bridge.

During one of those calls, Kamal told Layla that he had been diagnosed with lymphoma. The thought that her father might die before she was able to properly reconcile with him broke down Layla's resolve. The reality of his condition began to chisel away at her defenses, for deep within her remained a longing to reconnect with the man who had left her when she was a little girl. To establish a new foundation for an honest relationship, however, required closing past wounds. All she wanted from him was to acknowledge the hurt he had caused her over the years. It would have meant everything to her—it was all she needed to completely forgive him.

But this he could not do. Instead, he chose to avoid any mention of the past. It was obviously too painful for him to revisit, and too painful for her not to.

"Mummy," she asked me, "why is it so difficult for him to say he's sorry?"

I had to think carefully before giving her an answer. I needed to be honest, while being as fair to him as I possibly could. It was easier for me to do that now since the pain he had caused me had subsided. However, it forced me to revisit the past with different eyes to help my daughter understand what had happened.

"Your father loves you and your brother very much," I said, "but more than us, more than his family, he loves his country. After he left Libya, the only thing he lived for was to see Gaddafi gone so he could return. He did whatever he had to do, even if it meant sacrificing us. Right or wrong, it was a choice he has to live with. I don't think he can live with it if he has to admit his mistakes..."

Sadly, I could see from her expression that my answer was not enough. I secretly suspected that Kamal had also become more fundamentally religious as a result of his association with Wafa and Qatar. His behavior towards Layla had become more and more erratic. His rigid criticisms of her, and even me, pushed her further away from him until, finally, his hypocrisy and anger alienated her.

One year later, in the spring of 2009, Layla finally saw her father again. He wanted her to meet him in Washington D.C., so she flew up for a three-day visit. Their reunion was warm and Kamal seemed happy to see his daughter.

Kamal was there with Wafa and a female relative, both of whom were on a frenzied shopping spree. The entire three days were spent in an upscale shopping mall. Layla and her father sat in the food court of the mall talking and waiting while the women shopped, but the subject she needed him to address never came up. Instead, he talked about himself, his collection of watches, places he had been, and, incredibly, even boasted of taking some of his nieces and nephews on vacations around the world over the years. He did not sound like the man I had known.

Kamal decided to fly back with Layla through Atlanta on the same flight on his way to Tallahassee to visit his old friend Ismail, who was dying. Layla later told me that the short plane ride to Atlanta will always be one of the most cherished memories she has of her father. For the first time in all those years, it was just the two of them. He talked a lot during the flight, about Libya and his family there, and especially about Ali, and how he wished he had never left. The conversation was laden with sorrow, regrets, and a weary hope for a better future. For the first time in her adult life, Layla saw a glimpse of the man he once was—the man I had married—and her heart was touched by his passion and sincerity. She felt sorry for him, and prayed that the moment would be a turning point in their relationship.

With tears in his eyes, Kamal turned to his daughter and said, in a voice choked with pain, "I would give the past ten years of my life for one week in Libya..."

Layla took her father's hand and held it for a while before he took it to his lips and kissed it.

"I am so proud of you, *Habibti*," he said. "Your mother has raised you to be a good woman, and you are still the most beautiful girl in the world..."

I reminded my daughter that it was the song he had always sung to her when she was little.

Layla saw Kamal for the last time the following year, when he was at the Institut Gustave Roussy, a cancer treatment center in Villejuif, outside of Paris. She flew to France to spend a week with him at his request. When she met the doctor who had been treating her father for over ten years, she was shocked and saddened that he had no knowledge of her existence.

She sat with her father every day for hours, talking to him, feeding him, and sometimes even cleaning him. His mood grew darker towards the end of the week as his condition worsened. When the time for her to leave approached, he covered his face with a scarf. Layla never knew for sure the reason. Perhaps he was too ashamed to face his daughter, or perhaps he was frustrated at himself for being unable to communicate with her more honestly, even when he knew he was dying.

All those days, Wafa sat quietly in the corner of the room reading her gold-encased Koran, barely acknowledging Layla's presence. When she did, it was with condescension, repeating on several occasions that it was shameful Layla did not speak Arabic and was not a Muslim.

Finally fed up with the hypocrisy, Layla one day turned to look her straight in the eyes, and calmly replied: "Unfortunately, I did not have a father around to teach me."

Layla did not find the closure with her father she was hoping for in France, and once again I saw her frustration at being unable to capture the elusive dream of a genuine reconciliation. She almost wished she had not gone, cherishing instead the last intimate moments they had shared together on the flight from D.C. to Atlanta.

I know that Kamal loved his children very much, but I am sure his daughter reminded him too much of me, and of his own weaknesses. I think his anger at me was the disguise he used to cover his guilt and shame. I believe that deep down, because he was once a man of principle and integrity, he could never forgive himself for what he did, and for whatever reasons he thought he was doing it. I suspect he realized too late, that in the end, the only thing that truly matters is the love and respect of your family and friends.

Several months later, Tarek also flew to Doha to see his father, who was by then in a coma and not expected to recover. Tarek was only there for a few days, but was thankfully able to say goodbye and find the closure he needed. Sadly, Kamal never knew that his only son had travelled all the way from America to pay his last respects to a father whom he hardly knew.

In 2010 Kamal passed away in Qatar.

When I heard of his death, all I felt was sorrow. I knew that more than anything, he would have preferred to have died and been buried in his beloved Khums. Instead, he is buried in a land where he will always be known as a foreigner, the Libyan.

Tragically, Rogaya's prophecy of a son dying in a foreign land came true for two of her boys. Thankfully, she and Ibrahim did not live long enough to know that Kamal had also died abroad.

After his release from prison Amir escaped to Cairo, where he lived in self-imposed exile. About a year later, he died quite suddenly and alone, from a heart attack. Sadly, no one ever saw Ali again after he was sent to Abu Salim prison. Of the four Ben Ramadan sons, only one survived Gaddafi's reign of terror.

Three months after Kamal's death, I received a letter postmarked Paris, France. Inside the envelope was a note attached to another envelope. The note read:

Dear Madame,
Dr Ben Ramadan instructed me to mail this to you upon his death. Please forgive the delay.

With sincere condolences,
Dr Jean Matthey-Doret
Institut Gustave-Roussy
Villejuif, France

The other envelope was simply addressed *Stora*, and the handwriting was undeniably Kamal's. It took me a while to collect the courage to open it, not knowing what to expect, but knowing whatever it was, it would be the last time I would hear from him. This, I realized, tenderly fingering the paper he had once held, was the end of our journey together. Gingerly, I opened the envelope, and saw the familiar writing inside, strong but shaky.

I have lived my life without color or taste. I have spent it running to you and away from you. Even if God forgives me for what I have done, even if you forgive me, I will never forgive myself.

Gifts from the past ignites our memory and feeds our soul. Sitting in the stillness of my lush garden, with only the sounds of birds singing, I quietly shed my farewell tears for the Libyan...

EPILOGUE

After eight months of civil war, forty-two years of terror in Libya finally came to an end with the extremely violent killing of Gaddafi in Sirte, where he was born. Pitifully, his last words were:

"What did I do?"

Three days later, on 23 October 2011, the liberation of Libya was declared in Benghazi, where the seed for the revolution had been planted.

When I first saw the news of protests in Benghazi on CNN, my reaction was shock. I had given up hope of ever seeing the day when Libyans would collectively dare challenge the regime. Fear of repercussions on family and clan members had always been a strong deterrent in opposing Gaddafi. I expected the protests to end quickly, as soon as arrests were made and the protesters publicly hung. However, as the days went by and the protesters grew in numbers and persistence, I began to feel hope for the first time since leaving Libya thirty-two years ago. I followed Anderson Cooper's nightly report, applauding his role in introducing the world to Libya and the Libyan Revolution.

These young Libyans were not like their fathers, hindered by fear of change and reprisals. They amazed me with their daily acts of defiance and heroism, and my heart filled with pride for their spirit and courage. Unlike their fathers, they were actually daring to put words and thoughts into action, and risk the ultimate sacrifice for their country. The sight of some of them in flip-flops battling Gaddafi's army touched my heart. I cheered them on every day, praying for it to be over quickly. The wealth from oil is what kept Gaddafi in power, but the youth of Libya, not as susceptible to his seductive charisma, was what would finally bring him down.

In June 1996, at the height of his madness, Gaddafi did the unthinkable. On his direct orders, and under the supervision of his hated intelligence chief and brother-in-law, Abdullah Senussi, over 1,200 men were shot to death in the central courtyard of Abu Salim prison in Tripoli. Sitting on thirty acres and surrounded by twenty-three-foot-high walls, the prison was impenetrable; a torture chamber for anyone who posed any real, imagined, or trumped-up threat to the regime. For years wives, parents and family members of those who had already been murdered continued to make monthly visits with food and necessities for their loved ones, not knowing they were already dead.

In September 2011, a mass grave was unearthed by revolutionary forces outside Abu Salim prison, giving proof to the horrific massacre. Abu Salim was one of Gaddafi's most heinous acts of lunacy, and it was also the catalyst for the outrage that ultimately ended his brutal regime.

I couldn't help but remember how my own life had also been affected by this man, described by one Arab scholar as half-monster, half-clown. Like most dictators Gaddafi possessed an insatiably egotistical need for adoration at any price, never recognizing nor caring when adoration turned to terror.

Then I think of one man, Kamal Ben Ramadan, my Libyan, whose dreams were shattered and his life eventually destroyed by this lunatic. He was hindered by fear of Gaddafi's reprisal, futilely waiting and hoping that change would come from inside Gaddafi's own circle or the military. Ultimately, even his support and alignment with the opposition outside Libya did not bring him the results he had worked so hard to achieve. He had severed his association with the NFSL long before his death, unhappy with their evolving policies and the direction they were going.

As the events in Libya quickly unfolded, I felt sorry that Kamal was not alive to see it happening, sorry that he had died only months before, in a world where he did not belong, with so many broken dreams, sacrifices and mistakes scattered along his journey. He would have found light again in his life and he would have been there in Benghazi and Tripoli.

Kamal once told me that he would never forgive himself for what he did. Wherever you are now, Kamal, just know that I forgave you long ago. In your own way, you thought you were trying to do what those brave people were doing on the streets of Benghazi, Tripoli, Misrata, and all over Libya. Your dreams finally became reality. You told your daughter that you would have traded ten years of your life for one week in Libya, but really, you never left. The man who left Tripoli that morning in 1979 left behind his heart and his soul.

Ironically, it was the death of Kamal and the liberation of Libya that took my children back to their roots in the country. The veil of deception had been lifted, and years of secrets and lies were revealed and forgiven. My children have been reunited with their family in Libya. Their only sadness, and mine, is that Ibrahim and Rogaya were not alive to see their grandchildren again.

No matter what happened, I have no regrets, and feel honored to have been a part of this passage in Libyan history.

I pray that Libya will one day become a model state for the Arab world, the way Kamal had envisioned. It is my dream to go back there with my children before I die. I would like to stand with them at the ancient ruins in Leptis Magna and say a prayer for all those who have gone before me, to meet the descendants of my Libyan hero, Ibrahim, and to savor once again the wonderful dishes a beautiful woman named Rogaya once cooked for me on Libyan soil. Most of all, I want to breathe the air of freedom in a new Libya.

It is my belief that fact overrides propriety, and that truth always emerges, even if not in our lifetime. One of the qualities that I most admired in the Libyan culture was the outspokenness, something I was instilled with in my own upbringing. It is my sincere hope that no one undeserving has been offended by the story of my journey.

After the initial jubilation of a Libya free from Gaddafi, the country has sadly fallen under another type of fear and tyranny. Freedom and rebel fighters who were once united to destroy a common enemy have now fractured into militias, strongly reinforced by weapons acquired during the revolution. Each militia, divided by region or tribe, is now seeking dominance as a reward for their role in deposing Gaddafi.

Extreme Islamists, who were imprisoned by Gaddafi, are now supported by Al-Qaeda and ISIS in Libya. Entry into Libya, bordering six countries, makes it easily accessible by rogue groups as well as migrants and refugees.

At one time, Gaddafi was the recognizable enemy, but now there are many, and the country is devoid of any law and order. Thefts, blackmails, kidnappings, and murders by certain groups and opportunistic thugs have brought the country to its knees again. Indeed, 2014 and 2015 have been brutal years for Libya. Severe damage was done to countless existing infrastructures, including airports and oil terminals, and thousands of Libyans have been killed in violent as well as politically motivated attacks.

The struggle continues, and the freedom so many Libyans fought and died for has not yet been realized.

God help Libya...